SPQR IX

THE
PRINCESS AND
THE PIRATES

SPQR IX

THE
PRINCESS AND
THE PIRATES

JOHN MADDOX ROBERTS

THOMAS DUNNE BOOKS
ST. MARTIN'S MINOTAUR
NEW YORK

THOMAS DUNNE BOOKS.
An imprint of St. Martin's Press.

www.minotaurbooks.com

Library of Congress Cataloging-in-Publication Data

Roberts, John Maddox.
    SPQR IX : the princess and the pirates / John Maddox Roberts.
        p. cm.
    ISBN 0-312-33723-X (hc)
    ISBN 0-312-33724-8 (pbk)
    EAN 978-0-312-33724-7
    1. Metellus, Decius Caecilius (Fictitious character)—Fiction.
2. Cleopatra, Queen of Egypt, d. 30 B.C.—Fiction. 3. Rome—History—
Republic, 265–30 B.C.—Fiction. 4. Private investigators—Rome—
Fiction. 5. Mediterranean Area—Fiction. 6. Pirates—Fiction. I. Title:
SPQR 9. II Title: Princess and the pirates. III. Title.

PS3568.O23874S677 2005
813'.54—dc22   2004051436

First St. Martin's Minotaur Paperback Edition: January 2006

10 9 8 7 6 5 4 3 2 1

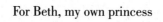

For Beth, my own princess

SPQR IX

THE
PRINCESS AND
THE PIRATES

1

Let me say at the outset that Cleopatra was not beautiful. People of deficient wit fancy that only a woman of the most extravagant beauty could have bagged both Julius Caesar and Marcus Antonius, the most powerful Romans of their day. It is true that both men had a taste for beauty, but men of great power and wealth have their pick of beautiful women and it took far more than mere beauty for the queen of Egypt to enthrall that pair of jaded old warriors, each of them a long-service veteran of the campaigns of Venus as well as those of Mars.

Of course, it didn't hurt that she was heiress to the most fabulously wealthy nation in the world. For the riches of Egypt even the most discriminating connoisseur of lovely women might overlook an extra half inch of nose, eyes a little too close set, a receding chin, or protruding front teeth, or, for that matter, a hunched back, bowed legs, and lion-faced leprosy.

Not that Cleopatra was ugly. Far from it. She was quite attractive. It was just that the qualities for which great men loved her were not entirely those of the flesh nor even those of her great wealth. The simple fact was that any normal man who stood in her presence for a few minutes loved her desperately *if she wanted him to*. No woman ever had greater control over men's feelings toward herself. Whether it was grand passion, fatherly fondness, doglike loyalty, or fear and trembling, if Cleopatra wanted it from you, she got it.

And love for Cleopatra was not the infatuation of a youth for some shapely, empty-headed girl. When Cleopatra wished a man to love her, he loved her as Paris loved Helen, without limits and forsaking all judgment, all sense of proportion or decency. It was a serious illness from which even the gods could not deliver him.

But I get ahead of myself. That was years later. When I first encountered Princess Cleopatra she was just a child, although a remarkable one. That was back during the consulship of Metellus Celer and Lucius Afranius, when I was an envoy to the court of Ptolemy Auletes at Alexandria.

The second time was a few years afterward on Cyprus.

"WHY," I ASKED, "CAN I NOT STAND FOR praetor immediately? I've served as aedile for two full years, which is unprecedented, and for which the people of Rome owe me not just a praetorship but the best propraetorian province on the map. Everybody loved my Games, I got the sewers scoured out, I fixed the streets, rooted out corruption in the building trades—"

"You are not going to stand for praetor just yet," Father said, "because we are already supporting our candidates for the next elections, as we agreed before we knew your aedileship would be prolonged for an extra year. Besides, the people prefer their praetorian candidates to have put in more time with the legions than you can boast."

"You're just trying to put off returning to Gaul," Creticus said. He was perfectly correct.

"And why not?" I answered. "Nobody is getting any glory out of that war except Caesar. You'd think he was fighting all alone up there to read his dispatches to the Senate."

"The people don't require glory," Father said. "They require service. They're not going to hand imperium to a man who has no more than five or six years with the eagles to his credit."

"They elected Cicero," I muttered.

"Cicero is a New Man," said my kinsman Nepos. "He reached the highest offices on his reputation as a lawyer because he's a novelty. From

2

a Metellus the people expect what we've given them for centuries: leadership in the Senate and on the battlefield."

It was, as you might have guessed, a family conference. We Metelli got together from time to time to plot strategy. We fancied ourselves the greatest power bloc in the Senate and the Popular Assemblies and we did control quite a few votes, although Metellan power had declined from its peak of a generation previously, just after the dictatorship of Sulla.

Creticus laced his fingers over his substantial paunch and studied a flight of birds overhead, as if searching for omens. "As it happens," he said, "we've really nothing to gain by sending you back to Caesar."

My political antennae stood up and quivered. "A shift in family policy, I take it?"

"Everyone feels that Caesar already has too much power and prestige," Nepos asserted. He was a longtime supporter of Pompey and detested Caesar. His "everyone" meant most people of good birth. Caesar, despite his patrician birth, was overwhelmingly popular with the commons, whereas we Metelli, though plebeian, were of the aristocratic party.

"Still," Father said, "there is important military work to be done that doesn't involve fighting the Gauls. Work that can be proclaimed to your credit when you stand for praetor and, in time, consul."

"It would be glorious to make the Parthians return the eagles they won from Crassus," I said, "but since everyone who can lift a sword is in Gaul these days, I don't see how I—"

"Forget about land warfare," Creticus said. "There has been a resurgence of piracy in the East. It must be put down, and quickly."

My hair commenced to prickle. "A naval command? But *duumvir* is an imperium appointment, and I haven't held—"

"You won't be *duumvir*," Father said, "just commodore of a flotilla of cutters. No triremes, nothing bigger than a Liburnian."

My stomach knotted at the prospect of a sea command. "I thought Pompey stamped out the pirates."

"Nobody eliminates piracy any more than they eliminated banditry," Creticus told me. "Pompey crushed the floating nation that controlled the sea in the old days. But we've been distracted in the West for some time now, and a new batch of nautical rogues are taking advantage of the fact. It's time to crush them now before they build back up to full fleet status."

I didn't have much time to think about it. I had to do *something,* and the prospect of fighting in the dark Gaulish forests was infinitely depressing.

"Is the command conferred by the Popular Assemblies?" I asked, resigned and now considering the votes.

"It's a senatorial appointment," Father said. "But one of our tribunes will submit it to the *consilium plebis,* and it will pass without resistance. You are a popular man, and Clodius is dead. It will be to your credit that you've chosen an ugly, thankless task like pirate hunting instead of a chance for glory and loot in Gaul."

"Speaking of loot—" I began.

"If you can find where they keep their hoard," Creticus said, "well, it would be a nice gesture if you returned some of it to the rightful owners. Of course, in most cases that would be impossible. A respectable contribution to the public treasury will ensure a favorable reception from the Senate. Aside from that, why not help yourself?"

"When you stand for praetor," Nepos said, "it will go all the better if you're standing beside a pillar decorated with the rams of ships you've captured." (This was the traditional way to commemorate a naval victory.)

I sighed. "I want to take Titus Milo with me."

Father slapped the table in front of him. "Absolutely not! Milo is in exile. He's in disgrace."

"He used to be a fleet rower," I said. "He knows ships and sailors, and he wouldn't need any official appointment. He'd be of enormous help to me."

"As long as he stays away from Rome there should be no problem," Scipio said. "And he'll probably be happy for a chance to get away from Fausta." This raised a chuckle. My old friend and his wife were on the outs. She was the Dictator's daughter, and much of Milo's charm in her eyes had lain in his incredible rise from street-level gangster to the praetorship. His equally precipitate fall had failed to win her approval. He had had the consulship in his grasp, and now he was twiddling his thumbs on his estate in Lanuvium.

"This is what comes of allowing the scum and riffraff of the streets to participate in politics," grumbled Father, who had helped and protected a number of such men himself when it suited him politically. After all, *somebody* has to do the dirty work for aristocrats who cannot afford to soil their own hands.

"Where is my base of operations to be?" I asked.

"Cyprus," said Creticus. "Consult with Cato. He can brief you on the place. He spent better than a year sorting out their political mess."

"Who is in charge there now?" I asked.

"One Aulus Silvanus," Creticus said.

"Silvanus? Isn't he one of Gabinius's cronies?" At one time Gabinius had been a rival to Caesar and Pompey for military glory, but his promising career had come to little, and he'd been tried for extortion shortly before this time. Despite a spirited defense by Cicero, he'd been found guilty and exiled. When Cicero couldn't get you off, you had to be as guilty as Oedipus.

"He is, and report has Gabinius living in comfortable retirement on Cyprus," Scipio affirmed.

"It sounds cozy. When do I depart?"

"As soon as the proper senatorial documents can be drawn up. The Tribunician vote will follow automatically so you needn't wait for that." Father was as abrupt as usual.

"Very well," I said, sourly. "I'll begin making arrangements."

AS I WALKED BACK THROUGH THE CITY, my mood was moderately elevated. This appointment did not displease me nearly as much as I pretended. Like most Romans I abhorred the very thought of sea duty, but this was one of the rare occasions when I was looking forward to getting away from Rome.

My aedileship had won me great popularity, but it had been incredibly burdensome and expensive. I was heavily in debt and would be for years if I didn't do something about it. Caesar had offered to cover all my debts, but I would not be indebted to him. He had covered a portion of them, ostensibly as a gift to his niece, Julia, but in reality because I had extricated him from some difficulties, so we were even there. I owed him no political favors. A quick, profitable campaign against these pirates might just solve all my fiscal problems, if I could avoid drowning or death in battle in the course of it.

And I was tired of Rome. The place was quiet for the first time in years. With the death of Clodius and the exile of Milo, the powerful gangs that had enjoyed aristocratic support were leaderless. During his near-dictatorial sole consulship Pompey had scourged the City of its disorderly elements, setting up courts of savage disposition. The thugs quickly heeded the attractions of faraway places or took refuge in the gladiatorial schools from which most of them had come in the first place. The ones too slow to take the hint found themselves testing their pugnacity unarmed against lions, bears, and bulls in the Games.

Almost for the first time in my memory, Romans walked the streets in safety and nobody went armed. People went about their business in an orderly fashion, obeyed the rulings of the curule aediles, and were even polite to one another. Foreign merchants arrived in unprecedented numbers, knowing their lives and goods would be safe.

For years I had complained of the disorder of the City, and now that it was gone, I found that I missed it. All the peace and quiet seemed unnatural. I did not expect it to last. My fellow citizens were, after all, Romans; and we have always been an unruly, obstreperous lot. Forget the pretty myths about Aeneas and the brothers Romulus and Remus. The sober fact is that Rome was founded by outcasts and bandits from a dozen Latin tribes, with a few Etruscans, Sabines, and Oscans thrown in for good measure if the names of some of our older families are anything to go by. Our power and fortunes have waxed mightily, but time has done little to improve our disposition.

Getting across the City was a slow process for me because I was extremely popular and had to stop and exchange greetings from citizens every few steps. Romans felt no awe toward their ruling classes in those days, and some of the more old-fashioned sort were liable to run up and plant a big, garlicky kiss on your face if they were especially fond of you. This was a major failure of the well-known Roman gravitas.

I was pleased to note that the last signs of the rioting that had followed the funeral of Clodius were gone. The fires had been extensive, and the whole City was smudged and stank of soot for months afterward. Rome wasn't to see its like again until Antonius delivered his famous rabble-rouser over the corpse of Caesar many years later. Roman funerals were livelier than most peoples.

My mind was occupied with the usual problems that came with a foreign posting: what to take, what business to settle, how to break the news to my wife, that sort of thing. She should be happy enough about this, I thought hopefully. I wasn't going to a province at war, so I could take her along. Cyprus was reputed to be a beautiful place. It had, until recently, been home to a royal court, so she would find company congenial to her patrician station. Surely Julia would be happy with this posting.

Julia was not happy.

"Cyprus?" she cried, with a mixture of incredulity, scorn, and disgust. "After all you've done, they've sent you chasing pirates in Cyprus? They owe you better than that!"

"An ex-aedile is owed nothing at all. Technically, the office isn't even on the *cursus honorum.*"

She made an eloquent gesture of dismissal. "That old political fiction! Everyone knows the aedileship makes or breaks a political career. Yours should have earned you a dictatorship! Cyprus! It's an insult!"

We were so alone in the triclinium you'd never have guessed that the house was packed with slaves, hers and mine. They knew to keep their distance when she was in one of these moods. She was a Julian and a Caesar, and at times like this it showed.

"If you can't stand immediately for praetor, you ought to return to Gaul. It's there that reputations are to be made."

"Caesar's officers tend to get killed for the sake of Caesar's reputation," I pointed out.

"Caesar likes you. He would make you a *legatus.*"

"The Senate has to approve *legati*, not that Caesar cares much about Senate approval these days. And it would make me an enemy of Labienus, which I don't need. He's an unforgiving man."

"Labienus is nothing. Caesar is a far greater man, and soon he will be the only man who counts for anything. You should be with him."

I didn't like the way this conversation was going. "In Cyprus," I said, "there's an opportunity to accumulate some real wealth."

"That would be nice for a change," she admitted. "We could clear off all our debts." Her brow unfurrowed as the advantages began to sink in. Like all her family she was intensely political, but the charms of solvency made a powerful lure. "And Cyprus does have a famed social life."

"And with this service behind me, with a tidy treasure to boot, I'll stand for praetor next elections, You'll be a praetor's wife for a year, then I'll be posted to a really valuable province like Sicily or Africa. Wouldn't you like that?" Plus I'd be staying out of the legions. But I didn't say that. She would have thought it unworthy of a Roman official.

"Well, if it's unavoidable." Then she turned to the practicalities. "How are we to arrange travel? I'll need to take my personal servants, no more than five or six, and my wardrobe, and—" this went on for some time.

"I'll take a fast Liburnian as soon as I can," I told her. "That means I'll have such luggage as I can wrap up in a spare toga and sleep on deck. I'll take Hermes."

"I am not sleeping on any deck," she said.

"The grain fleet sails for Egypt next month. Those ships are huge, and they have plenty of passenger space. They always stop at Cyprus before proceeding on to Alexandria."

"And what will you be doing for a month?" she asked ominously.

"Why, chasing pirates," I answered, innocence oozing from every pore. Somehow, rumors of that German princess had reached her. We weren't even married at the time, but that made little difference to Julia.

"Does your family have any *hospitium* connections in Cyprus? I'm sure mine don't."

"I doubt it," I said, "but I'll look through my tokens just in case. We have hospitia just about everywhere else in the Greek world, but I don't believe any of my family have ever visited Cyprus. Of course, it's the birth-place of your ancestress, so the place must be littered with your cousins."

"I've warned you," she said, ominously. The Caesars traced their descent from the goddess Venus who was, of course, born on Cyprus, just off the coast of Cyprus at any rate. Her uncle Caius Julius traded heavily on this supposed divine connection, to much mirth from the Romans. It infuriated Julia when I tweaked her for this bit of Caesarian bombast, but anything to get her mind off that German princess.

While she was busy with her preparations, I called in Hermes. He was just back from the *ludus,* where he trained with weapons most days. I was training him in all the skills of a politician's assistant, which in those days included street brawling.

"Draft me a letter," I ordered, and he sat at the desk, grumbling. With a fine career ahead of him, with freedom for himself and, perhaps, sons of his own in the Senate some day, he would have preferred the life of a common gladiator. He loved the fighting part, hated the writing. Well, there were days when I would have preferred a life in the *ludus* myself. At least there your only worry was surviving your next fight, and your enemy always struck from in front.

"To Titus Annius Milo from his friend Decius Caecilius Metellus the Younger, greetings," I began. I saw Hermes's eyebrows go up. He liked Milo. "I have been posted to Cyprus to chase pirates. I am a total dunce at sea and need your help desperately. Cyprus isn't Gaul, which alone makes it a desirable place to be. There is a chance for some real money in this, and, besides, we'll be away from our wives and have loads of fun."

"I heard that!" Julia said, from deep in the house. The woman had ears like a fox.

"By the time you receive this," I went on, "I will be on my way to Tarentum. If you have not arrived by the time I sail, I will leave orders that you are to have a fast Liburnian. I know you are bored to death in Lanuvium so don't bother to pretend otherwise. We could both use some moderately safe excitement in agreeable surroundings. I look forward to seeing you in Tarentum or, failing that, on Cyprus."

"Sea service?" Hermes said unhappily. He was even more nautiphobic than most Romans.

"Just a bit of coastal sailing," I assured him. "We shouldn't have to spend a single night at sea or ever sail out of sight of land. You're an accomplished swimmer now; you'll be perfectly safe."

"I don't mind the sea," he said. "It's being out on it in a ship I don't like. The waves make me sick, storms can blow you to places where Ulysses never sailed, and even in good weather you're in the middle of a bunch of sailors!"

"You'd rather go back to Gaul?" That silenced him. "Pack up."

2

THE TRIP TO CYPRUS IS AN EASY SAIL
when the weather is good, and ours was perfect. At Tarentum I had made
a more than generous sacrifice to Neptune, and he must have been in an
expansive mood because he repaid me handsomely.

From Italy's easternmost cape we crossed the narrow strait to the
coast of Greece, then south along that coast, stopping every evening at little ports, rarely straying more than a few hundred paces from shore. Even
Hermes didn't get seasick. We put in at Piraeus, and I took the long hike
up to Athens and gawked at the sights for a few days. I have never understood how the Greeks built such beautiful cities and then could not govern them.

From Piraeus we sailed among the lovely, gemlike Greek islands,
each of them looking as if it could be the home of Calypso or Circe. From
the islands we crossed to the coast of Asia, then along the Cilician shore,
keeping a close watch there for Cilicia was a homeland for pirates. From
the southernmost coast of Cilicia we crossed to Cyprus, the longest stretch
of open water on the voyage. Just as the mainland disappeared from view
behind us, the heights of Cyprus appeared before us, and I breathed a

little easier. I have never been able to abide the feeling of being at sea with no land in sight.

One reason that I dawdled was that Milo had not met me at Tarentum. I hoped that he was close behind and would catch up soon. I already had a feeling I was going to need him.

The problem was my flotilla, its sailors and marines, and my sailing master, one Ion. The deeper problem was that I was a Roman, and they were not.

For a Roman, service with the legions and service with the navy were as unalike as two military alternatives could possibly be. On land we were supremely confident, and over the centuries we had become specialists. Romans were heavy infantry. We held the center of the battle line and were renowned for feats of military engineering, such as bridge building, entrenchment, fortification, and siege craft. Roman soldiers, when they weren't doing anything else, passed the time by building the finest roads in the world. For most other types of soldiery: cavalry, archers, slingers, and so forth, we usually hired foreigners. Even our light infantry were usually auxiliaries supplied by allied cities that lacked full citizenship.

At sea we were, so to speak, over our heads. Everyone knows how, in the wars with Carthage, we created a navy from nothing and defeated the world's greatest naval power. The truth is, we accomplished this by ignoring maneuvers, instead grappling with their ships, thus transforming sea battles into land battles. We were still wretched sailors and kept losing entire fleets in storms that any real seafaring people would have seen coming in plenty of time to take action. And the Carthaginians repaid our presumption by raising the most brilliant general who ever lived: Hannibal. And don't prattle to me about Alexander. Hannibal would have destroyed the little Macedonian dwarf as an afterthought. Alexander made his reputation fighting Persians, whom the whole world knows to be a wretched pack of slaves.

Anyway, our navy consists of hired foreigners under the command of Roman admirals and commodores. Most of them are Greeks, and that explains the greater part of my problems.

My first run-in with Ion occurred the moment I stepped aboard my lead Liburnian, the *Nereid*. The master, a crusty old salt dressed in the traditional blue tunic and cap, took my Senate credentials without a greeting or salute and scanned them with a barely repressed sneer. He handed them back.

"Just tell us where you want to go, and we'll get you there," he said. "Otherwise, keep out of the way, don't try to give the men orders, don't puke on the deck, and try not to fall overboard. We don't try to save men who fall overboard. They belong to Neptune, and he's a god we don't like to offend."

So I knocked him down, grasped him by the hair and belt, and pitched him into the water. "Don't try to fish him out," I told the sailors. "Neptune might not like it." You have to let Greeks know who the master is right away or they'll give you no end of trouble.

My other two Liburnians were the *Thetis* and the *Ceto.* Liburnians are among the smaller naval vessels, having only a single deck and two banks of oars, usually forty or fifty oars to a side, with only a single rower at each oar. I suspect that the ships of Ulysses were very similar, for it is an antiquated design and a far cry from the majestic triremes with their three banks of oars and hundreds of rowers. The small ram at the prow, tipped with a bronze boar's head, seemed to me more like a gesture of defiance than a practical weapon.

These three little ships with their tiny complement of sailors and marines seemed totally inadequate even for the humble task of hunting down a pack of scruffy pirates, and I hoped to secure reinforcements as I traveled. Ion curbed his insolence, but he remained abrupt and churlish. I was a landlubber and he was a seaman and that was that. The common sailors were little more respectful. The marines were the scum of the sea, hoping to win citizenship by twenty years of sea service. I suspected that some of them had been expelled from the legions and degraded from citizenship for immorality, and you have to know the sort of behavior that was tolerated in those days to appreciate the magnitude of such an offense. With such men at my back, the pirates ahead of me held little to fear.

"Hermes," I said, on our first day at sea, "if any of these degenerates gets too close behind me, lay him out with a stick of firewood."

"Never fear," he answered. Hermes took his bodyguarding duty seriously, and he had dressed for the role. He wore a brief tunic of dark leather girded with a wide, bronze-studded belt that held his sheathed sword and dagger. At wrists and ankles he wore leather bands, gladiator fashion. He looked suitably fierce, and the sailors gave him a wide berth.

We saw no pirates, but there was plenty of other shipping, most of it consisting of tubby merchantmen with their short, slanted foremasts, triangular topsails, and swan-neck sternposts. It was the beginning of the sailing season, and the whole sea was aswarm with ships full of wine, grain, hides, pottery, worked metal and metal in ingot form, slaves, livestock, textiles, and luxury goods: precious metals, dyestuffs, perfumes, silk, ivory, feathers, and other valuable items without number. Ships sailed bearing nothing but frankincense for the temples. From Egypt came whole fleets loaded with papyrus.

With all these valuable cargoes just floating around virtually unguarded, it was no wonder that some enterprising rogues simply couldn't restrain themselves from appropriating some of it. There was no way that a slow, heavily laden merchantman with a tiny crew could outrun or outfight a lean warship rowed by brawny, heavily armed pirates. Best simply to lower their sails, and let the brutes come aboard and take what they wanted.

Lucrative as this trade was, though, the pirates committed far worse depredations on land. They struck the coastlines, looted small towns, and isolated villas; carried off prisoners to ransom or sell in the slave markets; and generally made themselves obnoxious to all law-abiding people. There were countless miles of coastline, and only a fraction of it could be patrolled by coast guards.

I suppose this nefarious trade had been going on since the invention of the seagoing vessel. If we are to believe Homer, piracy was once a respectable calling, practiced by kings and heroes. Princes sailing to and from the war in Troy thought nothing of descending upon some unsuspecting village along the way, killing the males, enslaving the women and children, sopping up the wine, and devouring the livestock—all just a fine bit of sport and adventure for a hero back in the good old days. Perhaps these pirates I was to chase weren't really criminals. Perhaps they were merely old-fashioned.

Anyway, we didn't see any of them, which doesn't mean that they didn't see us. They would never attack a warship, even a small one. That would mean only hard knocks and no loot. So they kept to their little coves, their masts unstepped, all but invisible from a few hundred paces away.

Another thing I didn't see were warships. Much of the Roman navy was tied up ferrying supplies and men to Caesar in Gaul, of course, but I had expected to see the ships of our numerous maritime allies in evidence. Rhodes still had its own fleet at that time, for instance. It looked as if everyone had decided that, since Rome was grabbing all the land, Rome might as well do all the coastal patrolling as well.

From a line of mountain peaks, Cyprus grew into a recognizable island, and a pretty fair one, though not as beautiful as Rhodes. Its slopes were cloaked in fir, alder, and cypress, and probably myrtle and acanthus as well. At least, that is the sort of vegetation the poets are always going on about. It looked fine to me at any rate. Put me at sea long enough and a bare rock looks good.

The harbor of Paphos lies on the western coast of the island, and it proved to be a graceful city of the usual Greek design, which is to say that it conformed perfectly to the shape of the land, with fine temples on all the most prominent spots. Here, at least, the Ptolemies had restrained their usual love for outsized architecture and kept the temples beautifully scaled, like those on mainland Greece and in the Greek colonies of southern Italy.

Coming in past the harbor mole, we passed a naval basin surrounded by sheds for warships of all sizes, but these were empty. The commercial harbor, on the other hand, was full of merchant shipping. Cyprus lies within a great curve of the mainland with Lycia, Pamphilia, Cilicia, Syria, and Judea each but a short sail away. This convenient location made it a natural crossroads for sea traffic, and it has prospered greatly since the earliest settlements there. Before the Greeks the Phoenicians colonized the island, and Phoenician cities still exist.

"Bring us in to the big commercial dock," I told Ion. "Then take the ships to the naval basin."

"Looks like we'll have our pick of accommodations there," he observed.

The rowers brought us smoothly alongside the stone wharf, which jutted out into the harbor for at least two hundred paces. I climbed a short flight of steps to the top of the wharf, and sailors carried up our meager baggage, all under the watchful gaze of the inevitable dockside idlers. Aside from these there was no reception party, official or otherwise. Ordinarily the arrival of Roman vessels with a Roman senator aboard brought the local officials running to the harbor with their robes flapping. But then, Cyprus was now a Roman possession, so perhaps the governor thought that I should call on him rather than the other way around.

"Where is the residence of Governor Silvanus?" I demanded of one of the louts. He just blinked, so I repeated the question in Greek.

He pointed up a gentle slope behind him. "The big house across from the Temple of Poseidon." I could barely understand him. The Cyprian dialect differs from the Attic as radically as the Bruttian from Latin.

"Come, Hermes," I said. A couple of porters leapt to take our bags, and we strode along the wharf, picking our way among the boxes, bales, and amphorae that crowded every available foot of space. Everywhere lay stacks of brown metal ingots in the shape of miniature oxhides. Since the time of the Phoenicians the copper mines of Cyprus had been a major source of the metal, and it remained the basis of the island's prosperity.

Above the pervasive sea smell twined the scents of herbs, incense, and spices, along with an occasional vinegary reek where some ham-fisted porter had let an amphora drop and smash, wasting perfectly good wine. This gave me a thought.

"Hermes—"

"Yes, I know: find out where the good wineshops are." I had trained him well.

There is this to be said for a small, colonial city like Paphos: you never have to walk far to get where you are going. The Temple of Poseidon was a graceful structure of the simple Doric design, and I made a mental note to sacrifice there as soon as possible in gratitude for my safe arrival and wonderful sailing weather.

The residence of Silvanus was a two-story mansion of a size available only to the wealthiest in crowded Rome. The slave at the door wore fine Egyptian linen. He called for the major-domo, and this dignitary proved to be a cultured Greek of impeccable dress and grooming.

"Welcome, Senator," he said, bowing gracefully. "Senator Silvanus was not expecting a visit from a colleague, but I know he will be overjoyed and will be stricken that he was not here to greet you personally."

"Where is he then?" I asked, annoyed as always by domestics whose manners are better than my own.

"He visits today with his friend, the great General Gabinius, whose villa is just outside the city. He will return this evening. In the meantime please allow me to put his house at your disposal." He clapped his hands and a pair of slaves took charge of our bags while Hermes tipped the porters from the wharf.

"While your chambers are prepared, please avail yourself of some refreshment in the garden. Or perhaps you would rather bathe first?"

This was a bit of luck. Usually, the worst house is better than the best inn. This did not look like the worst house in town.

"I'm famished. First something to eat, then a bath."

"Certainly. I trust your voyage was not too arduous?"

I prattled on about the trip as he led us through the atrium and into a large, formal garden completely surrounded by the house, the way a gymnasium surrounds the exercise yard. Houses were not built this way in Rome. In the center was a lovely, marble-bordered pond with a fountain in its middle. It looked as if I had lucked into prime accommodations.

"We entertain several distinguished guests today," said the major-domo. "No person of note comes to Paphos without enjoying the hospitality of Silvanus."

"Admirable," I murmured. Everywhere, fine tables sat beneath beautifully tended shade trees, and roses bloomed in big, earthen pots. At one such table sat a young woman dressed in a simple but gorgeous gown of green silk. The dress would have bought a good-sized estate in Italy. Her hair was reddish brown, not at all a common color, and her skin was an almost transparent white. Strangest of all, she was writing in a papyrus scroll and had several others stacked beside her. Standing around her were a number of learned-looking fellows with long beards and dingy robes.

She looked up at me, and I was transfixed by a pair of astonishing green eyes. She asked, "Do Germans sing?"

I had seen those eyes once, years before, in a child's face, but one does not forget such eyes. "Princess Cleopatra! I was not expecting to find you here! Nor to encounter so odd a question."

"I perceive that the senator and the royal lady know one another," said the major-domo.

"Senator Metellus and I met several years ago, Doson, in Alexandria."

"Then, Senator, I shall attend to your accommodations." He bowed himself away. Slaves set me a chair at Cleopatra's table, poured wine into a fine Samian goblet, and set out a plate of bread, fruit, and cheese with a quiet, unobtrusive efficiency at which I could only marvel. Why couldn't I ever find slaves like that?

"You were in Gaul with Caesar until a bit over two years ago," Cleopatra observed.

"You are amazingly well informed." The wine was superb, but by this time I was expecting it to be. "My services were somewhat less than heroic."

"Distinguished, at the very least," she said, smiling. She had a marvelous smile. "And you were involved in the early campaigning, against Ariovistus and his Germans. That is why I asked. There is so little really known about the Germans, and I can find nothing at all about their musical accomplishments."

"I can't say that they really sing, but they make a sort of rhythmic, barking noise in which they take a certain satisfaction. It's nothing a Greek rhapsode would consider melodic. The Gauls, on the other hand, sing all the time. It grates on the Roman ear, but by the time I left I had learned to appreciate it in sheer self-defense."

"That is surprising. Romans seldom appreciate other people's customs and way of life." This was all too true. "But then, you have the reputation of being a surprising sort of Roman." She introduced her companions who were, as I had suspected, boring old scholars, both local and Alexandrian.

"Cyprus was the home of the philosopher Zeno," she said, "as I am sure you already know."

"Never heard of the fellow." I was lying, but the last thing I wanted was to get drawn into a philosophical discussion.

"I don't believe you."

"Princess, in Rome, when a man shows an interest in philosophy, it's taken as a sign that he is planning to retire from public life. Too much scholarly accomplishment means that you spent your youth in exile in places like Rhodes and Athens. For the sake of my reputation and my political future, please allow me to remain my uncultivated self. My wife will be here before long, and she will talk philosophy, poetry, and drama until your ears turn to bronze."

"I've heard that well-born Roman ladies are often better educated than the men."

"It depends on what you think of as educated. Men study war, politics, law, government, and the arts of public speaking. It takes long study to become proficient in all of them."

"Caesar seems to be the master of all of them. Is this a step toward becoming master of all the Romans?"

This conversation was taking all sorts of wild detours. "Of course not. Rome is a republic not a monarchy. The closest thing to a master of all the Romans is a dictator. Only the Senate can elect a dictator, and then only for a period of six months at the most. The Senate and Caesar do not get along well at all." This was stating it mildly. Caesar treated the Senate with a contempt not seen since the days of Marius.

"Egypt is a monarchy," she said, "and has been for thousands of years. Your republic has existed for—what, about four hundred and fifty-two years, if tradition is correct about the expulsion of Tarquinius Superbus?"

"About that, I suppose." I tried to figure how many years that had been but gave it up. "But we've done rather well in our short history."

"You have indeed. But a government appropriate to a city-state is rather inadequate when extended to a vast empire, is it not?"

"It works superlatively," I protested, lying through my teeth. Our rickety old system was coming apart under the demands of empire, but I wasn't about to admit it to a foreign princess, however beautiful her eyes.

"I think your Caesar has different ideas. He seems to be a most remarkable man."

"Just another general," I assured her. "He's done all right, but look at Gabinius. I understand he's here on Cyprus. Until a couple of years ago he was as successful as Caesar and Pompey. Now he's twiddling his thumbs on Rome's latest acquisition, all because he flouted the laws. No mere soldier is greater than the Senate and People." A sanctimonious statement, but it was a sentiment I made a strong effort to believe in, despite all evidence to the contrary.

"That is another thing I do not understand," she said. "How can any nation prosper when its generals prosecute and exile one another? It was behavior of that sort that destroyed Athens."

"Oh, well, they were Greeks after all. How do you happen to be in Cyprus, Princess?"

"There have been some legal questions to sort out since you Romans deposed my uncle and drove him to suicide. I am here as my father's representative. He was understandably reluctant to come in person."

"I can't imagine why. You Ptolemies kill each other at such a rate he can hardly object to our getting rid of his brother for him." I had no personal animosity toward Cleopatra, but I was nettled by this unwonted anti-Romanism.

Her face flamed. "And took Cyprus from Egypt in the process!"

"That, of course, is negotiable. Cato tells me that Cyprus may be returned to Egypt if your father continues to adhere closely to our treaties."

"When did you Romans ever give back land once you had seized it?"

"I can't think of an instance right off," I admitted, "but I'm not here on a diplomatic mission. I'm chasing pirates."

"Oh, how exciting!" The animosity dropped from her like a discarded garment. "May I come along?" Now she sounded like what she was: a girl of perhaps sixteen years.

"That might not be wise. Most of my men are only marginally members of the human race, and a Liburnian is not a royal barge or even a halfway decent trireme."

"I have my own yacht here. It's a Liburnian for all practical purposes, fully armed, and my men are all experienced marines."

"Well, ah—" my resolve was crumbling.

"You probably need every ship you can get."

"That is true, but—"

"There, you see? And there is precedent. Queen Artemisia of Halicarnassus commanded ships at the battle of Salamis."

"So she did," I murmured. "Got out of it by a spectacular act of treachery, as I recall."

"A queen does what she must for the good of her kingdom," Cleopatra said. I should have paid more attention to that remark.

"Well, I have been instructed to continue the most cordial relations with your father, King Ptolemy." That was another whopping lie, "but you must understand that I am commander of this little fleet and your royal status gives you no military standing."

It may seem that I gave in rather easily, but it was by no means the beauty and famed charm of Cleopatra that caused me to do so. No, my motives were strictly military. Her yacht would give me four ships instead of three, and her hired thugs were undoubtedly at least as good as my own.

"That is understood," she said, beaming happily. "I'll just be another of your skippers." I have observed upon other occasions that royalty often display the most unaccountable fondness for playing the commoner. Kings sometimes don common garb and hang around the taverns; queens go to the country, pick up a crook, and pretend to be shepherdesses; princes and princesses don the chains of recalcitrant slaves and insist upon being ordered about for a while, discreetly. It is all very puzzling.

Shortly thereafter I retired to the bath and luxuriated for a while, being rubbed with scented oil, scraped with golden strigils—well, gold-plated, anyway, and stewed in an extremely hot *caldarium*. A couple of hours of that and I was ready for dinner. I sensed that I would not be living this well for long, so I was determined to make the most of it.

Dried off, smelling faintly of perfume, I was led to the main triclinium, of which this mansion had several, another departure from the Roman model. Slave girls draped me with garlands of flowers and placed a wreath of laurel leaves on my brow to ward off drunkenness. The need for such precautions boded well for the festivities to come.

Silvanus himself rose to greet me. He was a plump, sleek-looking man with crisply curled hair, the product of a hot iron and a skilled hairdresser. This was the sort of Oriental frippery we frowned upon in those days, but this was his house, he was laying on the feast, and he could dye his hair green for all I cared.

"Decius Caecilius Metellus the Younger," he proclaimed, "you bring great honor to my house! Please take your place by me. I trust you have been shown the most careful attention? I am so sorry that I was not here to receive you."

I flopped down on the dining couch next to him, and Hermes, who was already in place, took my sandals. I lay to Silvanus's right, the place of honor. He introduced me first to the man on his left.

"Decius, I believe you must know Aulus Gabinius?"

"All the world knows General Gabinius," I said, taking the proffered hand, which was big enough to envelop my own. "But we've never met personally. I've heard you speak many times in the Senate and on the Rostra, General, but in the years when I've been in office you've usually been off with the eagles."

"I've heard wonderful things about your double aedileship," he said, in a sonorous voice. "It's about time somebody used that office to get rid of the scoundrels instead of acquiring wealth."

Gabinius had one of those great, old-Roman faces, all crags and scars, with a huge beak of a nose flanked by brilliant blue eyes beneath shaggy, white brows. Except for the intelligence in those eyes and the trained orator's voice, he might have been one of those martial peasant ancestors we revere.

"It's how the job is defined by law," I said modestly. "I trust that your stay here will be short, pleasant as it must be to enjoy the company of our host. With all the glory you have brought to Roman arms, surely you'll be recalled from exile soon and put at the head of another army."

"My military days are over, I'm afraid," he said, with equal modesty. "I'm content to spend whatever days are left to me in retirement. Perhaps I'll write my memoirs, like Sulla and Lucullus."

Lying old bugger. No man who has sought supreme power ever really gives up his ambition, as witness Crassus and Pompey, who tried to be field generals long after they were too old for the job. It was clear that

Silvanus trusted him. If the position to the right of the host is the place of honor, allowing the host to serve the guest with his own hands, then the position to his left is the place of trust. This is because, in Roman-style dining arrangements, you present your back to the weapon hand of the man on your left.

Cleopatra was to my right, at the next table and couch, which were at right angles, as was the one opposite hers. This, at least, was in accordance with Roman custom. Next to the princess reclined a lady of great beauty and expensive tastes, the latter evidenced by her many jewels and her attention-grabbing gown, woven of the costly Coan fabric, which is light, soft, and all but transparent. The censors rail against it for its extravagance and immodesty, but I have always rather liked it. Assuming, of course, that the lady thus draped has a body worth viewing. This one did. Next to her was her far less prepossessing husband.

"Since you already know our royal guest," Silvanus said, "allow me to introduce Sergius Nobilior, chief of the Banker's Association of Ostia, now charged with putting the deplorable finances of this island in order. With him is his wife, Flavia."

They declared themselves honored to make my acquaintance, and I replied with equal insincerity. The custom of having women recline at table with the men was still rather new, and it was one of which I heartily approved. On the couch to my right, at least, beautiful women outnumbered ugly men two to one, and that is an improvement by anyone's standards, except perhaps for Cato's.

The remaining table was a different story. Two of the places were occupied by a pair of Cleopatra's tedious scholars, whose names I no longer recall. The final guest was a roguish-looking young man with a homely face and an engaging grin. Silvanus introduced him as Alpheus, a poet from Lesbos. He looked like more interesting company than any of the Romans present.

"What occasion are we celebrating?" I asked, waving an arm to indicate the many statues, which were draped with garlands.

"Just dinner," Silvanus said.

"I can't wait to see what the real banquets are like around here."

The first course was served. It was the traditional hard-boiled eggs, but these were from a vast variety of birds, lightly tinted in different colors and sprinkled with rare spices. The courses that followed were far more lavish as to ingredients, with items such as peacock brains, flamingo tongues, camel toes, honeyed ibex ears, and so forth, prized for their exotic origins rather than their savor. Others were both more substantial and delicious: Danube sturgeon, brought to the island in freshwater tanks; roast gazelle from Judea; and Egyptian geese baked in pastry stand out in my memory. All of this was served with numerous wines, each chosen to complement the course being served. Soon the wreaths and garlands were being put to the test.

"Commodore," Alpheus said, using my semiofficial title, "when do you propose to begin your pirate hunting?"

"Immediately," I said, then thought it over. "Actually, I need to receive word of their next depredation. That will give me a starting point and a locale to investigate. I also intend to recruit a few ex-pirates for their expertise."

"A wise move," Gabinius affirmed. "You may wish to begin by examining your own crew. If they're like other naval crews of my experience, half of them will have been pirates at one time or another."

"I suspect so, but none will admit it. They all claim they were part of Pompey's pirate-conquering navy, even the ones who were infants at the time."

"I recommend a tavern called Andromeda," Alpheus said. "The wine is passable, and the company is the lowest imaginable. If ever there was a pirate hangout, that is the one. I'm there most nights." Alpheus definitely sounded like my sort of man.

"I'll give it a try as soon as possible," I said.

"I'll go along with you," Cleopatra said.

"Respectable ladies do not frequent such places!" cried banker Nobilior, scandalized.

"I'm not respectable," Cleopatra told him, "I'm royal. Royalty do not have to observe these tedious little social rules. We are above them."

Gabinius chuckled. "Still, Princess, those places can be very dangerous. I advise against it." Silvanus nodded agreement.

"Nonsense," she said, with her dazzling smile. "Should the valiant Metellus and the brilliant Alpheus prove insufficient protection, I have my personal bodyguard." She gestured toward the door, where a young man lounged against the wall, arms folded, one sandaled foot propped against the wall behind him. He had Sicilian features and was dressed much like Hermes, in a brief leather tunic with matching wrist straps and hair band and girded with weapons. He looked half asleep, but so does a viper just before it strikes.

He looked rather familiar, then it came back to me. "Apollodorus, isn't it?"

The youth nodded. "Your Honor has an excellent memory."

"You were watching little Cleopatra's back when I saw her in Alexandria a few years ago."

"All that politician's training is good for something, eh, Metellus?" Gabinius said. "Caesar can call every man in his legions by name, and they say Crassus could not only put a name to every voter in Rome but could name the fellow's parents as well."

"In the Greek nations," Alpheus said, "we memorize poetry rather than names. I can't name one man in ten in my own city, but I can name every man slain by Achilles and where he came from."

This raised a good laugh, which shows how drunk we were all getting. When the eating was over and the serious drinking started, the ladies took their leave. I noted that Hermes and Apollodorus faced one another truculently, each taking the other's measure.

"There's a likely pair of fighting cocks," Gabinius said. "Who do you think would win?" It was an inevitable speculation. We were, after all, Romans.

"Cleopatra's boy was trained in the *ludus* of Ampliatus in Capua," Silvanus said. "Yours, Decius?"

"The *ludus* of Statilius Taurus in Rome. I've paid extra for the best trainers: Draco of the Samnite School, Spiculus of the Thracians, Amnorix of the Galli."

"You don't suppose—" Silvanus began.

"No," I said firmly. "I won't let Hermes fight professionally. It's not that he'd object, but that it's exactly what he'd like, and I've other uses for him. And I'm certain Cleopatra would never allow it."

"Just a friendly bout," Silvanus persisted, "a little boxing or wrestling, perhaps a match with wooden swords. No worse than a few broken bones, surely."

"Look at those two," said Gabinius. "It would be death for one of them if it came to blows between them." He was right. Their faces were studiedly indifferent, but if the two had had fur, it would have been standing up. It is the nature of aggressive, superbly trained young men to challenge one another and test themselves.

Silvanus sighed. "Too bad. It would be a fight worth seeing."

Then Alpheus diverted us with some extremely scabrous songs by the more disreputable Greek poets. Included among these was the poet Aristides. When a Parthian general found a volume of Aristides among the effects of an officer slain at Carrhae, he used it as proof of the depravity of the Romans. If some barbarian should ever go through my war chest, the reputation of Rome may never recover.

I don't remember much about the rest of the evening, which may be taken for the mark of a really successful party.

3

I ROSE RATHER LATE THE NEXT DAY. AFTER a substantial breakfast, bath, and rubdown I was almost ready to face direct sunlight. A little fresh air in the garden finished the job, and by a little past noon I was ready for anything—ready for a cautious walk through the town, at any rate. With Hermes at my back I descended the principal street. My destination was the naval docks, but where the street emerged onto level ground there was a charming market, laid out in the artlessly casual yet orderly fashion you only see in Greek colonial cities.

It was arranged in an irregular quadrangle, surrounded by tile-roofed stoas supported by gleaming white pillars, their rear walls decorated with beautiful paintings of historical and mythological subjects. In the shade of the stoas, small merchants offered their wares while farmers sold produce beneath colorful canopies scattered about the square.

In the center of the square stood a wonderful marble statue of Aphrodite in the act of tying up her sandal. The white marble was so perfectly polished that it seemed transparent. Save for the hair, which was gilded, the statue was not tinted in the usual fashion; and I found this to be an improvement. Painting of statues is too often overdone, and the effect is garish. The people of Paphos, at least, had excellent taste.

"May I interest you in a fine gown for your lady, Senator?" The voice belonged to a little, white-bearded fellow who looked Greek except for his pointed Phoenician cap. "These are of the finest silk, brought by camels all the long way from the land of the Seres, said to be produced in the mountain fastnesses of that land by giant spiders fed upon human flesh."

"I've heard it's made by worms," I said, feeling the weave of a Greek-style peplos. It was as smooth as water. Silk was still something of a rarity in Rome.

He shrugged. "There are many stories. Nobody has ever seen the land of the Seres. What is undoubted is that it is the finest fabric on earth: stronger than a ship's sail, light as a breath, so comfortable that a lady can go decently gowned from neck to toes and feel that she's naked. They find this most stimulating."

"That's the last thing my wife needs." Something occurred to me. "Isn't there some sort of Parthian monopoly on the silk trade these days?"

"King Hyrodes claims that privilege, but the caravaneers are adept at avoiding his customs collectors. Just now the trade lanes are open, courtesy of your General Gabinius."

No doubt, I thought, a large piece of the trade stuck to his fingers, too. Gabinius had been quite successful in the East, although he had not gained the sort of renown that Caesar and Pompey had acquired; but our generals were accustomed to enriching themselves at the expense of the barbarians, and Gabinius had done well out of his proconsulship.

I bade the silk merchant good-bye and continued my explorations. As one might expect in a sea-lanes emporium like Paphos, wares from the whole eastern sea were on display, some for domestic sale but most to attract other merchants who might buy in bulk for transshipment farther west. If a merchant had one fine glass vase on his table, he was sure to have a warehouse full of them down at the docks, ready to load up for you, cheap.

I stopped in the Temple of Poseidon and made the promised sacrifice and admired the wonderful statue of that maritime god, executed by Praxiteles more than three hundred years before. In the great days of the Greek colonies, each city had competed with all the others to commission the finest sculptures and paintings from the greatest artists. Paphos, it seemed, had done especially well.

"Where now?" Hermes asked, as we left the temple.

"The naval docks. It's time to act like an official."

The naval basin of Paphos lay to one side of the commercial harbor, just within the long breakwater built to protect the ships from the worst effects of storms. It was an artificial harbor forming a half circle lined with low-roofed stone sheds to accommodate thirty ships. Inside the sheds the floors sloped upward so that the ships could be floated in, their masts and oars removed, then hauled up out of the water for repairs: to have their bottoms scraped, tarred, and painted, or for other work. During the stormy season, the ships were stored in these sheds, high and dry.

This facility turned out to be in the care of one Harmodias, a retired naval shipmaster who took his time about responding to my shouts and door pounding. His office was a little house situated among the warehouses for naval stores next to the sheds. He opened the door, blinking his one eye and scratching in his beard, wrapped in a moth-eaten garment that was also the blanket he had been sleeping in.

"What's all this racket?" he demanded, last night's wine still strong on his breath.

"I am Senator Decius Caecilius Metellus the Younger," I announced grandly. "I bear a senatorial commission to scour this area for pirates."

He removed his hand from his beard and scratched his backside. "Well, good luck." He walked to a small fountain that bubbled into a shell-shaped basin near his doorway and plunged his face into the water, shook his head and blew a while, then straightened, wiping his face with a corner of the disreputable robe.

"I expect your cooperation," I said.

"If I had any to give, you'd be welcome to it," he assured me. "But, as you can see, Roman naval power on Cyprus is diminished since its days of glory."

"I noticed. What happened to the ships?"

He sat on a stone bench and worked his toes against the pavement as if they were numb. Clearly this man woke up a part at a time. "Well, let's see. Five years ago I had ten fine triremes, ten Liburnians, and five penteconters, perfectly immaculate and with all their gear. Then General Crassus wanted them for his Parthian war. After that, General Gabinius wanted them for his campaigns in Syria and Egypt. Last year, General Pompey requisitioned them and sent them out to support General Caesar's war in Gaul. That's where they are now, if they're still afloat."

"Generals put a high demand on Rome's military resources," I commiserated.

"You've got that right. When I first went to sea, it was admirals used the ships for sea battles. Now all the navy does is ferry supplies for the legions, get them across water obstacles, run errands for them, anything but cruise and fight. It's no work for a real sailor, I can tell you."

"Well, I've work for you now. I'm here with three ships—"

He snorted loudly. "Ships! I saw them yesterday. Senator, your ships are cockleshells, and your crews are scum. Go sacrifice to Poseidon and ask him to keep a wide stretch of water between your little fleet and those pirates."

"I've already sacrificed. I asked for good cruising weather, and Neptune is cooperating so far. I'll be needing arms and provisions, so if you'll kindly unlock your storehouses I will inspect what you have."

"That won't take long," he grumbled, getting up and lurching back into his house. He returned with a ring of massive, iron keys. He had straightened his clothing somewhat and now wore a patch over the ruin of his left eye. Fully awake and walking steadily, he looked more like my idea of an old salt relegated by age to shore duty.

"As you might imagine," he said, as he strolled toward the smallest of the storehouses, "our squabbling generals got most of the stores as well. I didn't want to be totally stripped, so I hid some of my stores on a farm inland. That way I'd have a little something should we have to deal with an emergency."

He twisted a key in one of the large, double doors and tugged it open. "I mean, if you have to, you can press a merchantman into service, even build a serviceable ship in a few days out of green wood if you've the carpenters for it. But try to come up with one of *these* on short notice." He slapped a hand down on a massive bronze object that rested waist-high on wooden supports. It was molded in a rough semblance of Neptune's trident, but it probably weighed four or five hundred pounds. It was a ship's ram, and there were ten more like it, each of a different shape: boar's head, eagle, thunderbolt, crocodile, and so forth, each of them capable of ripping a great hole in a ship's hull and sending it to the bottom.

"This is the arsenal. Shields are over there on that wall." He pointed to a wall covered with perhaps two hundred shields. "They used to cover all the walls and the ceiling beams. Swords are on those racks in the back. Bows and arrows are stored in chests in the rear room, along with barrels of lead sling pellets."

"Catapults?" I asked. "Ballistae?"

"Not a one. Gabinius got the last of them." He shrugged. "Those things deteriorate fast in storage anyway. Best to build new ones for each season's fighting."

The next building held spars, masts, oars, and other woodwork; another held sails and awnings; another chains, ropes, and other cordage. The whole lot: arms, wood, cloth, rope, and iron work would have fit easily into one of the buildings and left plenty of room to spare.

"What about provisions?" I asked, without much hope.

"Not a bite. What the generals didn't get, the mice did. Not so much as a sack of raisins left. I've plenty of good jars, but you'll have to fill them with wine, water, oil, and vinegar yourself. There are plenty of ship's victuallers in the town. I can tell you which of them are the least dishonest."

"I was afraid of this." As I pondered my dismal situation, I noticed a small storehouse separated from the others by some distance. "What's in there?"

"Pitch, paint, and naptha," Harmodias said. "That's why it's kept at a distance. One spark in there and the whole harbor could go up."

"Let's have a look at it."

"Whatever you say, Senator."

We walked to the small storehouse. Like the others it was stoutly built of massive stone, roofed with red tiles, its small windows covered with bronze grates. Even before the Greek got the door open, I could smell the contents. Even the pungency of the pitch and paint was overwhelmed by the powerful odor of naptha.

"Is the naptha for making fireballs?" I asked.

"Right. That's what these are for." He walked past the huge jars to a wooden bin, reached in and pulled out something that looked like a wad of hair the size of a man's head. "This is tight-packed tow, specially made in Egypt, where they grow all the flax. It's already had a light soaking in pitch. Just before you row into a fight, you soak it in naptha, put it in the catapult basket, touch it with a torch, then let fly. It really blazes in the air, a very pretty sight. Hit your ship right, and you can set it ablaze from stem to stern." He dropped the thing back in the bin, which held several thousand of them.

"You're fully supplied with these," I observed, "and with naptha, to judge by the smell. Why didn't Gabinius or one of the others take all this?"

31

He grinned. "Lots of skippers won't have the stuff on their ships," he said. "Scared of it. They'd rather fight it out hand-to-hand than risk setting their own ships on fire."

I walked along the rows of huge jars. "They got most of the pitch, I see." I paused among the jars of red and black paint, all of them full. "But they didn't take the paint. Why is that?"

"For all I know, Caesar wanted to paint 'em green or yellow. They took what they wanted and left me what they didn't. What I've got is at your disposal, Senator."

I walked out into the fresh air. "Well, it's not much, but you've done well to keep what you have. Generals with imperial ambitions are like locusts. They devour everything in their path. My crews are skimpy. I'll need to hire experienced men for this job. Have the generals swept up all of them as well?"

"Sailors we have plenty of, Senator. If you like, I'll pass the word and we can hold interviews right here. If you'll allow me to advise you, I'll know which are the real sailormen and which are idlers."

"That will be most helpful. I would like to begin tomorrow."

"You don't waste time."

"While we've been talking, a ship has been plundered or a coastal village attacked. I intend to put a stop to it."

"They'll be here at sunup, Senator."

"I'll be here a good deal after sunup," I told him, "but a little waiting won't hurt them." I took a look around, noted a long, low stone shed near the water, and pointed to it. "I take it that is the slave barracks. You should have a staff of more than a hundred public slaves. Where are they?"

"Take a guess."

"They went along with the fleet."

"Needed for maintenance and general labor, I was told. I'm supposed to get them back when the ships are returned. I'm not wagering my savings on it."

"I'll find skilled carpenters and at least one good smith in the city and send them here to build us some catapults. Can you direct them in the manufacture?"

"Easily. Get us some seasoned hardwood and the best cordage you can find. Weak rope is no good for ballistas."

I took my leave of him and turned my steps toward the waterfront. It was lunchtime, and I found a small tavern with tables in front beneath a grape arbor. Seated and starting on my first cup of wine, I said, "I can tell you're bursting to say something, Hermes. What is it?"

"No rations," he began, "no wine, no oil, not a single sack of dates or wheel of cheese. He hid arms and supplies, why not that? I'll tell you why: he sold it! As soon as Pompey's men were gone, every bite and sip of those provisions were in the market here and he's been getting drunk on the proceeds ever since. He's a rogue, and you shouldn't trust him."

"In all probability you are right," I told him. "But when generals and proconsuls act like thieves, why should we expect a low-level functionary to act any better? And he kept back something. It takes courage to keep something from the likes of Gabinius."

"If those storehouses had been completely empty, he'd have lost his job," Hermes groused, "so he had to keep something in them. Besides, he's a Greek."

"What else are we going to find in these waters? Until something better comes along, I'll put up with him, and don't you give him any of your insolence either—even if he is a Greek."

For a while I admired the sight of ships entering and leaving the harbor, which afforded a fine spectacle. The usual practice was to sail right up to the breakwater, then lower sails and run out the oars. The procedure was reversed when leaving. Unlike warships, which unvaryingly carried a single mast bearing a single, rectangular sail, merchant vessels often had two or even three masts and multiple sail plans. Where Roman warships were usually painted red and black, these were painted in a rainbow of colors, with fanciful bow and sternposts, the banners of many merchant companies and the protective devices of numerous gods.

"Look at that!" Hermes said. He pointed to where a sleek little vessel was raising its sail even though it was still within the harbor. It took me a moment to see what had surprised him so. The sail was bordered with purple. Not the cheap off-crimson tint that sometimes passes for purple, but the genuine Tyrian. It was an immense extravagance.

"That has to be Cleopatra's yacht," I said. "She must be aboard, drilling her crew. I fear that I'll regret allowing her to come along." I pondered the sight for a while. "She must have risen in her father's affections if he's allowed her a purple-bordered sail."

"I hear he's executed two of her sisters," Hermes said. "Maybe he values the children he has left all the more."

For the next hour, while we ate, Cleopatra's yacht maneuvered around the harbor, under sail and under oars, rehearsing all the actions of a naval battle and no doubt terrifying all the merchant skippers, some of whom almost suffered ramming. But the little ship was expertly rowed, its oars polished to such whiteness that they resembled ivory, flashing like wings as it darted about, nimble as a dragonfly.

"She's going to take some restraining when we sight real pirates," Hermes observed.

"All too true," I agreed. "In war there's nothing as dangerous as an enthusiastic amateur."

After lunch I called on the harbor master, a busy official named Orchus.

"How may I be of service, Senator?" His clothing was rich, his beard neatly curled and dressed with scented oil, an Oriental affectation coming into esteem in the eastern parts of the Greek world.

"From now on," I told him, "I want you to question the master of every incoming ship about acts of piracy in these waters: locations, dates, description of what goods or persons were stolen, and so forth. Have your secretary write up a daily report and deliver it to me at the house of Silvanus."

"It will be my pleasure to carry out your instructions," he said, "but I cannot vouch for the accuracy of the reports."

"You think the skippers would lie about this?"

"And why not? If a merchant captain is offered a cargo of fine wine at one third its market value, he will accept it and is not likely to speculate about its origin. On the contrary, he will sacrifice to Hermes in gratitude for this stroke of luck and will pray to encounter more of the same." Hermes is the god of thieves.

"But don't these merchants find it to be in their interest that Rome should scour pirates from the sea? Do the pirates not regard all shipping as prey?"

"Not always. They make certain not to alienate everyone. After all, they must sell their plunder somewhere."

"What about the captives? Surely they can report the sacking of their own towns."

"Here on Cyprus we do not deal in slaves. Almost all such are taken to the great market on Delos—if, that is, they cannot raise a ransom."

"This is scandalous," I said.

"Decidedly. It is also a tradition many centuries old, one with which Rome does not interfere, I might add. Rome needs slaves, too. And I am told the pirates are careful not to victimize Roman citizens."

"A sound policy. That was the sort of behavior that caused their downfall years ago. Well, get what you can out of them and send your reports on to me. I expect to be at sea a lot, but I'll send someone to pick up the reports at regular intervals."

"It shall be done."

"Let's go inspect our ships," I told Hermes.

"Haven't we had enough of them for a while?"

"I just want to see if Ion has sold them for firewood."

We found the ships hauled up onto a convenient stretch of sandy beach. The masts, sails, and oars were neatly laid out; the hulls propped up with timber balks; the sailors busily at work scraping the bottoms. Whatever his shortcomings, Ion was a thoroughgoing professional when it came to his vessels.

I found him squatting beneath one of the hulls, inspecting a plank that appeared to be nearing the end of its serviceable life.

"Why aren't you using the naval harbor facilities?" I queried.

"That's for bigger ships, and the sheds are for bad weather. If you want a good look at your ship, there's nothing like a good, sandy beach that won't scrape the bottom and bright sunlight to see by. I'd not have spotted the rot in this plank in the shade."

"Well, I won't advise you concerning your own work."

"Good. You'll need to buy pitch. All three hulls need treating."

"I see you didn't bother to go to the naval stores for it."

"Why bother? I haven't seen any naval stores in the last two years east of Piraeus. We need some cordage, and you might as well pick up some paint. It always makes the men feel better to start a cruise with the ships looking good."

"At least we have paint. Go to the naval yard and take all you need."

"Well, there's a miracle. Weapons?"

"Enough to take on another hundred marines and provide at least light weapons for extra rowers. We'll be looking over the available manpower tomorrow morning."

"I'll be there. Don't expect much."

"I've lived too long to expect much," I assured him, "but I want the best of what there is to be had in this place."

I spent an hour looking over the vessels and the men as if I knew what I was doing, a talent much needed by a man involved with politics. A Roman official is expected to be proficient in law, public speaking, administration, priestcraft, agriculture, and warfare. In reality, proficiency in law and rhetoric are sufficient. The rest can be handled by competent subordinates.

"Somebody's coming," Hermes said, pointing toward the water. A golden skiff manned by twenty rowers sped our way, oars flashing in perfect unison. When I say golden, I don't mean it was touched up here and there with gilding. The whole thing was gilded, a truly Ptolemaic affectation. It looked like a piece of the sun detached and come down to visit. In the prow stood a man in white livery trimmed with golden embroidery.

When the keel touched the beach, the rowers leapt over the bulwarks, grasped the boat, and lifted it onto the sand. They were a matched set, tall, long limbed, with skins just a little darker than the sand. Their hair was dressed like the square-cut Egyptian wig, and they wore the traditional linen kilt of that land—white as a candidate's toga. When there was no danger of getting his sandals wet, the man in the white tunic hopped ashore.

"Princess Cleopatra, daughter of King Ptolemy, sends greetings to the distinguished senator Decius Caecilius Metellus and invites him to join her aboard the royal galley *Serapis*." He had the high, fluting voice of a court eunuch. This did not mean that he was a gelding though. Sometimes court functionaries pitched their voices falsetto in order to sound like eunuchs, who enjoy special status at the Egyptian court. Greeks are unfathomable people to begin with, and the ones who run Egypt are stranger than most.

I climbed aboard, curious to see what sort of craft Cleopatra might consider a proper royal yacht. During my stay in Egypt I had seen the incredible river barges the Ptolemies amused themselves with: virtual palaces set atop two vast hulls, propelled upstream by thousands of rowers, like something the gods would travel in on their occasional forays to the world of mortals. Only logical, I suppose, when you consider that the Ptolemies, like the old pharaohs, tried to fob themselves off as secondrate gods. Divine or mortal, those barges impressed the common folk no end, and since most of the population of Egypt lives within sight of the Nile, they all got to see their resident god as he drifted past in splendor.

But I had paid little attention to the Egyptian navy. They own the greatest port in the world, but the Egyptians are not a seagoing people. Ships from every land that borders the sea and even those that lie on the ocean beyond the Pillars of Hercules send their ships to Alexandria to carry away grain and other goods, but few Egyptian ships ply the waters. I had always considered Egypt a naval nonentity.

The rowers set briskly to their oars, and we fairly flew out to the waiting vessel. As we drew nearer I saw that *Serapis* was a bireme of conventional design but higher of sides and wider of beam than most: neither as lean as a typical warship nor as tubby as a merchantman. Its ram was in the shape of a cobra's head, and the hull was painted crimson, trimmed with gilding. Along the rails I saw some serious-looking ballistas.

Cleopatra awaited me at the rail as a ladder was lowered to the boat. I scrambled aboard with little loss of dignity, closely followed by Hermes.

"Welcome aboard, Senator!" Cleopatra cried, as a little band of musicians shrilled on pipes, rattled sistra, and plucked harps. Slaves whirled small vessels of burning incense on golden chains, filling the air with fragrant smoke. A slave girl draped my neck with a wreath of lotus blossoms. Where they came from I have no idea.

"This beats anything the Roman navy has to offer," I told the princess. She wore a plain gown of white linen, almost as short as a hunting tunic and belted with a golden cord beneath which was tucked a small dagger with a golden hilt and sheath. On her feet were plain sandals of plaited straw.

"Would you like to inspect the newest vessel in your fleet?" she asked.

"I wouldn't miss it for anything. Lead on."

She led me along the narrow deck that ran the length of the vessel. To each side the heads of the upper-bank rowers poked above deck level. They sat at their oars perfectly still but sweating profusely. No wonder, considering the pace she had set tham that morning. They were powerfully muscled men with typically Egyptian faces, their heads shaven but protected from the sun by head scarves of white linen.

"Egyptians live on the river," Cleopatra said, "so we have an abundance of skilled rowers. These were chosen from the best, matched as to height and length of arm."

The deck beneath my feet was beautifully polished. All the workmanship I could see was far superior to what I normally saw on Roman ships. We climbed three steps to the forecastle, a small but crucial area of the ship where the ballistas were concentrated. Here stood about forty armed men in two ranks to each side.

"These are my marines. Their commander is Epimanondas. They are all Macedonians, chosen from my father's guard."

Macedonians, although they speak a dialect of Greek, are not to be confused with true Greeks, who are a degenerate and effeminate people. The Macedonians are primitive, ferocious, and probably much like our own Roman ancestors. These wore old-fashioned armor of bronze and layered linen and open-faced helmets of bronze, looking more like Homer's heroes than modern legionaries. This made sense, as a Roman mail shirt would quickly rust under seagoing conditions. They carried small, circular shields and held half-pikes at their sides. Their captain was a scar-faced veteran whose arms were a bit fancier than the rest but were still eminently serviceable.

"A fine pack of villains," I said approvingly. These men, at least, I was going to be glad to have with me on my pirate hunt.

"When do we commence operations?" Cleopatra asked. "I'm eager to begin." I had to remind myself that this queenly young woman was still little more than a girl. Only the very young or very stupid are anxious to go out and court death.

"I've alerted the harbor master to inform me the moment report of a pirate action comes to him."

"Well, you are the admiral, but it seems to me that the place to look for pirates is not where they've just been but where they are going to strike next."

"You are very perceptive," I commended her. "But we have to start somewhere. I hope that a pattern will eventually reveal itself and give us something to go on. In the meantime we will begin cruising. If nothing else, it will demonstrate Roman presence in these waters and drill our sailors in combined operations."

She smiled. "I'm ready now!"

"I can see that, but your rowers aren't. If you race chariots, you don't race the same team twice in the same day. Besides, tomorrow I plan to hire sailors and marines to fill out my crews. You are already splendidly manned. I suggest you rest your men tomorrow. We begin cruising the day after."

4

I ARRIVED AT THE NAVAL HARBOR EARLY, wide awake and clear-eyed. The night before, mercifully, Silvanus had decided to spend at the villa of Gabinius, allowing me to excuse myself from the evening revels without giving offense. I dined lightly in my chambers and rolled into bed early, all too aware of the rigors to come.

In the little plaza before the house of Harmodias, that worthy sat behind a wooden table with a scroll, ink, and reed pens before him. Beside him sat Ion. All around the plaza sat, leaned, or otherwise lounged a pack of nautical-looking men, perhaps two hundred of them. Some wore the brief tunics and caps of sailors, others had the sturdy physiques and multiple scars of professional soldiers. Some of the latter had arrived bearing their own arms and armor, and from the look of them they had deserted from every army in the known world.

"By Jupiter Best and Greatest!" I said to the two behind the table. "These look worse than the lot I already have!"

"Senator," said Harmodias, "if you're looking for schoolboys, we have an academy of decent repute right here in Paphos. Go over there and you'll find plenty of well-bred lads who can quote Pindar for you all day long."

"No need to be sarcastic," I admonished him. "I'm just expressing my disgust with the material, as has been customary with every recruiting officer since Agamemnon. All right, let's divide the labor. You two know sailors, so pick out what we need. I'll interview the marines. First, I'll address this pack and acquaint them with the situation."

I walked around in front of the table and looked over the assembled scum, letting them know how little pleased I was. They, in turn, looked less than impressed with me. I reached to one side, and Hermes slapped a sealed tablet into my palm. I held this aloft and proclaimed: "I am Senator Decius Caecilius Metellus! This is my commission from the Senate and People of Rome to scour these waters of the pirates that infest them! The job is pirate hunting; the pay is what every sailor in Roman service receives." The sour looks got sourer.

"On the other hand, I have wide powers of discretion concerning any loot obtained during this operation. I have drawn up a table of shares for every man who serves with me. What this means is that if you serve diligently, at the share-out—when we have bagged these pirates and their loot—each of you may depart with more money than you have ever seen." This was more like it. Grins began to appear on the villainous faces.

"All right!" Hermes announced. "I'm sure you've all done this before, so line up in front of this table, sailors to the left, soldiers to the right. Be ready to give your name and prior service, and no lies!" He sat and took his writing materials from his satchel.

The men shuffled into line and the first soldier appeared before me. He was typical of the lot: Macedonian helmet, Iberian cuirass, Gallic shield, Roman short sword, Greek tunic, Egyptian sandals. Physically, he looked like an African ape recently shaved.

"Name?"

"Leacus, sir. I'm from Thrace, most recently a light auxiliary in the army of General Gabinius." At least his speech was commendably military.

"Strip and let's have a look at you," I ordered.

"You're not buying a slave!" he said indignantly.

"No, but neither do I want to hire a cripple or a convict. Strip. To the skin."

He muttered, but he obeyed. It was only what every recruiter does if he has no one to vouch for a man. I was not really looking for the stripes of a runaway slave. Such men often as not make good soldiers. I was more interested in brands, notches, and other marks of the convicted felon, which are splendidly concealed by helmets and armor.

Unclothed, the Thracian even more resembled an ape, but I saw no incriminating marks, just battle scars on every unarmored surface. "You'll do. Next." Several men were already walking back toward the city, knowing that proof of their criminal proclivities would be exposed.

By midmorning I had picked nearly a hundred tough specimens. Before the naval base's small altar to Neptune, I administered the awesome oath of service to them and paid each the symbolic silver denarius. For the duration of their service they were immune from prosecution for past indiscretions, and any who attacked them were to suffer the punishment due to any foolish enough to take up arms against Rome.

Those who had no arms of their own were issued weapons from the arsenal, then we marched the lot, soldiers and sailors, to the beached ships. Men were assigned to each vessel; the sailors immediately set to the tarring and scraping, while I lectured the marines.

"If you are accustomed to normal naval operations, forget them. We won't be trying to sink our enemy's ships. Sunken ships can't be sold, and drowned pirates can't tell us where their base is. Keep that in mind. All the chasing around, looking for a few wretched raiders, has one real aim: we want to find out where their base is. That will be where they have whatever loot they haven't disposed of already. It's also where they'll have the captives they're holding for ransom. Some of these will be Roman citizens, and Rome wants them back.

"Finding the ships and catching them is up to the sailors. Once we're alongside, it will be up to you marines to capture them. Instead of the ram, we'll be using the *corvus*. Are you all familiar with this elementary device?" Most signaled they were, but I explained anyway because men tend not to admit to ignorance. "The *corvus* is a plank hinged to our ship at one end, with a big spike at the other. When we're close enough, we drop the spiked end onto the enemy's deck. At that time the two ships are effectively nailed together. We then walk across the *corvus* and proceed to kill or capture the pirates. The Roman Fleet used this tactic against the Carthaginians, and it worked splendidly. Our ships are not large, so our *corvus* can't be wide. We'll have to cross in single file. The first man on the *corvus* must be brave, but then he gets a double share of the loot, which is a great spine stiffener. Any questions?"

A Palmyrene named Aglibal spoke up, "It seems to me that the pirates may use the *corvus* to board our ship."

"There may be disputes concerning right-of-way on the *corvus*. I expect you men to win all such disagreements."

Once they grasped the essence of our tactics, I put them aboard the ships and drilled them in the intricacies of using the *corvus*. Crossing a plank may seem simple, but nothing is simple in battle. Interval is always crucial—keeping the men close enough together to support one another but far enough apart that they don't interfere with each other's fighting ability. Placement of the *corvus* would also be crucial, but that was up to the skill of the sailors.

With the ships beached, I drilled the men in disembarking over the bows. If we should be lucky enough to catch some pirates raiding a village, we would simply run our own ships up on shore and assault them, assuming, of course, that they did not greatly outnumber us. While we watched the men sweating through these exertions, Hermes voiced his doubts to me.

"You realize that many of these men have probably been pirates themselves?"

"Of course. It makes no difference. Loyalty to their former colleagues will weigh nothing against a rich payday in the offing. There isn't a man here who wouldn't cut his own brother's throat for a handful of coins. Our armies are always full of men we defeated in the last war. Professionals are always willing to change sides. Their loyalty is to their paymaster, and that's me."

"What about Cleopatra? She's just a girl playing at war. Suppose she doesn't like the look of the real thing? She might run at a crucial moment. That could mean disaster if we go in expecting even odds."

"I think there's more to Cleopatra than you see. She's grown up in a savage court, and she knows she'll need Roman favor in the future. If her little brother becomes king in accordance with our latest treaty with Ptolemy, she'll marry him. That will make her the real ruler of Egypt because he's an imbecile like most of his family."

"I hope you're right."

It may seem odd that I was having such a conversation with a slave, but I was grooming Hermes for better things. I had already determined to give him his freedom when we got back to Rome, and then he would be my freedman and a citizen as well as my aide and secretary as I assume the higher offices in Rome and the provinces. In a single generation our generals had nearly doubled Roman territory, with consequent increases in propraetorian and proconsular commands.

Things were reaching the point where, in some years, there were not enough consuls and praetors leaving office to staff all the new territories. Caesar's new conquests in Gaul, once pacified, would make at least two new proconsular provinces, and he had eyes on the island of Britannia. Soon, I thought, we should need to hold elections twice each year.

Late in the afternoon, Silvanus and Gabinius put in an appearance. They watched my men drill for a while, and Gabinius pronounced himself impressed that I had them shaping up so well in so short a time.

"I've no time to dawdle," I told him. "My best chance is to bag these pirates quickly before they get word that there's a Roman force after them. They'll hear about it in just a few days at the outside, so I want to take to the water after them as soon as possible."

"Very wise," Silvanus said. "I can see that you've been soldiering with Caesar. He acts faster than any general in Roman history. Even Sulla and Pompey were slow by comparison."

Gabinius snorted through his oversized nose. "If Pompey ever moved fast, he might arrive at the battle first and take some casualties. Can't have that."

I signaled to Ion, and he sounded a shrill blast on the silver whistle he wore on a chain around his neck. The men ceased their activities and gathered to hear me.

"That's enough for today. Starting tonight, you will all bunk in the naval facility. I want you ready to put to sea at a moment's notice, and I promise you it will be a short moment. You are to use only the taverns right here on the waterfront because I don't want to have to scour the whole city looking for you. Any man who fails to report for duty had better find a fast ship to some distant port because you have now taken the oath of service and I am empowered to administer any punishment I can imagine. You men don't want to learn about the depths of my imagination. Be here at dawn. Dismissed."

Silvanus had a litter big enough for the three of us, and I accepted his invitation to share it, leaving Hermes to make his way to our lodgings on foot. When the slaves picked up the conveyance and began their smooth pace, I learned what was on the minds of the two most powerful men on Cyprus.

"Commodore," Silvanus began, "you are the one with the commission from the Senate, and it is not my place to advise you, but I hope you will not be offended if I offer you some anyway."

"I am always happy to hear the opinions of men of distinction and experience."

"Then let me say that I believe it to be a grave mistake to allow Princess Cleopatra to join your flotilla. She is a charming girl and I have enjoyed having her as my guest, but she is no friend of Rome. She hides it well, but she bitterly resents our annexation of Cyprus and the death of her uncle."

"My flotilla is very small," I said, "and now I find that naval stores of all descriptions are in short supply or entirely absent, except for paint. Her ship is a fine one, better than any of mine, and its men, sailors and marines, are of the best quality. I need that ship."

"Then take it," Gabinius said, "but leave her ashore."

"It would be an intolerable insult to Ptolemy to commandeer his vessel and treat his daughter in such a fashion."

"Ptolemy is a buffoon and should be grateful for whatever bones get tossed his way from the Roman table," Gabinius said.

"Nonetheless, I want that ship, and I am inclined to humor Cleopatra." I was not sure why I was being so stubborn since the doubts they expressed echoed my own, but I had just been justifying myself to my own slave and exasperation was setting in. Also, I was not certain why they thought it to be a matter of concern to them, and such uncertainties quickly become suspicions in my mind.

"Let it be on your head," Silvanus said. "But, mark me, she will desert you in action or bring about some other mischief."

I found the lady herself waiting in my quarters when we got back to the mansion of Silvanus. She was dressed in a nondescript gown and behind her, as always, stood Apollodorus. With her was the merry-faced young poet, Alpheus.

"They've just arrived," Hermes said. He had reached the house ahead of us. "The princess says you have a previous engagement."

"Engagement?"

"Don't you remember?" Cleopatra said. "We are going out to the Andromeda to hire ex-pirates!" She smiled like a delighted child.

"I let it slip my mind. Anyway, I probably have more than we need. You should see the pack of villains I hired today."

44

"I'll bet you hired none who admitted to his old trade," Alpheus said. "And now they've taken your oath, they'll never own up to it."

"Come on," Cleopatra insisted, "join us. It will be far more fun than another drunken banquet."

"I like drunken banquets," I told her. "But since I agreed already, I'll go along." Actually, I didn't remember setting a specific date for this venture, but lapses of memory were nothing new to me.

"Good!" she cried, all but clapping her hands with glee. She stood and Apollodorus wrapped her in a voluminous cloak and drew its cowl over her head. Doubtless this suited her sense of drama, but it was not necessary. In plain dress and without her extravagant jewelry, she looked like any other lively Greek girl; attractive but not strikingly so, and with no visible clues as to her royal ancestry. I have noticed on many occasions that royalty often fancy that some look sets them apart from other mortals, as if their flesh shed golden rays, but I have never found this to be so.

I sent word to my host that urgent business called for my presence elsewhere and went out into the deepening dark with a pair of slaves, a poet, and the future queen of Egypt in search of the lowest sailor's dive in town.

The Andromeda was located near the docks, in a narrow street of low, single-story buildings, most of them devoted, in one way or another, to the maritime trade: warehouses, chandler's shops, the houses of ship-wrights and sailmakers, and, naturally, sailors' taverns. We knew we had the right place by its sign: the ever-popular image of a beautiful naked woman chained to a rock.

Inside it was typical of all such places all over the world. The ceiling was low, the atmosphere was smoky from the many lamps, and the predominant smell was that of spilled wine. Along one wall ran a long counter that held amphorae of wine, their mouths gaping invitingly. Several long tables ran the length of the room, and in the corners were a few smaller tables. There were probably fifty or sixty men in the room, most of them recognizable as sailors by their caps and their pitch-stained tunics, along with a few women of questionable station in life.

"May I find you a table, sir?" The barmaid was a good-looking young woman with the well-developed arms and upper body of one who hoisted heavy jars and pitchers all day long.

"You may," I said. "One of those corner tables, if you please."

As we wended our way toward the rear of the room, curious eyes followed our progress. Although on military duty, I wore a nondescript tunic and plain sandals. Nonetheless, nobody would take me for anything other than a Roman. Besides my classically Roman face, nobody else in the world stands or walks like a Roman. It is something drilled into us by the legions and the rhetoric schools, which emphasize stance and movement as much as voice, and there is no disguising it. Even Hermes, though born a slave of questionable ancestry, shared this bodily attitude, bestowed by his upbringing in Caecilian households.

Cleopatra, Alpheus, and I took our seats at a small, round table, while Hermes and Apollodorus stood behind us, each leaning against the wall, arms folded, one foot propped against the wall behind him, eyes scanning the room, studiedly ignoring the other.

"I've never been inside such a place!" Cleopatra said, her eyes sparkling beneath the cowl.

"I can well believe it," I said. "Ptolemaic princesses are gently if extravagantly reared. You may take it from me though that your father has been in many such." Gossip had it that old Ptolemy Auletes had made his living, when young, playing the flute in places far more disreputable than this one. Now that he was a king and a god, he sometimes missed the old days.

"Here," said Alpheus, "you have exposure to a different world. Heretofore your education has been that given by scholars and philosophers and courtiers training you for your future role as queen and mother of the next king. You know of the real world of the common people only from reading. It is not a bad thing for one who will one day rule to see at firsthand how most of the world lives."

This had a distinctly odd sound to me, but then the Greeks are different.

The barmaid arrived at the table with a large bowl divided down its middle into two halves. One held olives, the other parched peas and nuts: thirst-inducing snacks esteemed by tavern keepers the world over.

"Bring us a pitcher of Falernian," I said. "Don't bother with water."

"No Falernian," she reported. "We have Coan, Corinthian, Lesbian, Cretan, and we just got in some fine Judean. Have you ever tried Judean? It's wonderful." Having no reason to doubt her word, I ordered the Judean.

With my eyes adjusted to the dimness, I took a longer look at our surroundings. The walls were plastered white and covered with paintings and graffiti. The paintings were second-rate, mostly the usual sea-gods, tritons, nereids, and so forth. One wall had a depiction of the story of Perseus and Andromeda. The graffiti were no more than ordinarily scabrous, mostly of the cursing or blessing sort. Some, though, were in languages I could not read. I took some to be Persian, others Syrian. One of them, I swear it, was in Egyptian hieroglyphics.

"What do we do now?" Cleopatra asked.

"This is a tavern," I said. "We drink."

She frowned. "We can do that anyplace."

"We can't rush things. I can't very well stand up and announce my intentions. It wouldn't look right. We'll have to wait and be approached."

"How will anyone know who you are?"

"They'll know," I assured her. "They knew the moment I walked in here."

The wine arrived and the Judean proved to be as good as the girl had promised and of a pale rose color I had never seen before. Since Cyprus lay close to Judea, it could travel there without suffering the usual deleterious effects of a long sea voyage.

Alpheus regaled us with stories of the gods and how they had disported themselves on Cyprus and in its surrounding waters. He was a most ingratiating companion, and it was a good thing for him, since it was how he made his living. As the evening rolled pleasantly by, I saw a few of my own men, but they faded back out when they caught sight of me. No man feels comfortable carousing under the eye of his commander.

"Decius," Cleopatra whispered, touching my arm, "over there, that corner table opposite ours—doesn't that woman look familiar?"

I squinted in that direction. At a small table a woman sat between two burly, bearded men. From both sides they leaned close and spoke into her ears. I suspected they were not discussing the price of copper in the Paphos market. The woman had let her cloak fall back far enough to reveal a good-quality gown skimpy enough to reveal the greater part of her prodigious breasts. Nobody's hands were above the table, but they seemed to be busily employed. The woman's flushed, laughing face looked decidedly familiar.

"Isn't that Flavia," Cleopatra asked, "the banker's wife?"

I looked again. Her dark hair hung loose to her shoulders, meaning she had been wearing a blonde wig at the banquet two nights earlier. It was definitely Flavia.

"The lady seems to enjoy slumming," I said. "She wouldn't be the first rich woman I've known to supplement a fat, old husband's inadequacies with virile if lowborn company." I could have named a score of noble Roman ladies who could have given this one lessons in scandalous deportment, but it has never been my habit to gossip.

"Pretend we haven't seen her," Alpheus advised, relishing the whole business. "Otherwise she might be embarrassed next time we see her with her husband—was his name Nobilior?—at the house of Silvanus."

Moments later, while the princess and the poet were deep in conversation, I happened to glance toward the corner table and saw Flavia staring straight into my eyes. She wore a loose, lazy, slightly drunken smile as she shrugged a shoulder and let her gown fall, revealing one amazingly bulbous breast. It was quickly captured by one of her companions, who began to maul it mercilessly with a broad, calloused hand while she smiled at me triumphantly and her lips formed a word I could not understand. No, we were not likely to embarrass this woman.

"Are you the Roman sent out here to hunt pirates?"

My attention was distracted from the woman to a man who stood by our table, and he was a riveting specimen. Deeply tanned like all sailors, his powerful body was covered with old scars, and they were from battle not the public torturer. His tunic was even scantier than that worn by Hermes and exposed a great deal of this scarred flesh. Tucked into his rope cincture was a large, curved dagger. Most astonishingly for these waters, the man's short-cropped hair was pure blond, almost like a German's. His eyes burned a brilliant blue above his blocky cheekbones. His feet were bare.

"From the look of it, I've found one. Who are you?"

"Ariston," he said, pulling up a stool and sitting without waiting for an invitation.

"That's a Greek name, and you are no Greek," I said.

"You couldn't pronounce the one I was born with. It doesn't matter. I've been using this one for thirty years or more, and I'm used to it."

"Where are you from? I've never seen anyone quite like you, and I've traveled more widely than most."

"I was born on the steppe beyond Thrace, to the north and east. When I was a boy my tribe was wiped out by another, and the children were marched to the Euxine Sea and sold to slavers there. I was bought by a shipmaster and have lived on the sea ever since."

I gestured for the serving girl. "Bring us another cup." She returned with the requested vessel, and I filled it. Ariston took it, poured a small libation, and drank.

"You must be a Roman all right," he said, wiping his lips with the back of a scarred hand. "You can afford the best."

"And I can afford to pay well for the services I require. I presume you are interested in offering such?"

"If we can come to an agreement." He glanced at Cleopatra, raised almost invisible eyebrows. "You're that Egyptian princess, aren't you? The one who's been playing admiral out in the harbor."

"You don't seem greatly awed," she noted, flushing slightly.

"I've had princesses bent over the rail of a captured ship with their wrists tied to their ankles. They're much like other women, and they don't bring as much ransom as you'd expect. Kings produce lots of them and have plenty to spare."

Apollodorus began to uncoil from the wall, and Ariston glanced up at him. "Easy, boy. I'm no threat to your lady; and if she can't take the conversation in a place like this, she can stop her ears with wax like Odysseus or go seek company of her own kind."

"It's all right, Apollodorus," Cleopatra said. Slowly he relaxed, but his dark eyes burned. Hermes smirked faintly at his discomfiture. I glared at Hermes, and his face went aloof again.

"I take it," I said, "that you have sailed with these pirates I am looking for?"

"If I hadn't I wouldn't be of much use to you, would I? Yes, I sailed with them for a while. I won't give you the names of any towns we raided or ships we took because I don't feel like being crucified just yet."

"You'll be safe once you take my oath of service," I told him, "but I won't feel inclined to take you on without more than you've just told me."

"That is fair. To begin, fifteen years ago I was a sailor aboard the *Scylla* in the fleet of Admiral Lichas, based in Cilicia. When Pompey swept down upon us like a storm, I surrendered with the rest. We were taken inland to be settled in a new town in Illyria, but I was never meant to be a farmer so I made my way back to the sea and signed on to the first ship that passed.

"I've been plying the sea ever since, all over the Euxine, the Great Sea, and even beyond, all the way to Britannia. But it's a tame life once you've known pirating."

49

"I can imagine," I said. "Most soldiers I know complain about peacetime—no towns to burn and sack, no women to rape, no men to torture and kill to get at their belongings, no parades, dragging the captives behind you while the citizens sing of your glory."

He nodded. "It is tedious. Imagine how your soldiers would feel about fifteen straight years of peace."

"They would find it intolerable," I agreed. "So when the opportunity arose to go back to piracy, you didn't hesitate?"

"Not for an instant. I was in Piraeus when I heard that some men were setting back up in the old business. I knew they would be needing experienced men, so I took ship for Cyprus and made contact with them."

"Cyprus?" I said. "You mean they're based here?"

"This was six months ago. They had a base on the other side of the island then. The base changed three times just during the time I was with them: a place on the Lydian mainland called Pyrios, a little island near Rhodes, then a cove on Crete that the locals call the Beach of Crabs."

"Who is their leader?"

"Last I heard, a man named Spurius."

"That's impossible. Spurius is a Roman name."

"Well, it ought to be, since he's a Roman. I've always heard that Romans will steal anything, anywhere, so why not at sea?"

I had no good answer for that. As I have said, we are not a nautical people, but there was no reason why some Roman should not set himself up as a pirate chief.

"Ariston," Cleopatra said, "what made you leave these pirates? It sounds as if the life suits you well." She displayed not the slightest distaste for this seafaring murderer, only a lively interest. If she wanted to see real life, she was getting it by the bucketful in this place.

"The old life suited me well, but not this. You see, in the old days we were the kings of the sea. The pirate fleets ruled the waters from the Euxine to the Pillars of Herakles and beyond. We rowed right up to Roman ports and bared our buttocks at them. Kings of the land payed us tribute just to make us go away. We blockaded whole cities and made them ransom themselves. We gilded entire ships and hoisted sails dyed with Tyrian purple. *That* was living the way a pirate should!" He looked morose.

"This new lot are not worthy of the old fleets. With a few, miserable Liburnians they skulk about, raid small villages, and take merchantmen—as long as there's not another sail in sight. It's too paltry for me. In the fleet of Lichas I rose to command a trireme! We went ship-to-ship with the fleets of Bythinia and Rhodes and sent them scurrying back home."

"Until Rome came and swept the sea clean of you," I said.

"Rome ruins everything for everybody," he said, then grinned crookedly. "Well, that's how the wheel of Fortuna turns. Now Rome is at the helm, and I'd rather serve a first-rate power than despoil goatherds and take defenseless ships hauling wool. My pride won't take it."

"How do you propose we find these pirates?" Alpheus asked.

Ariston cocked his head toward the young man. "Who's he?"

"I am a poet."

"He's not sailing with us, is he?"

"No," I answered, "but she is."

He rolled his eyes. "This is going to be an interesting voyage."

Cleopatra smiled sweetly. "Don't expect me to bend over the rail for you, tied or untied." A bit of the murderous Ptolemy showed through her polish.

"Alpheus's question was a good one," I said. "Just how do you propose we find them? It's for just such advice that I will be hiring you."

He lifted his cup. "I think that should wait until after I've taken your oath and accepted your silver denarius."

I dipped into my purse and took out a denarius. "Here," I said, tossing it to him. "This is your provisional enlistment, as witnessed by Princess Cleopatra, who is now one of my officers. You are now under Roman protection. When we leave here, come with us. I'll find you a bunk in the house of Silvanus for the night. You've been seen talking with us, and your life is no longer worth that denarius in this port."

He grinned, showing not a single empty space among his white teeth. I considered it a good sign that a veteran brawler of his years still had all his teeth. Then his grin faded. "I'd feel better if you gave me the oath right now." He had a true sailor's reverence for the supernatural powers.

"We need an altar for that," I said. "You can take the oath tomorrow at the naval base."

"We pass the Temple of Poseidon on the way back to the house of Silvanus," Alpheus suggested. "Why not give him the oath there?"

"Good idea," I said. I picked up our pitcher and peered into its faintly damp bottom. "Time for more." I signaled for the barmaid, and she came scurrying over.

"Who knows?" said Alpheus. "We might have a whole crew of men like Ariston recruited before it is time to leave."

"I have a feeling there are very few men around here like Ariston," Cleopatra said, eyeing the man coolly.

He grinned again, "You have that right, Princess."

The wine arrived quickly, and we drank to our new recruit. Cleopatra asked for another song from Alpheus, but he protested that he was sung out for the moment and reeled off in search of the jakes. So, willful as a child, she demanded pirate stories from Ariston. He complied happily, and she gave him her rapt attention.

Alpheus slipped back onto the bench beside me and whispered, "Look over there." He nodded toward the corner where Flavia lounged, her gown fallen to her waist and no fewer than six sailors surrounding her. Her face was flushed crimson, and she laughed loudly as they took liberties with her. "Do you think she'll take them on each in turn or all at once?"

I pondered the logistics. "Common wisdom holds that a woman can properly entertain no more than three men at once, since the gods have bestowed upon her only that many orifices suited to the task. If she is dextrous with her hands in spite of such distractions, she may deal with two more. I've known certain wonderfully trained courtesans who can manage five to the satisfaction of all involved. But six? I would think that unlikely."

"I would like to watch just to find out," he said. "Do you think she would object if I were to go over there and suggest it?"

I considered this. The evening had reached the stage where this seemed like a reasonable proposition. "Best not," I said. "I may need to borrow money from her husband before my business here is over. The Senate has granted me its usual, niggardly budget for this project, and I may well exceed it soon."

"Pity," he said wistfully. "It would be a spectacle worthy of a poem in the style of Duris." He referred not to the Samian historian, but to the Ionian poet of the same name, whose works were not only forbidden in Rome but were regularly seized and burned even in Greek cities, and you can't get much more salacious than that. I had paid dearly in hard coin for my own collection of his works.

"What are you two talking about?" Cleopatra demanded.

"There are some aspects of real life," Alpheus said, "that should wait upon greater maturity and sophistication, Princess."

Before long it was clear that we would get no more recruits that night. The place began to empty, and soon I saw that even Flavia of the heroic appetites had retired somewhere with her six salty swains. Eventually, I stood.

"Time to go," I said. "We must be at the ships early. I want to take them out on patrol, even if we've had no word of a pirate strike."

"Are you sure you can walk?" Cleopatra asked.

"Princess," I replied, "a Roman officer can walk where other men can only crawl."

"That makes no sense whatever," she observed.

"He is a Roman," Alpheus told her. "He was trained in rhetoric, not logic."

I paid our score and bought a small jug of the best-quality wine to be had at the tavern. At the door Hermes and Apollodorus took small, oil-soaked torches from the jar provided by the management.

"Apollodorus," I said, "you walk ahead of us. Hermes, come along behind."

"My place is at my lady's back," the Sicilian boy said adamantly.

"You can't talk to the senator like that!" Hermes cried. "Get up front or I'll ram that torch up—"

"*I* shall lead the way," Alpheus proclaimed grandly, seizing a torch and lighting it at the door sconce, "as Orpheus led Eurydice from the realm of Tartarus."

"With happier outcome, I hope," Cleopatra said, giggling girlishly.

"Thanks," I whispered to the poet.

He winked. "How are we to teach our slaves manners if not by modest acts of diplomacy?"

We set off with the poet in front and the two slaves stalking along behind, stiff-legged as a pair of Molossian fighting hounds sniffing each other's backsides. I could see that I was going to have to do something about those two before much longer.

"His heart full of joy," Alpheus proclaimed as he stepped forth, "the Thracian made his way from the gloomy palace of terrible Hades, and close behind followed his beloved Eurydice, at whom he durst not gaze until both should stand beneath the blessed light of Apollo.

"Past the Three Judges their steps took them, and by the lovely song of Orpheus the eyes of Minos, Rhadamanthus, and Aeacus were dazzled and their souls were filled with bliss. Monstrous Cerberus laid his three heads upon his paws and allowed them to pass unharmed, his savage heart soothed by the divine music.

"Through the sad Asphodel Fields did Orpheus lead his darling wife, victim of the serpent's sting, and the jealous shades gathered round but hindered them not, for in the rapture of the Thracian's song their thirst for blood was slaked, and they remembered the joys of their mortal lives, and knew peace."

We turned a corner and climbed the main street, the voice of Alpheus echoing from the whitewashed fronts of the buildings to either side.

"At the shore of the Styx, that black river which is a terrible oath, the fingers of Orpheus drew from his lyre so sweet a tune that the turbulent waters calmed and became as polished bronze, and ancient, cankered Charon, drawn by the heavenly music, brought his ferryboat to shore, though never before had he fetched his passengers from the Tartarus shore, but only those unhappy shades destined to go there, never to return.

"From the prow of Charon's barge stepped Orpheus onto land, his beloved Eurydice but a pace behind, amid the batlike twittering of the hopeless shades gone thither with no coin beneath the tongue to pay the ferryman.

"Up the long, long cavern they climbed, Eurydice fallen behind in the gloom, unable to see her husband, guided by his wonderful music, sweet to her ears as light. In time before them, tiny as a star in the distance, lay the mouth of the cave, at Aornum in Thesprotis.

"At last bold Orpheus, he who dared enter the dread land of Hades, went forth into the holy light of Apollo, and with a final note ended his incomparable song, and turning to let his eyes drink in the sight of his beloved wife, saw to his horror that she still stood the distance of but a single pace within the mouth of the awful cave. Alas! But a moment's vision had he of his beloved, and with a despairing cry she faded from his view, to return to the home of the pitiless Lord of the Underworld, there to dwell forever."

Alpheus ended his song neatly just as we arrived before the Temple of Poseidon. We applauded him heartily, even Ariston, who didn't impress me as much of an aesthete. As lyric poems go it wasn't all that distinguished, a minor variation on a well-worn theme. Plus, as I remembered the sequence of steps to the Underworld, Cerberus stood on guard between the Styx and the Asphodel Fields, not between the fields and the home of Hades.

But, considering that it was composed extempore, in a fog of wine fumes, and timed perfectly to end at our destination, Alpheus had earned his applause.

"Now, Ariston, come with me. Princess, I take it that you have been trained in hieratical duties?"

"I am a priestess of Isis, an initiate in the Eleusinian Mysteries, the Cult of Dionysus, and—"

"We don't need anything that specialized. I just need you to act as witness and pour the sacrifice at the proper moment."

So we climbed the steps to the splendid altar that stood before the temple. With Cleopatra holding the wine jar, I borrowed Hermes's sword and, grasping it by the sheath, held it out toward Ariston, who placed his horny palm on its hilt. Then I administered the oath, which is a sacred thing and not to be written down. At the required moment, Cleopatra poured the wine onto the altar and we watched as it ran down the blood channel to the drain that would carry it to the earth below.

"That's that, then," I said, tossing the weapon back to Hermes. "Welcome to the service of Rome. Stay in the navy for twenty years, and you'll be rewarded with citizenship."

Ariston laughed loudly. "So that I can spend a few years of doddering old age privileged to vote some thief into office?"

"You could take up residence in some thriving little municipality, get elected to office, and line your own purse. Plenty of clever veterans have done that."

"The wonders of living in a republic," Cleopatra said bemusedly.

We began to stroll across the plaza toward the governor's mansion when I stopped in my tracks at an all too familiar sound: a triple slither of blades leaving sheaths. Hermes, Apollodorus, and Ariston had drawn in the same instant. I had heard nothing to alarm me, but that didn't slow me down. My hands dived into my tunic and emerged with my dagger in my right fist and the spiked, bronze bar of my *caestus* across the knuckles of my left. I scandalized my family by brawling with such low-bred weapons, but they had saved my life in too many dark streets for me to entrust it to any others.

"How many?" I asked.

"We'll know soon," Hermes said.

"Hold this," Apollodorus said, handing his torch to Cleopatra. She took it, eyes gone wide as he took his position just behind her to the right, where he could keep her in view and she would not interfere with his sword arm. He would ignore the rest of us, but nobody would touch Cleopatra while he was alive. Hermes stood back-to-back with me, and Ariston stood half crouched a few feet away, his eyes darting in all directions. Alpheus stood rigid, his torch held aloft, eyes bugged out in astonished terror.

All this was the work of an instant, and in the next instant they attacked.

With a hideous screech, they closed on us in a half circle. I had no time to make a count, but I knew they outnumbered us grievously. Well, I'd been in that situation before. The answer was to carve down their numbers as quickly as possible. I was surrounded by glittering metal and then the first of them was on me in a wash of wine-and-garlic breath. He cut high, going for my throat, and I ducked low, stepping in to drive my *caestus* into the bundle of nerves in his armpit. He squawked at the unexpected pain, and I drove my dagger in somewhere in the vicinity of his midriff.

The man dropped away from me just in time for me to see one dart past Cleopatra. Apollodorus thrust his sword out almost lazily, and the man stopped with a look of wonder as a great fountain of blood erupted from his throat. The really great swordsmen always seem to move slowly. Then I had no more time to appreciate his technique as another was on me. Meantime I could hear a series of grunts behind me and hoped that Hermes was coping well, as my back would feel terribly bare otherwise.

My new admirer wore a short coat of Gallic mail and had a curved sword in one hand and a small fist shield in the other. He had come ready for war, and here I was, half naked and slow with all the wine I had put away. The sword flicked toward my eyes, and I batted it aside with the *caestus,* but it was a ruse. His real blow came from the little shield. Its iron edge came down on my right forearm just behind the wrist, and I heard my dagger hit the pavement an instant before the shield came in a second time, driving into my ribs and sending the wind from my lungs in a great blast.

Lights flashed before my eyes as I fell. My back hit the pavement and I saw, upside-down, Hermes fully occupied with a man who swung an iron-tipped staff in both hands. No help to be had from that direction. I tried to draw my legs in for a desperate kick, but I knew it was too late: the curved sword was already drawn back for the deathblow. All I could think was: *It is good to die immediately after sacrificing. Neptune will intervene for me with the Judges.* My father would have commended such a pious last thought, though he would have cursed me for a fool for dying in such a fashion.

Then a broad shape came between me and my would-be murderer. Ariston, crouched low, thrust a massive shoulder into the fellow's midsection, bending him almost double. With a heave of powerful thighs, the ex-pirate sent him almost straight up, turning over end-for-end. Incredibly, Ariston spun and brought his broad-bladed knife down in a shearing blow, and the man landed on his back in a clashing of mail, half-beheaded.

Then there was silence until I heard a low whistle. "Will you teach me that move?" Hermes, naturally.

"I am glad," I wheezed, "that you are so solicitous of your half-slain master."

The boy helped me to my feet. "I've seen you half killed a dozen times. You don't get to see a move like that every day."

"Many thanks, Ariston," I said. "I can see already that I did the right thing recruiting you."

"What is going on here!" shouted someone. Then I saw Silvanus coming across the plaza with five or six slaves holding torches and staves. With him was Gabinius, accompanied by a grizzled man who had the look of a retired centurion. Both old soldiers held heavy, legionary swords in scarred fists.

"Just a small ambush," I said, "nothing to concern yourself about." My studied nonchalance was spoiled by the searing pain in my side. If I'd been fully sober it never would have happened.

"Princess!" Silvanus cried, "Are you well?"

"Perfectly unharmed," she said, her voice breathless and excited. "I don't believe this attack was meant for me." Beside her, Apollodorus cleaned his blade on the tunic of the man he'd killed. I felt a hand clap my shoulder and turned to see the elated face of Alpheus.

"That was splendid! I shall compose a poem on this fight!"

I wiped a hand down a half-numb face. "Poets sing of battle," I said, "not sordid little brawls like this."

"What do you think went on before the walls of Troy? Just a brawl." He smiled and shrugged happily, verses already running through his head no doubt.

Gabinius examined the carnage. "Looks like the Senate steps back to the old days." Five bodies lay there. I spotted the one Apollodorus had eliminated so elegantly, the one I had killed, and the one Ariston had eliminated. The staff man lay gurgling, bloody froth bubbling from a gaping chest wound. An unarmored man with a short sword had his hands full taking on a good man with a staff. Hermes had learned well.

"Who got this one?" I asked, pointing to an eviscerated man who lay nearby.

"He's mine," Ariston said. "And I sent another running with an arm cut half through. He should be dead by morning."

"Then you get a high score for tonight's work," I commended him. "How many were there altogether?"

"I counted eight," Alpheus said, "There were two who hung back and ran when they saw their companions bested."

"Did you see anyone just standing back and watching not taking any part?"

"No, but I wasn't looking back there in among the alleyways. I confess I was overcome with fear. I should have paid more attention."

"You did all right. I—"

"Metellus," Silvanus bit out, "how dare you risk the life of the princess like this? If the Senate heard—"

"Not here in front of foreigners!" Gabinius snapped. "Let's go inside and talk." This was eminently sensible advice.

A few louts from the night watch arrived, and Silvanus pointed to the staff man, who still breathed. "Take him to the lockup and put the hot irons to him. I want to know the name of whoever put these men up to this deed. Promise him a quick death if he talks."

"The one I cut must be leaving a trail like a gutted boar," Ariston said.

Gabinius turned to the grizzled man. "Take two of these men and follow the blood. Bring me back a live man or a dead one, but live by preference. You know how to make them talk." The old centurion nodded shortly, then pointed a blunt finger at two of the watch, "You and you. Come." Off they went like hounds on a scent.

We walked back toward the mansion, Silvanus bubbling apologies the whole way. "Princess, I cannot tell you how sorry I am that this has happened. Please assure your father—"

"Nonsense. All turned out well, and it was most exhilarating. Please don't concern yourself on my account. They were after the senator."

"You might've been the target," Gabinius said, bluntly.

"I don't see how—"

"You're worth a good bit of change now, with your older sisters dead and you set to marry your brother after the Egyptian custom. Auletes would pay handsomely to have you back."

"Exactly," said Silvanus, as if he had been thinking the same thing. "Naturally these rogues would eliminate your protection, first the senator and his guard and this ugly fellow I don't know, then Apollodorus, then just bag you and carry you off to their ship."

"Oh," she said, her face suddenly grave.

"Hermes," I said, "Take Ariston back to our quarters and find him a place to bunk down."

"Come along," Hermes said, regarding Ariston with a certain admiration. Well, it had been quite a feat, even though it galled me that I had needed another man to save my neck.

"And now, Senator," Silvanus said, "we need to talk."

All I wanted was a hot bath and a good night's sleep. The hot blood of combat had cooled, the wine I had drunk was causing my head to ache, and I was pretty certain that I had a cracked rib or two. But there was no help for it. Duty comes first for any servant of the Senate and People of Rome. I followed the two into Silvanus's study.

5

IN THE STUDY GABINIUS AND SILVANUS waited while the household physician examined me. My right wrist and forearm throbbed worse than my head, but there was no break. A great bruise was already spreading over my right side, and the man's probing fingers drew new pains from that vicinity.

"There may be cracked ribs," he reported, "but there is not enough movement to indicate complete fracture, so there should be no puncturing of organs. You will have to wear a tight bandage for a few days, but this should heal easily." With an assistant's help he wrapped me from hip-bones to chest with enough linen to keep a pharaoh safe for eternity, but at least he didn't insist on packing it with foul-smelling poultices like many physicians. Thus wrapped I was uncomfortable, but the pain subsided markedly.

"And now, Senator," Silvanus began, "perhaps you could tell us of your evening's activities." Pointedly, he did not offer me any wine. For a change I was not in the mood for any.

"First, let me make a few remarks. Silvanus, you are governor here and out of respect for your office I will cooperate with you. Aulus Gabinius,

I am a Roman official on duty. You are an exile with no legal or political standing. Like all of Rome I am in awe of your distinguished career and your great military services to the state, but you have no say in my activities here."

His face clouded, but he had no basis for protest. "That is understood. I will take my place in the Curia once more. In the meantime, I help my friend Silvanus in his duties as governor of Cyprus."

"Very well. This is what happened." And I gave them the story of the night's events. Of course, I felt under no compulsion to give them all the details. For instance, I left out the business about the lady Flavia and her drinking companions. I wished now that I had paid more attention to the men and less to the woman. It was not unthinkable that some of them were among my attackers. I had no good reason to suspect her, but at this point I considered everyone suspect, including the two sitting across from me. In those days it was no unusual thing for senators to plot murder against one another if there were any political or monetary advantage to be had. I was in a completely unfamiliar situation, and only a fool assumes a stranger to be a friend without plenty of proof.

"I'm no trained logician," I said, wrapping up my story, "but I've spent many hours in conversation with Cicero and he's taught me a bit about the subject, which is always helpful in legal cases. First, eliminate the most unlikely possibilities. It was not just a pack of thieves out for loot."

"Not likely," Silvanus said. "There are plenty of wealthy merchants reeling home drunk every night. No idiot is going to attack a band with trained bodyguards for what might be in their purses."

"The whole city knows you're here to crush the pirates," Gabinius said. "Most likely that's what they were—pirates who wanted to get you first."

"Or thugs who wanted to ingratiate themselves with the pirates," Silvanus put in.

"Or hirelings of some merchant who has been getting rich receiving pirate loot," I said. "Yes, the list of possibilities is a long one. Political motives, anyone?"

"Cleopatra wanting to do Rome a dirty turn?" Silvanus hazarded. "I'm still not clear on why she came here in the first place, and as her host I can't very well ask probing questions."

"I think that very unlikely," I said.

Gabinius grinned maliciously. "She got you out into the street at night, didn't she? None of this night's little adventure was your idea, if we're to believe you. She could've set the whole thing up."

That blow struck home. No man likes to admit he's been manipulated, especially by a mere girl, however royal. "Apollodorus killed one of them," I protested lamely.

"The boy may not have been in on it," Silvanus said. "In any case, he'll automatically kill anyone who gets too close to his mistress in a situation like that."

"Or she may've told him to kill one just to take suspicion away from her," Gabinius pointed out with some relish. "Maybe she figured seven would be plenty to deal with a half-drunk senator and his slave. She didn't bargain on that ugly villain you hired. Nobody expected him to fight like a damned champion gladiator."

It was all too true. "Well, there's plenty of suspicion to go around," I admitted.

"Feeling so keen about taking her out with you now, Senator?" Silvanus asked.

"Absolutely," I said, enjoying their perplexed expressions. "From now on I want her right where I can see her."

Gabinius laughed, that great Roman laugh that sounds like swords banging on shields. "You're Caesar's friend, all right! That's the way he thinks. I hear he keeps the sons of Gallic chiefs he's killed in his bodyguard."

"Senator," Silvanus said, "I know you need rest and you must be at your ships early, but bear with me a moment and let me explain a few things about the situation here."

"Please do."

"When we annexed Cyprus it was partly to sort out the usual dynastic bungling of the Ptolemies, but partly, also, to tighten the Roman hold over Egypt. It has not yet been decided what to do with Cyprus. We may wish to keep it. As a naval base, it would give us effective control of the whole eastern seaboard. Or we may decide, graciously, to give it back to Ptolemy. Or, perhaps, to his son, in recognition of certain treaty clauses and concessions."

"I understand all that," I said. "We've been propping up weak kings in Egypt for generations."

"I say conquer the place, make a province of it, and be done with it," Gabinius growled.

"You would," Silvanus observed. "If you were to, as you almost did a short time ago, how long before Caesar and Pompey dropped everything, pooled their strength, and marched against you?"

"About a day, maybe two."

Egypt was so rich that no Roman general would stand by to see another take the place. The man who conquered Egypt would immediately be the richest, most powerful man in the world, richer than Crassus. It was bad enough when Sertorius set himself up as independent ruler of Spain. At least he was no great threat there. A general with his legions based in Egypt could aspire to conquer Rome and become, for all practical purposes, the ruler of the whole world.

"So you see, Senator Metellus, my position here is not just that of Roman governor over a mixed pack of Greeks and Phoenicians. There is a balancing act going on here. Future relations between Rome and Egypt are in that balance."

"I spoke with Cato before I came here," I said. "He said he set things in order with no trouble."

"That's Cato," Gabinius said. "And he had little concern save the local population and local affairs. He gave them a taste of the Roman whip and, as usual, they settled down. That was while I was busy putting old Ptolemy Auletes' fat rump back on his throne. Now things are different."

"When Caesar finishes in Gaul," Silvanus said, "all of Rome's attention will be turned eastward. There are matters to settle with Parthia, and something will have to be done about those squabbling Jewish princes. They're disrupting trade and foreign relations in a crucial part of the world. We'll want Ptolemy's support in those operations: supplies, auxiliaries, garrison troops—he has them all to spare. So please try not to get his favorite daughter killed, even if she did conspire to have you murdered."

Gabinius clapped a hand on my shoulder. "I've accomplished plenty of work with men who've tried to kill me, every Roman of any stature has. I hear you even cooperated with Clodius on an occasion or two. Just do the work, never trust him or turn your back on him. If you can do that with a bloody lunatic like Clodius, surely you can hold your own with a girl playing at war."

The grizzled old centurion came in. "No luck. We found the man in an alley, dead. He'd bled out from that arm cut. Severed the big vessel. I'm amazed he got as far as he did."

"How about the other one?" I asked.

"Died before they got him to the lockup."

"Well, so much for that." Silvanus said disgustedly. "Senator, I think we've kept you long enough, and I hope you'll keep what we've said in mind."

"Gentlemen," I said, lurching to my feet, "rest assured that I shall give your words my closest attention. And now, I bid you good night."

I walked back to my quarters as steadily as I could and found Hermes waiting up for me, sitting with his sword across his knees.

"Sleep across the doorway tonight," I told him, "and keep your weapons handy. From here on in, we trust nobody."

"You mean we were trusting someone before?"

AS SOON AS THE SUN CAME UP, MY MEN put their shoulders to the hulls and pushed them into the water. They floated prettily, spruced up and repainted, ready to go out and ravage the enemies of Rome. The sailors swam out to them and worked them under oars to the long wharf, where the marines boarded and supplies were loaded.

Cleopatra's ship already floated out in the harbor, and to judge by her royal banner she was aboard already. The enthusiasms of the young are irrepressible.

"A message for Senator Metellus!" shouted someone. I turned from my supply tally to see a boy running down the wharf, holding aloft a bronze message carrier. "Harbormaster Orchus sends you this, Senator." I took the polished tube from his hand and twisted off the cap. Inside was a slip of papyrus.

To the Commodore of the Roman Fleet, I read, smiling at the grandiose salutation. *The grain ship* Hapi *has just put in on its way from Egypt to Piraeus. Its master reports that yesterday he passed a devastated village on the island of Salia.*

"Brief and to the point," I remarked. "Ion, how far is this place?"

"Half a day's sailing if the winds are favorable, which this time of year they won't be. But they've been there and gone. Won't do any good to look at burned houses and dead bodies."

"Still, it's a starting place. We may be able to quiz witnesses, and, in any case, with so many new men we need a shakedown cruise and plenty of drill before I'll feel ready to take them into a fight. This is as good an excuse as any."

He shrugged. "You're the one with the commission." It was about as sincere a gesture of respect as I was likely to get from him.

I dispatched a sailor to Cleopatra's ship *Serapis* with a message giving our destination. As soon as the last jar was loaded we pushed off and rowed to the harbor mouth. Once in clear water, all ships hoisted sail. The wind was favorable for getting us around the island of Cyprus, but after that we would probably have to row. That suited me well enough because the men needed exercise and I wouldn't have to pull an oar myself.

Once we were under way, Ariston walked up to me. Since he was shipping as a marine he had no duties at the moment. Like many of the sailors, he had lowered his tunic from his shoulders and wore it knotted about his waist. From arsenal stores he had chosen a close-fitting iron cap and a small, round shield of hippopotamus hide as his sole military equipment. I could not guess how that last item had found its way into the arsenal at Paphos, since it must have originated in Nubia. For weaponry, he stuck with his big knife.

"That man I cut last night," he began, "did they catch him?"

"They did. Bled to death within the hour. The big blood vessel was severed." I caught the look that crossed his face. "What's wrong?"

"I said dead by morning, and that's what I meant. I cut him here." He drew a ragged-nailed finger from the bulging triceps on the back of his upper arm across the equally bulging biceps in front. "Cut him hard and all the way to the bone—I felt my blade scrape it—but no deeper than that. I've seen plenty of men die in battle and duels and brawls from arm cuts. That big bleeder's on the inside of the arm, right next to the bone. I don't think my blade could've touched it."

"Well, well," I said, "why does this fail to surprise me? Keep this to yourself, Ariston."

"Whatever you say, Senator."

"Why didn't you draw armor and a better helmet? The men will take you for one of the sailors."

He smiled crookedly. "Wear a bronze shell that'll drag me straight to the waiting arms of Poseidon if I go overboard? Not buggering likely. If I have to swim for it, I want nothing on me I can't get rid of before I hit the water."

"At least a decent shield then," I suggested.

"This is the best combination for a deck fight: a little shield and a dagger or short sword. Anything bigger just gets in the way."

"You'll want a bigger shield when we come under arrow fire," I insisted, nettled by his confident expertise.

"Don't you know how to avoid arrows in a fight?" he grinned.

"How?"

"Just get behind someone else."

I gave up. "You're the pirate." This made me remember why I'd hired him. "How do they fight when they take a ship?"

"I wouldn't call it fighting. More like a sheep killing. But just in case, they're ready for one. Tangling with a fighting crew like this, they'd start with a few arrows—not many good archers among them—then javelins when the ships are in range."

"Will they grapple?"

"Not with us. They'll be trying to get away, remember? No loot to be had on these ships, just a bunch of them killed if they win and the survivors crucified if they lose—no incentive to come to grips in that prospect. If they have to fight, most will be armed like me. If any wear armor, it'll just be a piece of hide hung from the neck to cover the chest and belly, maybe a plain helmet that gives them plenty of air and vision, not the bronze buckets some of your marines wear. If we grapple them, they'll try to board first, and they'll fight like the Furies," he made a gesture to avert the evil one may expect from speaking that dread word, "because that's the only way they'll come out of it alive."

"And if we catch them on land?"

"For a shore raid they may use heavier weapons and armor. Some of them have fought in the armies and know how to do it right. But on shore, if it looks like they're losing, they'll think maybe they can run and hide. They may not fight as desperately."

"What real advantages do they have?"

He thought for a moment. "First off, numbers. You have four Liburnians. They have six to ten most times. And, ship-for-ship, their numbers are still superior because every man aboard's a fighting man. Rowers and sailors are all armed, and all fight when boarding time comes. Your *corvus* and Roman boarding tactics may tip the balance, but maybe not."

"Because their leader is a Roman and knows what to expect."

He nodded. "Spurius. He'd've made a good skipper in the old days when we were a floating nation."

"Tell me about him."

67

"I'll tell you what I know, but it's not all that much. I wasn't close to him, not even in the same ship. I saw him on shore from time to time and sat in on the councils. Pirates aren't organized like a navy, you know." He spread his nostrils and took a deep breath of the sea air. "It's a band of equals and everyone has a say. The leaders are just the toughest fighters, the best sailors, or the ones who are smartest about finding prey and getting safely away with the loot."

"Which of those was Spurius?" I asked, fascinated by this look into a life so foreign from anything I was used to.

"Well, he's no great seaman, as you might expect, being a Roman. But as a fighter he's qualified to go up against the best of them, toe-to-toe, and come out with his enemy's blood on his sword and none of his own on the ground."

"That's praise, coming from your mouth."

He smiled with satisfaction. "I was taught young, and I was taught right. Anyway, some say Spurius was a Roman deserter who threw in with Spartacus and got away before the end came. I don't know about that."

"How old would you judge him?"

"About forty would be my guess."

I thought about it. "The Slave War began in the consulship of Clodianus and Gellius twenty-one years ago and ended two years later. It's conceivable, if he deserted as a young recruit. Anyway, go on. Tell me what he looks like."

"Tall for a Roman, about your height, but wider built. Strong as an ox and quick as a cat. He wears a full beard and lets his hair grow long. Maybe he doesn't want to look like a Roman, with your clean-shaven faces and short hair."

"I don't suppose you'd know how to distinguish our regional accents? It might help to know if he's from Rome itself or some other part of Latium."

He shook his blocky head. "Never heard him speak Latin anyway, just Greek and some Aramaic."

"Aramaic? Did you go ashore in Syria or Judea?"

"We went there to sell loot once. I think that's where I heard him speak it. Greek will get you by almost anywhere, but Aramaic is handy to know in the eastern parts."

"Did he speak it well?"

"Better than me. Sounded as fluent as he is in Greek, and he speaks Greek like an Athenian. Why?"

I gazed off across the calm water. My weather luck was holding. "I'm just trying to build a picture of the man. I don't want to be fighting a total stranger when we've drawn swords on one another. Many commanders just assume things about their enemies and leave it at that. They tend to die with looks of great astonishment on their faces."

"That's shrewd."

"What is he like as a planner?"

"The best. He knows the trade routes, he keeps up on whose fleet is where, he knows the value of everything, and when, say, a load of fine glassware will fetch a better price in Berytus than in Jaffa. He's been called a small-minded merchant for it, but never to his face."

"Does he have regular contacts—shore-based merchants, for instance, who take his loot off his hands?"

"Certainly. But he always deals with them in private. It's one way he hangs on to his leadership."

"How did he get to be leader?"

"He organized one of the first crews, so he had his own ship going in. Any pirate may challenge the chief to a fight for leadership. I imagine that's how he got to be top dog in the first place. I saw him deal with two such challengers myself. It didn't last long either time."

"He sounds like a formidable man."

"He is that."

"Does he have a second? Anyone close to him?"

He shook his head again. "There's no second in a pirate fleet—just the chief and the individual skippers. As for friends, he acts like every man of the fleet is his brother, but I never saw anyone who seemed closer to him than the rest."

"Does he have a woman or women? Boys?"

"He takes a woman sometimes, after sacking a town. Never more than one and never keeps her more than a day or two, then passes her on to whoever wants her. I never heard that he fancied boys." He shifted, cat-like, to a roll of the ship. "And now, Senator, you know as much as I do about Spurius. He's not a chummy sort, and I doubt anyone knows more than I just told you."

"You are a gold mine of information, Ariston. I will be quizzing you further, but that's enough for now. If you should remember anything else about Spurius, even a tiny detail, please tell me at once, even if it seems unimportant."

He nodded and sauntered off, moving easily with the motion of the ship, which was beginning to make me uncomfortable. My short stay ashore had already robbed me of much of my seaworthiness.

Ariston paused for a second, then turned back. "One other thing: his ship is the *Atropos*."

That was something to mull upon. There are three Fates: Clotho, Lachesis, and Atropos. Clotho, with her spindle, spins the thread of each man's life. Lachesis, with her rod, measures it. Atropos, with her scissors, cuts it. Atropos is known as "She Who Cannot Be Avoided."

Ion came up to me. "We'll be running out oars soon." He looked at Ariston's retreating back. "Where on Poseidon's great domain did you find that one?"

"About where you'd expect. Why? Don't you like him?"

He shrugged. Greeks shrug a great deal. "He's a sailor all right. But hard as it may be to credit, he's too rough even for my pack of villains. I plan to sleep lightly while he's on my ship."

"I'm glad to hear it. I want everyone to sleep lightly from here on. I want to get these pirates, and I don't want to waste a lot of time at it. Once we're under oars I want to begin formation training with the other ships. While you're seeing to that, I'll be drilling the marines on deck. And I want a sharp lookout kept. It's unlikely we'll spot the pirate fleet so soon, but stranger things have happened, and I won't spurn any gifts the gods throw my way. It's a sure way to draw down their wrath."

"As you command, Senator." He walked away, barking orders.

Now I had some idea of whom my enemy was. How strange to be coming all the way out here, into alien waters, and be facing a fellow Roman. If he was a Roman. It would not be that difficult to fake among foreigners. But somehow I had a feeling that the man was the real thing.

He kept himself aloof from the rest and trusted no one close to him. It was only wise, considering his murderous companions. I allowed myself a moment of identity with him. I, too, was surrounded by people whose loyalties were suspect even where hostility was not absolutely certain.

But what else could be made of him? Fluency in languages is no uncommon accomplishment. But "Greek like an Athenian"? That could be the mark of a Roman of the better classes. Almost everybody knows some Greek, and a traveler or trader has to know it well; but common trade Greek is very unlike the polished language taught in the rhetoric schools, and that is invariably the Athenian dialect. It was something to ponder.

Aramaic is the language of Judea, Syria, and the surrounding territories, a merging and simplification of several related languages spoken in that part of the world, rather as the old dialects of Faliscian, Sabine, Marsian, Bruttian, and so forth have in recent generations merged into the Latin spoken today. Anyone who lives or trades between Antioch and Egypt needs to be proficient in that tongue.

The full beard and long hair could be a disguise, making him nearly unrecognizable to any who knew him in his earlier life. It could mean as well that he hoped someday to return to that life, rich with ill-gotten loot, and settle down into respectability. Get rid of the hair and beard and nobody would know him as the terrible pirate chief. I myself had seen a number of hirsute Germans who had come over to the Roman side. Shorn of their shaggy locks and decently barbered, they looked exactly like normal human beings, except for their odd coloring.

And his past? A blank. I dismissed the tale of his having fought beside Spartacus. Any prominent, enigmatic man who refuses to divulge any information about his history invariably has one invented for him. Always, it will be lurid and colorful and will often associate him with famous personages. We had done the same with Spartacus himself: he was the disgraced son of a fine Roman family; he was an allied chieftain who had learned the Roman art of war and turned it against us; he was a renegade son of that old bugger, Mithridates; and so on.

In truth, nobody knows who Spartacus was. In all likelihood he was born a slave, or was some Thracian sheepherder drafted into the *auxilia*, deserted, and sold into a *ludus* in Capua to fight in the games. The fancied history is always far more gratifying than the commonplace reality.

At least, now, my enemy had a face.

For a few hours we had the men sweating at the oars, practicing fleet maneuvers, changing swiftly from the cruising formation, with the ships one behind the other, to the battle-line formation, in line abreast, or in a shallow crescent. There are many other formations, but I wanted this single maneuver mastered right away.

I had been doing a good deal of reading about naval tactics on the journey to Cyprus and was happy to learn that some of what I had read actually worked in practice. While the rowers practiced their evolutions, I drilled the marines on the ballistae: crew-served crossbows that shot a heavy iron dart with enough power to skewer three armored men like quails on a spit.

We did not have nearly enough of these weapons. I had counted on getting more from the naval stores at Paphos, which shows how inexperienced I was in this regard. *Never* count on resupply at your destination, even if it means passing heroic bribes at the Ostian or Tarentine naval depots before setting out. It would be several days before the new ones I had arranged for would be completed.

Some of the men professed to be expert archers, but I never met a soldier who professed to be less than expert at anything that involves killing people. Only five had arrived at the hiring with bows, and there were a few more bows and some crates of arrows aboard my ships. The problem was I could not hold archery practice at sea, where the arrows would all be lost. That would have to wait.

We saw the smoke before we saw the island.

In midafternoon the watch at the masthead called out that he saw a cloud of smoke in the distance, and the helmsman adjusted his steering oar at Ion's order. The yard had been lowered against the unfavorable wind, and the watch clung to the top of the mast like a monkey, with nothing but a twist of rope about the mast to help support him. He seemed perfectly comfortable though. I suppose you can get used to anything if you do it long enough.

Within the hour we saw the island, a low hump of brown and green, undistinguished and in no way as lovely as the Aegean islands. Its name meant nothing to me, which was a good indication that nothing was produced there that was marketed in Rome. Most islands produce at least a local wine, an exceptional type of pottery, marble of a special color, something of the sort for which it may be famed. Not this one.

"What do the people here do?" I asked Ion, as we drew near enough to distinguish the remains of the village.

"Fish, farm a little, and raise sheep, last I heard. I suspect they do nothing at all now if the raiders have been thorough. In all my years of sailing, I was here only once, to take on some dried fish. And they trade a little wool. They are poor even for island people."

The timekeeper, whose flute gave the rowers their pace, slowed his fluting as the leadsman in the bow dropped his weighted line and called out the depth of water beneath the keel. When we were almost alongside the rickety little wharf built out into the water, Ion ordered down oars. The rowers plunged their blades into the water, braking the ship's way so that we halted alongside the wharf, the ram barely nudging the gravel of the beach. My other three vessels ranged themselves just offshore.

"Well," someone said, "that's a pretty sight."

The village had once been a fairly attractive and decent place by the remaining evidence: mud-brick houses with whitewashed walls and thatched roofs; a temple the size of a small Roman house dedicated to some local god; a line of boatsheds by the water; long, horizontal poles supported on posts for drying nets; big, wooden racks for drying fish.

It had probably been home to about two hundred poor-but-not-starving people before it was destroyed almost as thoroughly as Carthage. The thatch was ashes, collapsing most of the mud-brick walls in the heat of their burning. The boat sheds were cinders, and the boats splinters of wood. The drying racks, even the nets themselves, had gone onto the bon-fire built inside the little temple.

And there were bodies, some of them impaled on the posts that had supported the net-drying poles. Others just lay on the ground or smol-dered within the houses, many of them dismembered. The stench was appalling; but if you have lived through battle, siege, and the more dis-reputable Roman streets, it takes a lot of stink to turn your stomach.

"They've been thorough all right," Ion said, a touch of wonder in his voice. This was unexpected. "Why such destruction? They couldn't have put up any sort of fight."

"That thought has crossed my mind as well. Ion, call everyone ashore. Beach the ships, nobody is going to come on us unawares here."

"Let me send *Triton* around the island first before we bring the ships in. It won't take an hour. It's not likely, but someone could be hanging about on the other side."

"You're right. Best to be cautious. Order it so, and tell them to be on the lookout for survivors. There are always survivors in my experience, and I'd like to question any such."

While the ship went about its mission, I walked through the village, Hermes close by me. A brief survey confirmed my first impression: all the dead were old, crippled, or looked like they had tried, pathetically, to put up a fight.

"They made off with all the good slave material," Hermes observed.

"Raiders usually do," I affirmed. I saw Ariston looking bemusedly at the ruined temple and called him over.

"Is this how they commonly behave?" I asked him.

He shook his head vehemently. "Never saw anything like it. It makes no sense. You don't kill sheep you don't intend to eat. You shear them."

"Exactly. They took everything of any use to them: food, wool, women, the young to sell, and able-bodied men who showed no fight. Then they went through this unnecessary butchery and burning. It merits some thought."

A short while later *Triton* returned and reported no ships lurking about and no survivors visible from offshore. I had everyone, sailors and marines, assembled where I could address them.

"I want this island scoured," I told them. "Bring me anyone you find alive. These unfortunate people," I waved an arm, taking in the ruined village and its late inhabitants, "must be given burial and funeral rites, lest their shades follow our ships and bring us bad luck." Actually, I rather doubted the power of the dead to do mischief to the living, but it is the custom and would make me feel better at any rate. "Get to it!"

There wasn't enough wood left on the island to make a decent funeral pyre, so the men scraped a shallow grave in the sandy ground and the bodies were placed in it and covered over. Atop the grave a small cairn was built, and with Cleopatra's assistance I performed a burial rite and poured offerings of flour, wine, and oil over the cairn.

The princess was sickened by the stench, but the sight of all the carnage did not terrify her as I might have expected. I commented upon this.

"The women of my house are schooled in controlling their emotions. Among the descendants of Alexander, great rage is the only emotion that may be displayed on public occasions." The founder of her line, Ptolemy Soter, had married a sister of Alexander. Her name, not coincidentally, had been Cleopatra.

"Is this what war looks like?" she asked.

"Sometimes," I said. "But this is very extreme. Sometimes we Romans destroy a town as thoroughly, but only to make an example, as when people who have accepted our terms treacherously repudiate a treaty and attack us."

"Clearly, that was not the case here."

"No, and I intend to learn why this was done."

The search party returned; and as I had expected, they brought in survivors: Three women and two men, all of them too stunned to feel

74

terror. They did not look like Greeks but rather like some archaic survival of an earlier age, dark of skin with ink black hair that fell in snakelike locks to the shoulders of the men, to the waists of the women. Their clothes were filthy and ragged, their skins bruised and scratched. They had broad faces and might have been handsome had it not been for the brutish stupefaction of their expressions.

"What happened here?" They said nothing, did not indicate that they so much as heard my words. A marine began to handle them roughly, but I put a stop to it. "No. They've suffered enough. Let them rest. Give them food and drink; let them know they will come to no harm. No further harm anyway. I'll question them later. Ion."

"Yes, Senator?"

"It's too late to return to Cyprus. We'd be overtaken by nightfall. We'll stay here the night and go back at first light."

Soon cooking fires were burning and sails were turned into tents for the men. The sights of the day had turned everyone somber, and there was little of the usual chatter. The sailors, who had worked the hardest, ate in silence, then turned in and slept like exhausted dogs. The marines, charged with security, sat up longer and conversed in low voices.

Cleopatra had brought her own tent, naturally, complete with all its furnishings. It was ringed with guards who stood at attention, spears erect as if this were a parade ground in Alexandria.

"Come join me, Senator," she said, and I was nothing loath. Before the tent a fly was stretched and beneath this I sank into a folding chair with a seat and back of leopard skin. Cleopatra reclined luxuriously on a couch that was furnished with plump cushions. From what I could see, the tent was furnished with equal lavishness, and under it all were splendid carpets. I accepted a cup of wine from one of her slave girls. The cup was solid gold; I could tell by the weight.

"To hold all this," I commented, "Your ship must be bigger on the inside than on the outside."

She smiled. "It's all in knowing how to pack." She turned serious. "So have you come to any conclusions about this?"

"I am entertaining some possibilities. I would like to talk with those survivors before I try any conclusions."

"Join me in some dinner. Maybe soon they'll be recovered enough to tell us what happened."

Cleopatra's larder was decidedly superior to anything available on a Roman warship. It was not opulent, but everything was of the highest quality, and it included items such as honeyed figs and dates, fine seedcakes, and ducks brought that day from Cyprus and prepared by her amazingly efficient cooks.

"Take some of this over to those poor people," she ordered a slave. The man loaded a tray with delicacies and disappeared.

"They'll eat better than they have in their lives," I said, "but it is a dear-bought meal."

"How lost they must be," she said. "Their whole world was destroyed."

When our dinner was finished, it was fully dark. Cleopatra and I rose and went to where the survivors sat at a little fire. Four of them were eating, but from the look in their eyes it was an automatic action. They did not even know what they were doing. Ion and a couple of the marines stood by watching. The shipmaster pointed to the woman who was not eating. She sat a little apart.

"A little while back that one went down to the shore and washed her face and arms. She must be coming out of it."

With her face scrubbed clean of soot, dirt, and tear streaks, I could see that the woman had vertical lines tattooed from her lower lip to her chin, and a circle within a circle in the center of her forehead.

"Woman, can you understand me?" I asked, as gently as I could. Romans are not trained in gentle speech, but after what she had been through I was unlikely to terrify her. She looked up at me, so at least she was aware of her surroundings. She spoke a few words in a language unlike anything I had ever heard.

"Ion, do you think any of the men might know this language?" I asked.

He frowned. "I have sailors from all over, but an earthquake wouldn't wake them, what with the way you worked them today."

"I can understand her," Cleopatra said.

I turned to gape at her. "Princess, your linguistic skills are renowned, but I'll wager the tongue this woman speaks is unique to this island."

"It's spoken all over the world," she said. "It's Greek. But it is the most archaic dialect I have ever heard spoken. This tongue was ancient when Homer composed his poems. I think it's a variant of the Cycladic language, dead for a thousand years. I've only seen it written in some very ancient texts, and those copied from earlier writings."

Cleopatra could always surprise you.

"Ask her to describe what happened."

Very slowly, considering each word carefully and with many repetitions at the woman's puzzled expressions, she got the question across. The woman began to speak in a gush of words but Cleopatra, by gestures, managed to slow her down. Finally she turned to me.

"Her name is Chryse. The village has no name and she knows no place but this island. The day before yesterday, five ships appeared offshore in the late morning. The people thought they wanted to trade for fish and wool so they rushed to the shore. But the strangers came ashore armed and began herding them together, tying the women and children with ropes, binding some of the younger men, killing others, and cutting down all the old people. With some others, she ran to the interior. She hid under a rock overhang she knew about. She does not know how these others managed to conceal themselves. She does not know what became of her man and her children."

"Ask her about the attitude of these raiders."

She looked at me. "What do you mean?"

"Were they angry, as if these islanders had done them some harm? Were they joyous, laughing as they killed, raping and having a good time? How did they look and sound?"

Once again Cleopatra managed to get her meaning across, and the woman answered, having to repeat herself many times for full comprehension.

"She says that they were grim, but they showed no anger, as if they were doing a job. 'Like men gutting fish for dinner' is how she put it. She saw no rape."

"Did she see their leader?"

Once more the byplay, which was growing quicker. "She saw a big man by the shore, with long hair and a beard, and the others seemed to defer to him. But he scarcely glanced toward the islanders, and she was too terrified to notice much beyond that."

"Can she describe their ships?"

Cleopatra asked. "Like yours, but the same color as the sea."

"Thank her. Tell her we will take her and the others to Cyprus and find a place for them. They will not suffer further."

The woman spoke and Cleopatra turned to me. "She does not want to go to Cyprus. She does not think the others will either. This island is all they know."

"But there is nothing left for them here. Tell her that even if they find food to eat, they will die here alone in time."

Cleopatra tried. "She wants to stay."

We went back to Cleopatra's tent.

"Ready for some conclusions now?" she asked, handing me another cup.

"This was an example," I said. "It's the only explanation. Those raiders were ordered to devastate this place utterly. That is why they went about it so methodically. It was just a task—a disagreeable one, perhaps, but a task to be carried out nevertheless."

"For whom was this example intended?" she asked. "For you?"

"You can't intimidate a Roman with slaughter, and this Spurius knows it. No, this was intended to let everyone in the eastern sea know what will happen to anyone who cooperates with us. Word of this butchery will be all over Cyprus when we return, and that means it will be all over the eastern sea in days. It's a very efficient system of communication."

"That means this Spurius knows you are here and hunting him."

"He struck this place two days ago. He must have heard of my arrival and my mission as soon as I set foot on Cyprus. I would like to know how that happened."

The next morning we set sail from the blighted island. None of the survivors would come with us, despite our fervent urging. We left them there, relics of a lost world. It was sad, but the world is full of sadness.

6

IT WAS LATE AFTERNOON WHEN WE GOT back to Paphos. Ariston came up to me just as we pulled into the naval harbor.

"They'll strike very soon now," he said. "They may be hitting someplace this very hour. When word of what we saw on that island spreads, you can expect little cooperation even from the people you are trying to help."

"Where?" I asked him.

"Anywhere they want to go," he assured me.

I could have tried swearing everyone to silence, but I knew the futility of that. Several hundred men cannot keep a secret, even if they are all Romans and honor the same gods. Here I had the sweepings of the whole sea, not to mention Cleopatra's Egyptians and her gaggle of servants. Even to try such a thing would start rumors far worse than the truth.

A small crowd of citizens, sailors, and dockside idlers had come to view our return; but the little throng quickly dispersed when it was clear we were coming back without pirate heads, freed captives, and heaps of loot. It was a little early for that. An elaborate litter remained on the wharf as I stepped off the gangplank, its liveried bearers squatting patiently by its poles. A delicate, multiply ringed hand drew its curtain aside.

"Senator! Did you have a pleasant voyage?" It was Flavia. She wore an expensive but relatively modest gown, and the elaborately dressed blond wig was back in place. She looked every inch the noble Roman lady, and it was hard to believe that I had seen so many more inches just two nights previously.

"It was a tolerable outing, no more than a shakedown cruise really."

"Did you see any pirates?"

"No, but we saw where they'd been. It was instructive."

She slid over to one side of the litter. "Please join me, Senator. I am sure that your labors have given you an appetite. An early dinner at my home will do you a world of good." She caught my raised eyebrow and smiled. "My husband would like very much to talk with you."

"Then if you will allow me to make a few arrangements here, I will be most honored."

"Go right ahead. I like to watch sailors at their work."

I told Hermes to haul our gear back to our quarters at the house of Silvanus and wait for me there. He didn't like it but knew better than to argue. I left orders with my captains to be with their ships and crews at dawn, ready to sail at my orders. Out in the harbor, I could see Cleopatra's gilded barge carrying her to the commercial wharf. I left word with Harmodias where I would be for the next few hours should I be needed.

Then I crawled into the litter beside Flavia, and she dropped the curtain. Immediately I was enveloped in a cloud of her perfume. I was not unaffected. Of course a man of my station should properly be repelled by a noble woman who wallows with the lowest dregs of society, but then I have never been very proper. And there is something undeniably exciting about such a concentration of raw, animal appetites and energies.

But, to my credit, I retained my distance. Bitter experience had taught me that many of my personal catastrophes had been brought about through my weakness for very bad women. And I had known some of the worst. Clodia, for instance. And then there was that German princess, Freda. She wasn't really evil, just a savage like all her race, but fearsome for all that. I had encountered the younger Fulvia and a score of less famous but equally shameless women, and I had been involved with some of them and attracted by all. A bronze founder had once explained to me that glowing metal was beautiful, mysterious, and exciting; but one should never touch it with bare hands. It was sound advice.

She laid a warm hand on my arm. "Everyone says that you are a man of the world, Decius Caecilius. You are a friend of Caesar, and the old bores like Cato consider you degenerate."

"I have been so complimented," I admitted.

"Wonderful. The moralists are so tedious. I would appreciate it though if you would not bring up the subject of my nocturnal escapades when you speak with my husband."

"Flavia, your pleasures are your own business and I will seek to advise neither you nor your husband, but he must be more than a bit obtuse if he does not know already."

"Oh, he knows perfectly well how I amuse myself. It is something we have simply agreed not to discuss in the company of our peers. He has his own pastimes, and I do not interfere with them. It is a comfortable arrangement, don't you think?"

"The world would be a happier place if other couples were so understanding," I assured her. In truth, such liberal marital arrangements were not uncommon in Rome. Flavia was just more extreme than most in pursuit of gratification.

The house of Sergius Nobilior was only slightly less grand than that of Silvanus. Roman *equites* of that day, which is to say the wealthiest plebeian families, dominated banking, finance, and other businesses. Though most of them were perfectly happy to make money and stay out of the Senate, with its endless duties and burdensome military obligations, they formed a very influential power group and they dominated the Popular Assemblies. This was the class to which Sergius Nobilior belonged.

The man himself greeted me in his atrium.

"Senator! You do my house great honor. When we heard your ships had been sighted my wife swore that she would bring you back, and she usually catches her man." He said this without seeming irony. "Please join us for some dinner. Living on ship's food is tedious."

"It wasn't much of a voyage," I told him, "but I gladly accept."

We went into the beautifully decorated triclinium and confined our talk to inconsequential things while we ate. There were no other guests, an uncommon thing in a wealthy man's household, so I assumed he had some sort of business he wished to discuss privately. I therefore drank cautiously. So, I noted, did the two of them.

"Was your voyage productive?" he asked, as the fruit was brought out.

So I told them about the island we had visited with its devastated village and its few stunned survivors.

"How terrible!" Nobilior said. "What inhuman beasts they must be to do such a thing. I cannot believe this report that their leader is a Roman." Flavia, on the other hand, sipped sweet Egyptian wine and did not seem unduly shocked by such goings-on.

"Well, if we Romans are nothing else, we are versatile. Personally, it seems to me that no one but a Roman could cause so much trouble with so few ships and men."

He chuckled. "You are certainly right about that. Sometimes I think that the rest of the world makes it too easy for us. Have you heard how Ptolemy got his throne back?"

"I was in Gaul much of that time, but I heard rumors concerning the passing of heroic bribes."

"More godlike than heroic," he said. "It seems that his subjects thought him remiss in allowing us to annex Cyprus. When his brother committed suicide, the subjects drove Auletes from his throne. After all, he had taken the surname Philadelphus: 'he who loves his brother.' The Egyptians thought that a bitter irony. But they must have some sort of Ptolemy so they put his daughter Berenice on the throne. According to Ptolemaic custom, a queen cannot rule by herself, so she cast about for a royal husband and eventually chose Archelaus of Pontus.

"Auletes immediately fled to Rome, where he petitioned the Senate to restore him to his throne. Do you know by what right he made this petition?"

I thought back. "He'd been voted the status of 'friend and ally' a few years earlier, hadn't he? I think it was during the consulship of Caesar and Bibulus."

"He had. He paid handsomely to get that title, too. Pompey and Caesar guaranteed him the title, but they told him it would be expensive— no less than six thousand talents."

"Six thousand!" Even by the standards of the time that was an enormous bribe.

He nodded. "Six thousand. That represents, roughly, half a year's income for Egypt. But Auletes is a beggar and everyone knows it, so where do you suppose he came up with the sum?"

This was his story and I'd just eaten his dinner so I played along. "Where?"

"He borrowed it from Rabirius Postumus. Do you know him?"

"I met him once, several years ago, at a party at the Egyptian embassy. He'd just been appointed Ptolemy's financial advisor. Surely even Rabirius wasn't rich enough to lend six thousand. Crassus couldn't have come up with that much in one lump sum."

"Rabirius is an old friend of mine," Nobilior said complacently. "He took a number of us on as partners in this enterprise. Of course, that was just to have the title so that the Senate would have to back his claims. Getting Rome to provide him with the military force he needed was going to cost a further ten thousand. Mind you, at this time he still owed for part of the original six."

"I think I see where this is going," I said. "He agreed to pay, but first we had to restore his throne so he could start looting his own country to pay it off."

Nobilior smiled. "Exactly. Caesar isn't the only one who knows how to use indebtedness to his own advantage. Now, by this time, Caesar himself was busy in Gaul, and Pompey had affairs of his own to manage, but there was our friend Aulus Gabinius, waging war in Syria with a perfectly good army at his disposal. He couldn't break off his war against the Parthians and go to Egypt with his whole force, but Caesar sent him a strong force of *auxilia*, Gabinius recruited others locally, and off he went, accompanied by Rabirius to keep an eye on everyone's money."

"I wonder," I said, "how the voters would feel if they knew that so many of our wars are just business arrangements? A lot of them still think that things like the glory and honor of the Republic are involved."

He shrugged. "Nobody objects to the heaps of loot and the cheap slaves our victorious generals bring back. That's what they really care about. That and keeping the barbarians as far away as possible. There are plenty of voters now alive who remember the Cimbri and Teutones camped a few day's march from Rome, before Marius crushed them. Remember, kings all over the world bankrupt their kingdoms through foolish wars even when they don't suffer conquest themselves. Should the Roman people complain because our own wars are so profitable?"

"You have a point." I wondered what other point he had but suspected that he would get around to it sooner or later.

"A versatile man, our Gabinius," Flavia observed. She may have had multiple meanings here, but I had too little information to sort them out.

"A Roman statesman has to be versatile," I pointed out.

"Do you remember how Pompey got his extraordinary command against the pirates?" Nobilior asked.

I thought about it. "That was when Piso and Glabrio were consuls, wasn't it? It was four years before my quaestorship. My family had me in Campania that whole year, administering a training camp for recruits to be sent to Crete for Metellus Creticus's army there. I was out of touch with Roman politics that year and most of the next."

"Pompey's imperium was to last three years," Nobilior said, "and it encompassed the entire sea and fifty miles inland, overriding the imperium of every provincial governor. And it was conferred by a *lex Gabinia*."

"Gabinius was the tribune who got that law passed?" I had forgotten that.

"After a good deal of fighting, yes. The tribune Trebillius interposed his veto and was supported by Otho. There were weeks of brawling."

"I'm sorry I missed it."

"They were lively times. In the end the Senate had to bring in a whole rural voting bloc to break the deadlock. The country people were great supporters of Pompey, of course, so the law got passed."

"Are you telling me that Gabinius is Pompey's man?"

"I am telling you that war, politics, and business are very complicated in this part of the world. As to his current affiliation"—he made an eloquent gesture with his hands—"these things change. The *lex Gabinia* was many years ago, and Pompey's sun is in eclipse."

"Here in the East," Flavia added, "the people have a different view of Rome. The current politics of the Forum mean little to them. In the West, Caesar is the man of the hour. Here he is all but unknown. The great names in the East are still Pompey, Gabinius, even Lucullus. Their paid-off veterans and mercenaries are settled all over the islands and seaboard, many of them active in the various armies of the region."

"In Egypt," Nobilior said, "a sizable contingent of the king's forces bear the name 'Gabinians.' Some are Romans, but most are those *auxilia* sent by Caesar—Gauls and Germans, many of them."

Here, it seemed, he was coming to the crux of the matter.

"And not only those," Flavia added. "He picked up recruits from a lot of settlements in Cilicia and Illyria."

"Including," I asked, "those settlements founded by Pompey to separate the erstwhile pirates from the sea?"

"That I could not say," Nobilior asserted. "It would have been in violation of the surrender terms after all. These men were not to take up arms again. Still, few laws lack flexibility where power and ambition are concerned."

"All too true. Well, then, it may be that this man Spurius is one of those paid-off veterans now set up in business for himself."

"Quite likely." Nobilior nodded. "Would you care for some of this excellent Lesbian?"

I left his house no more than pleasantly tipsy. Flavia saw me to the door personally.

"You must visit us again soon, Senator," she said.

"I would not forego the pleasure," I assured her. Her parting kiss was far more ardent than commonly sanctioned by the rules of etiquette, but at least she kept her clothes on.

As I walked away I reminded myself to steer a wide course around that woman. Julia would, after all, be here soon, Flavia was a deterrent to clear thinking, but I managed to draw my thoughts upward from my nether regions sufficiently to ponder what I had just heard.

Nobilior implied that these pirates were Gabinius's men. But, if so, where did that leave me? Gabinius had no imperium, was no more than an exile like many others, awaiting his chance to go back to Rome and resume his Senate seat. If some of his veterans turned outlaw, that did not mean he had put them up to it, although the implication could not have been clearer.

When I reached my quarters at the governor's mansion I sent Hermes to fetch Ariston.

"How do the accommodations here suit you?" I asked him when he arrived.

"Fine so far. The serving girls here have taken a shine to me. When you consider the quality of the men they usually have to put up with, that's not too surprising. The food and wine and the room are all better than I can afford at most times." He stretched his powerful arms. "It would get boring as a steady diet, but for now I like it just fine."

"Good. Ariston, when you were in Spurius's little fleet, did many of the men speak of serving with Gabinius on his Egyptian expedition?"

He nodded. "Several of them did, as I recall. They said his recruiters had come to the villages where they were settled and offered them the chance to do something more congenial than trudge along behind an ox, and they'd jumped at it."

"Did these recruiters say why their oath not to take up arms again had been suspended?"

He shrugged. "I wasn't there. But Rome is always raising *auxilia* from defeated people, right? And that oath specified that we never take up arms *against Rome*. If a Roman general wanted them to fight an enemy of Rome, what could be wrong with that? Anyway, Pompey was mainly concerned that we keep away from the sea."

"Quite so. But did any of these men perhaps hint that he still served Gabinius in some fashion?"

Ariston's gaze sharpened. "You mean you think he may be behind this?"

"It is one of many possibilities I am exploring."

"Nobody said so. Anyway, if a man that highly placed wanted to do such a thing, he would treat with only one person, and that would be Spurius. Even then, he might not see the man personally. He'd probably use an emissary."

"Yes, I know how it's done." I remembered innumerable dealings between prominent candidates and officeholders in Rome and the street-gang leaders whose support they needed. Some freedman always acted as go-between. "Go on back to your quarters. Mention to nobody what we've spoken about."

"Come, Hermes," I said, when he was gone, "let's call upon Princess Cleopatra."

We found her in a beautiful little nook of the formal garden, well illuminated by torches and braziers, accompanied by her scholars and listening to Alpheus, who stood before them declaiming a lengthy poem concerning the birth of Venus, which, according to the myth, had occurred not far from the spot we occupied. Upon coming ashore in her scallop shell, she founded her first temple right there in Paphos, where the ancient, rather modest structure remained the center of her cult.

Of course, the Greeks call her Aphrodite, "the foam-born." Among the Greeks she is a gentle goddess, lacking the more alarming qualities of the Roman Venus. This does not keep us from identifying the two goddesses though. Among other advantages, it allows us to steal Greek statues of Aphrodite and set them up in our Temples of Venus without impropriety.

I am told that, in the old days before we came under Greek influence, our gods had no form, and we didn't even know what they looked like. It is difficult now to think of Jupiter without picturing Zeus, or Mars lacking the image of Ares, but once this was so.

I waited in the shadows of the fruit trees until Alpheus had finished his song, and while I waited I noticed the man seated next to Cleopatra. He looked decidedly familiar—a pudgy, round-faced man with a bald head, wearing a great many Egyptian rings on his fat fingers. The Egyptian jewelry jogged my memory. It was Photinus, First Eunuch to the court of King Ptolemy. When I had seen him years before in Alexandria, he had worn the Egyptian dress, complete with wig and cosmetics, favored by that court's functionaries. Despite that he was a Greek like the rest of them, and here he was dressing the part.

"Good evening, Princess," I said, as the applause died down and Alpheus took his bows.

"Ah, Senator, there you are," she said, smiling. "We tried to find you earlier."

"I have been enjoying the hospitality of Sergius Nobilior," I told her.

"You remember Photinus, I am sure," said Cleopatra.

"It is so good to see you again, Senator Metellus," he said heartily. Our previous relations had been of a decidedly hostile nature, but the present moment is all that counts to courtiers and diplomats.

"An unexpected pleasure," I assured him. "What brings you to Cyprus?"

"Some trivial matters concerning the transfer of authority to Rome. A great many Egyptian noblemen have extensive landholdings on Cyprus, and their anxieties must be set at rest."

"We wouldn't want them worrying," I said. "I'm sure all will work out to your satisfaction. We Romans are punctilious about property rights, especially in regard to land and slaves."

"You mean," Cleopatra said, "that having stolen the whole island, you will respect all the deeds and titles?"

"Exactly," I affirmed. "It's the way the world works, if you hadn't noticed, Princess. After all, you Ptolemys stole the island from someone else, didn't you? And I'll wager you simply deposed the previous possessors, too—killed them or sent them packing without a drachma. Our way is better. Everyone agrees that our taxes are far lighter than the ones their old native rulers levied on them. It doesn't take long for people to get used to it."

"Rome's lordship is the admiration of the whole world," Photinus said.

"Come, sit with us, Senator," Cleopatra said. "You have missed a marvelous presentation."

"I caught the final verses," I told her. A moment later Alpheus joined us. Cleopatra presented him with an olive wreath, as if he had won in the Olympics.

"You flatter my modest verses," said the poet.

"Is this a new poem of yours?" I asked.

"I have been working on it for some time," he said, accepting a cup from one of the servers. "It was commissioned by the Temple of Aphrodite here in Paphos for the great festival. It will begin on the next full moon, ten days from now. Have you visited the Temple of Aphrodite, Senator?"

"I intend to, but I'm not on a sight-seeing expedition so it will have to wait until I have leisure."

"Do we sail out again tomorrow?" Cleopatra asked.

"If we have word of another raid."

"Then we will just get there too late again," she pointed out.

"The next raid or two should establish a pattern," I told her. "Once I have a pattern nailed down, I may be able to anticipate where they will strike next. In the meantime the men are far from perfectly drilled, and these outings will improve their performance."

"But what if there is no pattern?" she asked. "What if they attack on whim or just cruise about at random until they spot some likely, undefended place?"

"If these were ordinary sea robbers that would be a consideration," I admitted. "But their leader seems to be a Roman of military experience, and I think his mind will work in a more orderly fashion. He knows the business procedures of the islands and coastal ports, and I believe his raiding will be conducted with an eye toward maximizing his profits. With enough information about his activities, I should be able to anticipate his actions."

"You are depending heavily on these stories of the man's Roman origins," she said. "Suppose they prove to be wrong? It is easy enough to take a Roman name and allow others to make up stories about you."

"Even so," I said, "he is no brainless criminal following the pirate's trade for lack of a better. If he is not a Roman, I'll wager he has served with the Roman forces in the East. I understand Gabinius enrolled quite a large number of foreigners into the army he took to Egypt to set your father back on his throne."

"Yes," she agreed, "it contained only a core of Roman soldiers. The rest were every sort of Greek and Syrian. Then there were Cappadocians, Judeans, Lycians, Dardanians, and so forth. It was like the roll of the ships at Troy. There were even some Gauls and Germans. Those were the first Germans I ever saw."

"Why didn't you ask them if they sang?"

She smiled. "My father would never let me go near those soldiers. He considers only the Macedonian household guard fit to stand near a princess."

"Many of these soldiers stayed behind in Egypt, did they not?" I inquired.

"Many of them did," she said. "People grumbled about a Roman occupation, but they were just mercenaries. They took their oath to my father and are no longer part of any Roman army."

"Are there Romans among them though?"

"A few. But they are time-served veterans, not deserters or part of a Roman force. Their services are theirs to sell. Why are you so curious?"

"I am just trying to gain a clear idea of the military situation in these parts. In the West it is simple. There are the Roman legions and not much else except for our enemies. Here it is complicated. I am told that among these mercenaries are a number of the pirates resettled inland by Pompey."

Cleopatra shrugged. "If so, I am sure that it was all done quite legally. After all, it was a Roman general who arranged matters."

"So it was."

"Senator," Alpheus put in, "if you have no alarms to distract you in the morning, would you allow me to show you the Temple of Aphrodite? It is well worth the visit, and I have a feeling that, once your pursuit of Spurius begins in earnest, you will have very little time to devote to the finer things."

"That sounds like a splendid idea," I said. "Ion insists that those lazy sailors need some rest. If duty doesn't call, I will be more than happy to accept." The truth was, I felt the need of some rest myself. The wine was working on me, making the urgency of pirate-chasing seem more and more remote as the evening wore on. I looked around. "Where is our host? Off carousing with Gabinius again?"

"He is conferring with a delegation from Alexandria," Cleopatra said. "They arrived today with Photinus."

"Would General Achillas be among them?" I asked. I had been at swords' points with that martial gentleman during my stay in Alexandria. The thought of meeting with him on Roman territory was not without a certain charm.

"Oh, no!" Photinus said. "If it were an Egyptian delegation, I would be with them right now. No, these are Roman citizens resident in Alexandria who have anxieties concerning their property in Egypt and here on Cyprus."

"The duties of a Roman governor are tedious," I said, gazing about the beautiful garden, "but they have their compensations."

"Our host has done well for himself, I suppose." Photinus sniffed. He and Cleopatra lived amidst luxury that made the mansion of Silvanus seem little more than a hovel.

THE NEXT MORNING ALPHEUS ACCOMPA-nied me to the naval docks, where I learned that there was no word of new depredations. I ordered my skippers to keep the men in or near the barracks, ready to board and sail instantly. In the arsenal I checked on the progress made on the catapults and ballistas, which were coming along nicely. Then I went with Alpheus to visit the Temple of Aphrodite.

"The temple," Alpheus explained, as we drew near the complex of sacred buildings, "is one of the most ancient in the Greek-speaking parts of the world. Even if the tale of the goddess's arrival here and personal founding of the temple is untrue, it is far older than any Temple of Aphrodite on the mainland. It was built by people who still respected human scale."

Human scale was something of an exaggeration. It looked more like a temple built for Pygmies, no larger than a common farmhouse, constructed of large, ragged blocks of local stone and roofed with the inevitable red tile. The pillars of its portico were clearly stone replacements for wooden ones hewn from single logs.

Oddly, I found this pleasing. I have always preferred the very ancient, small Italian temples to the grandiose structures we have built in recent generations. The proportions of this temple were exquisite, and its setting was as charming as one could ask: a garden of ancient and lovingly tended trees in which bees hummed and birds sang as they had for who could tell how many centuries. Smoke from the morning sacrifice rose from the altar, and the scent of pure frankincense perfumed the air.

"The Ptolemies and the other successors of Alexander," I noted, "were in the habit of building colossal temples and enlarging the ones already in their domains. Have you ever been to Sicily?"

"I confess I've never been that far west," he said, "although I have heard of its temples."

"They built temples for giants. In fact there is one that has caryatids in the form of Atlas-like Titans. The Temple of Ephesian Diana is immense and, of course, the Serapeum in Alexandria is tremendous. The kings of Cyprus have never been poor. Why is their most famous temple so humble?"

"The priestesses have never allowed the temple to be enlarged. They say that the goddess founded it this way, and this is what she wanted. The kings have found other ways to embellish it. This garden, for instance, is entirely man-made. Early kings built great retaining walls and hauled in earth for the plantings. But the temple itself, and the image of the goddess, are as they have been since the days of legend."

I could find no fault with this, having seen too many bloated temples erected to the glory of the rich and powerful rather than in reverence to a god.

White-robed priestesses were everywhere, speaking with the numerous visitors. Most of the latter had come to Cyprus to attend the *Aphrodisia*. As usual, many of the more prominent visitors brought gifts for the temple. To my astonishment there was a familiar face among the priestesses.

"Flavia!"

The woman turned and smiled. She had been speaking with some prosperous-looking people in Roman dress. She took leave of them and came to join us.

"So you have found time from your duties to pay the goddess honor, Senator?"

"Indeed. But I did not expect to see you here dressed as a devotee."

"At home I am a priestess of Venus of the Mariners. We enjoy reciprocal status with the sisterhood here. Aphrodite of Paphos is primarily a sea goddess, with beauty, love, and fertility as her secondary traits. The connection between our temples goes back for centuries, before the time of the Etruscan kings. Come along, I'll show you the regalia."

Nothing loath, we followed. Since the temple was so small, most of its belongings were in outlying buildings, most of them larger than the temple itself. We entered one of these, a low, one-story structure faced with a finely painted portico, its roof supported by severely plain Doric pillars. Inside, a number of visitors stood admiring a wall covered with nets. It was not what I expected.

"Looks like a fisherman's storehouse," I remarked.

"Look more closely," Flavia advised.

So I went closer. The nets were extremely fine, almost like if over-sized spiderwebs. They also glistened brightly in the light that streamed through the portico windows and door. Then I saw that they were made not of twine but of fine, golden chain.

"At the climax of the *Aphrodisia*," she explained, "the priestesses will wear these nets when they go down to the sea to bathe and be renewed."

"In the old story," Alpheus said, "Hephaestus used a golden net to snare his wife, Aphrodite, in bed with Ares, her lover."

"On the mainland," she said, "Aphrodite lost most of her aspect as sea-goddess. You'll recall that it was Poseidon who offered to marry her himself when he saw her in the golden net. Here in her most ancient shrine, the net was hers, not her husband's."

"Will you be participating in the festival rites?" I asked her.

"Only as an attendant. A pity, really. I would love to bathe in the sea in full view of thousands of worshipers. Roman religious practice is so stodgy these days."

"How true," I commiserated. "Have you considered joining the Cult of Dionysus? It's forbidden throughout Italy but still greatly esteemed in the Greek parts of the world."

"I highly recommend the Samian rite," Alpheus said. "It is very an-cient, supremely orgiastic, and considered to be the holiest of all the Dionysian sects. The priestesses of Samos are renowned for their piety."

"Sergius would never agree," she said, sadly. "He is a banker, and Samos is not a particularly wealthy island. We'll probably never go there. Come along and let me show you the image of the goddess. It isn't what you might expect."

This proved to be true. The interior of the tiny temple was dim, and wisps of incense smoke made graceful volutes in the air. As my eyes grew accustomed to the light, I beheld the goddess taking form at the rear of the chamber. She was represented in white stone, probably marble, but she

92

could not have been more different from the polished, lifelike sculptures so familiar to us. The stone was roughhewn and porous, shaped in the vague semblance of a human form, its arms not separated from the body, nor the legs one from the other. An indentation midway up suggested a waist-line, two large but indistinct swellings represented breasts, and an ovoid shape at the top was her head. There were no discernible facial features.

I gazed upon this extraordinary image for a long time, somehow moved by it as I rarely was by the more famous statues of Aphrodite. With those, the observer was always conscious of them primarily as works of art rather than as objects of devotion. This seemed to me the cult object in its purest form. Gradually it came to me what I was seeing.

"This is the goddess still rising from the sea, still composed of sea-foam!" I said. "She has not yet achieved her full, divine form."

"You are perceptive—for a Roman."

It was not Flavia who had spoken. The voice reminded me of honey lightly flavored with smoke. I turned to see a woman of regal bearing, per-haps fifty years of age, once of a beauty to compare with Helen, and still wonderfully handsome. Her hair was black, parted simply in the middle, and her features bore the straight-lined perfection of the pure Hellene. Her skin was almost white, with the faintest olive tinge, and her eyes the clearest blue. I could see these things because she stood in the shaft of light admitted by the doorway. Her gown was purest white, and the light shone right through it, revealing a body unmarred by the years.

"I have been accused of many things but never an abundance of perception. Do I address the high priestess of this temple?"

"I am Ione," she said. I took this for affirmation.

I bowed. "I extend the respect and reverence of the Senate and Peo-ple of Rome, my lady."

She accepted this gravely as her due. "And I give you welcome to this holy place. I did not mean you any disparagement. It is just that Greeks un-derstand this aspect of the goddess instinctively, while Romans usually just see a crude piece of stone. You are not a Roman of the usual sort."

"I am told so by many of my fellow countrymen but never as a compliment."

"I think your country values the wrong sort of man. Please come with me."

Mystified, I followed her outside. Before her, the visitors parted hastily, some of them bowing almost as deeply as Orientals. Flavia and

Alpheus fell in behind us, and we picked up a following of the younger priestesses, some of them visibly pregnant. Unlike Vesta, Aphrodite is not served by virgins. Ione led us to a rather small but gnarled tree of a sort I had never seen before.

"This is the oldest tree in the garden," Ione said. "It was ancient when the kings first erected the terrace and planted the other trees. It is said to have sprouted from the stone when Aphrodite came here to found her temple. It is a myrrh tree, and there is no other like it on Cyprus, nor on the surrounding islands, nor on the nearby mainland. Kore, come here." A beautiful girl of perhaps seventeen attended and drew from her girdle a small pruning knife, its blade shaped like the crescent moon. Ione took the knife and with it cleanly severed a twig from a lower branch. This she presented to me solemnly. Somehow I knew that this was an act of deep significance.

"Please accept this and with it the favor and protection of the goddess."

I took it. "I accept this honor, reverend lady, but I do not understand why you do this."

"A man like you needs the protection of the gods far more than most." With that she turned and walked away, trailed by her beautiful, fruitful priestesses. The visitors who had been watching this strange ceremony regarded me with wonder and envy. Flavia's expression was more one of fear.

As Alpheus and I walked back to the harbor, he rattled on about what an extraordinary honor had been bestowed upon me. I still have that twig. It rests in my family shrine with the household gods; and in the many years since I received it from Ione's hands its leaves have dried and shrunk, but none have fallen off. Has it protected me? No one I knew in those days is still alive, so perhaps Paphian Aphrodite has watched over me. But, if so, it has been as much a curse as a blessing.

When we reached the harbor, word had just arrived of a pirate attack on a town on the other side of the island, so I took my leave of the poet and sailed off. Of course, we found no pirates, only a town where they had recently been. This time the looting had been of the conventional sort, with only salable goods and persons seized.

When we got back to Paphos, I learned that Governor Silvanus had been murdered.

7

THE MESSENGER THRUST THE BRONZE
tube into my hands the moment my feet touched dry land. "Extremely urgent business at the governor's mansion," he said, before I had a chance
to open it. "You are to come with me immediately, Senator."

"It can't be all that urgent," I told him. "I have things to attend to,
not least of which is reading this." I opened it and read. It was a marvel of
baldness:

Senator Metellus:
There has been murder here. Come at once.
A. Gabinius

"Truly Caesarian brevity," I remarked to no one in particular. Since
the note was signed by Gabinius rather than Silvanus, I already had an
idea of just who had been murdered.

"Ion!" I shouted. The man came running up.

"Sir?"

"Don't let anyone turn in until the ships are readied for instant launch. The practice cruises are over. Next time we'll be serious. We won't come back to port until we've bagged some pirates. Hermes, Ariston, come with me."

Already Cleopatra was rushing from her ship to join me. From the look of it, another messenger had delivered the same summons to her.

"This sounds serious," she said, when she arrived, slightly out of breath. She had not waited for her slaves to assemble her litter. "Come on. I may be a princess, but I haven't forgotten how to walk. I'm not going to wait to travel in state."

"No sense arriving tired," I advised, setting a leisurely pace. "Believe me, whoever's dead will still be dead whan we get there."

Doson, the majordomo, received us at the door. He was pale but composed. "Please come inside, Princess, Senator." He waited until we were all inside and the door shut behind us before going on. "Forgive this irregularity, but General Gabinius has given instruction that this matter not be made public immediately."

"Since General Gabinius is giving the orders, I take it that Governor Silvanus is deceased?" I said.

"Sadly true. It is terribly tragic and very, very strange. I—ah, here is the general now."

Gabinius entered the atrium, his craggy face more than ever like that of a battered eagle's. "My friend Silvanus is dead," he said. "I have not allowed word to spread yet. We must discuss this matter. Come with me."

We walked through the house, in our progress passing several tough-looking armed men of military bearing. One of them was the grizzled old centurion I had seen on the night we were attacked outside. From someplace came the muffled sound of many voices wailing.

"Those are the household slaves," Gabinius explained. "Of course it's their duty to mourn the master, but I've made them do it where they won't be heard outside." We entered the room where I'd conferred with the two senior Romans after the street fight.

"Who are those thugs?" I asked him, as we took chairs.

"Old soldiers of mine who've thrown in their lot with me. If you are ever exiled, you'll be well-advised to keep a picked band of such men close to you. In exile you'll have few friends and a great many enemies. Just now they're keeping the other guests quiet."

"You behave high-handedly, General," Cleopatra observed. "Had the governor no deputy?"

"No. One was to be sent out from Rome, but whoever the Senate has picked hasn't shown up yet."

"Then it seems to me," she said, "that Senator Metellus is the ranking Roman official here." I wished she had kept her mouth shut. My situation was precarious enough, and the last thing I needed was to get into a dogfight with Gabinius.

"The senator," he said, "has a commission from the State to deal with the pirates in the adjacent waters. That is going to keep him fully occupied for a long time. He has never held an office higher than aedile. I have served as praetor and consul together with the attendant promagistracies, as you well know, Princess."

"But you are an exile!" she said heatedly.

"That means only that I may not set foot in Italy until my exile is rescinded. Exile does not diminish my status."

I held up a hand. "This does not help things. I am quite willing to attend to my naval duties and leave administration here to an experienced magistrate until a replacement arrives from Rome. Cyprus does not yet have provincial status, and its government is still provisional. This is as good an arrangement as any, for now. There are more immediate matters to attend to."

"Exactly," Gabinius said. "I am glad that you are being so sensible, Decius Caecilius. We should work well together. To begin with, I was a close friend of Silvanus, so I shall undertake all the funeral arrangements and have his ashes sent to his family. They have a vault on the Via Appia, I believe."

"Will you deliver the eulogy?" I asked.

"I have been composing it all morning. It is a shame there are so few Romans of rank here to attend, but I will send the text to Rome to be recited at the tomb site. I will also write his family concerning his slaves and other property here. I presume his will is filed in Rome. It may contain manumissions for the senior slaves, and there will have to be some sort of disposition for the rest. I will see to all this."

"Agreed," I said. "Now I would like to know the circumstances surrounding the governor's death. You used the word 'murder' in your note, so I presume he died violently and that you've ruled out accident."

"Decidedly. I've seen men killed in a great many fashions, but this one is unique in my experience. I think you should view the body."

"An excellent idea," I said, standing. Cleopatra got up as well.

"No need for you to see this, Princess," Gabinius said.

"But I wish to. I have seen people die in great variety, too, General, some of them close relatives."

He shrugged. "Suit yourself." He led us from the room. "The body was discovered early this morning by the chamber slave who was supposed to wake Silvanus at sunrise. He had an early meeting scheduled with those wretched businessmen from Alexandria."

We found the late Governor Silvanus reclining upon his bed, his face blackened, eyes wide and protruding, mouth agape as if gasping for breath. Any such breath was precluded by the amorphous, yellowish mass that filled his mouth, spilling onto the pillow. It didn't look like something regurgitated in his death throes. Rather, it had the distinct aspect of something forcefully crammed into his mouth, causing the cheeks to bulge like a trumpeter's.

I picked up a particle from the pillow and examined it closely. It was a golden crystal, semitransparent. It looked almost like stone, but when I squeezed it between my nails it shattered. "What is this stuff?" I mused.

"You know what it is," Gabinius growled. "You've seen it all your life."

Cleopatra picked up a few grains and rubbed them between her fingers, then sniffed at the resulting powder. "Frankincense," she pronounced. "He choked on frankincense. What an amazing way to die."

"I don't suppose," I hazarded, "that our host was in the habit of experimenting with exotic foods? I have known others to sample inappropriate foodstuffs to their detriment."

"Not likely," Gabinius said. "Look at him. I'd say this was done by at least two strong men, more likely three. Someone held him down while someone else jammed his gullet full of frankincense. Then he had to be held there for a while. A man doesn't choke to death quickly, you know that."

"All too true. Have the slaves been examined?"

"Doson got them together and made a count. They're all here. There are a couple of porters strong enough to have accomplished it, but surely they would've fled after murdering their master. I don't think the household staff were involved."

"That's a relief," I said.

"It would make things simpler," Cleopatra said.

"Too simple," I told her. "Under Roman law, when a slave murders a master, all the slaves are crucified."

"What was it you said about my family's homicidal habits?"

"There are far easier ways to kill a man," I noted. "Stifling him with frankincense must have some sort of significance. Is there a large amount of it in the house?"

"The steward tells me there is some kept in the family shrine for the household gods," Gabinius answered. "There is never more than about half a pound of it on hand. I looked and there is about that much still there. Silvanus has at least a pound jammed down his throat. The killers brought it with them."

"Who was the last to see him alive?" I asked.

"After dinner he dismissed his slaves and went to bed it seems."

"And who were his guests?" A wealthy and important Roman almost never dines alone. Failure to entertain nightly means a reputation for miserliness, which is death to a political career.

"Most were those Roman businessmen from Alexandria," he said with distaste. "A despicable lot of moneygrubbers if you ask me." He had the true aristocrat's distaste for people who earned their own money instead of stealing or inheriting it. Gabinius had stolen and inherited quite a bit of it in his time. All quite respectably, of course. There is no shame attached to plundering the conquered and squeezing treasure out of desperate allies. His conviction for extortion and subsequent exile was just political bad luck not lasting dishonor.

"Were you here last night?"

"Eh?" he asked angrily, "what's that?"

"I merely want to establish who was present," I said.

"As a matter of fact I was at my house outside the town. When the murder was discovered, Doson locked the doors and sent a messenger to fetch me."

I ran a hand over my face, deep in thought. This was a complication I surely did not need. Pirates were a nuisance; this could be a disaster. "We need to assess the state of anti-Roman sentiment on the island. If this was done by a disgruntled pro-Ptolemy faction, we could be looking at the start of a war."

"I hope you do not imply that I was involved in this sordid business!" Cleopatra said hotly.

"Just now I can dismiss no one from suspicion. This is a matter of utmost seriousness."

"I will conduct the relevant investigation," Gabinius said. "There is no need for this to distract you from your duties."

"But there is," I said. "I was his guest."

There was little he could say by way of objection. Hospitality is more than mutual entertainment; it involves sacred obligations. I was eating his food and sleeping beneath his roof. And ancient, ritual law decrees that if a host is slain, it is the duty of his guest to avenge him. Silvanus was a man I had not known well and did not particularly like, but that is of no significance to religious law. Failure to seek out his killers and bring them to justice could draw the wrath of the gods, and I was not about to risk that.

For a while I examined the bedchamber but found nothing of significance. There was little evidence of struggle other than a slight disarray of the bedclothes. I assumed that Silvanus must have been asleep when the killers struck, allowing them to pinion him securely before he had a chance to resist.

"When will you make the announcement of his death?" Cleopatra asked.

"I see little point in concealing it any longer now that we have been informed," I said. "Aulus Gabinius, why don't you go ahead and inform the city council and post notice of Silvanus's demise? For now there's no need to say that he was murdered. This isn't Rome, and we don't owe these people a rigorous legal accounting. They may as well have the impression that he died of natural causes or misadventure. If anyone challenges that, it will be evidence of a conspiracy."

He nodded. "It makes sense. With all that stuff cleared out of his mouth, he'll look presentable enough for his funeral, except for the color of his face. How shall we say he met his end?"

I shrugged. "People drop dead all the time, and nobody can say why. But you might as well simply say he choked to death. It's not an uncommon cause of death. I've known men of great distinction and accomplishment who have choked on peach pits or chicken bones. It will account for his blackened face."

"I shall do it then," he agreed.

"How many of the household know for certain that he was murdered?" Cleopatra asked.

Gabinius thought for a moment. "Doson, Androcles the steward, and the slave who discovered him; and she's spoken to no one but Doson, he's assured me. My own men, and I've instructed them to keep silent about it. For the rest, they just know the master's dead."

"Let's see how long we can keep it that way," I advised. When will you notify Rome?"

"It's too late for a ship to sail today. I'll compose a letter to the Senate this evening and dispatch it to Rome at first light. I can't detach any of your ships, and Caesar's stripped the naval base as you learned. I'll hire a ship to row hard to Tarsus. There is a naval base there, and the commander is a friend of mine, Lentulus Scaevola. He'll detach a fast cutter to take the letter to Brundisium or Tarentum. A rider can carry the letter to the house of Cicero in Rome, and Cicero can present it to the Senate."

I thought about it for a moment. "I probably can't get word there any faster. Are you and Cicero on good terms these days?"

"Excellent. He'll call a special meeting of the Senate for this." He was all but grinning, and I could see the wheels turning in his head. Cleopatra looked from one of us to the other, clearly mystified.

"Let's do it that way then." Finished with my examination of the area around the bed, I straightened. "And now, if you don't mind, the princess and I are overdue for dinner and some rest."

"Go ahead. I'll see to things here. Doson!" He bellowed the name, but the majordomo had been waiting just outside the bedchamber door. He hurried in. "General Gabinius?"

"You may release the household staff, but none of them are to leave the house or talk to anyone outside until I say so. They are to attend to their late master's guests as always. Begin preparations for a funeral and tell everyone to mourn quietly. They can wail as loud as they like at the funeral."

The majordomo bowed. "It shall be as you say, General."

We left and repaired to the garden. Slaves appeared and efficiently set about making us comfortable and getting us fed. Despite swollen eyes and tear tracks, they didn't appear especially grief stricken, merely anxious in the usual fashion of slaves when the master is dead and their future uncertain.

"Is this the way you Romans always do things?" Cleopatra asked. "I find it difficult to believe that a serving Roman official is deferring to a mere exile! Why did you not take charge and arrange affairs to your own liking?"

I took a sip of the excellent wine and selected a seedcake. "Rome is a republic, not a monarchy," I reminded her. "I am not a viceroy, and Gabinius is not a powerless nobody, like someone your father would exile, stripping him of lands, wealth, and influence. Rome is governed by great families whose leading members hold the consulships and praetorships. Their supporters comprise Romans of all levels. There are the bulk of the senators, who are men who have held the lesser offices; the class of *equites,* who have money and property but who don't go into politics, like our friend Sergius Nobilior the banker; and the great bulk of the citizenry, who vote in the Plebeian Assembly. There is also the Centuriate Assembly and the Tribunician Committee, but these days real power lies in the Senate and the Plebeian Assembly."

I dipped the seedcake in honey. "Politics consists of a constant rearrangement of support and power blocs, as each of the great families seeks to place as many of its own members and supporters in high public office as it can. Yesterday's deadly enemy becomes today's staunch ally. An exile voted by an indignant Senate may be rescinded by a friendly tribune passing a law in the Plebeian Assembly."

She shook her head. "It sound like anarchy. It's political chaos."

"It can be confusing, but it works well for us. For instance, the nearest naval base is at Tarsus. The commander there is Scaevola, and he is a supporter of Pompey, who detests the Metelli. If I were to send that letter under my own seal, he'd put it on the slowest scow on the sea.

"I *would* send the letter to Cicero to read to the Senate. Cicero has always been friendly with me and usually with my family as well. He once attacked Gabinius in a lawsuit. As I recall, he characterized Gabinius as 'a prancing, effeminate dancing boy in hair curlers.'"

"That is difficult to imagine," she replied.

"Nothing is too scurilous in a Roman lawsuit. A few years later, he ably defended Gabinius in a lawsuit for extortion; but Cicero was no longer so popular in Rome, and Gabinius was exiled. Gabinius is a strong supporter of Caesar though. So when Caesar returns from Gaul, he will have Gabinius recalled and restored to all his honors. This sort of thing happens all the time."

She sipped at her wine and said nothing for a while, then declared, "You people are insane. That is no way to run a petty city-state, much less a great empire. Can you really administer *anything* on a basis of friend-ships and feuds and temporary pacts of assistance between families and individuals? Can anything of importance be decided when four separate assemblies have to take a vote? When one consul can overrule the other and a decision of the Senate can be blocked by the veto of a single trib-une? It is madness!"

"We've done rather well with it," I said, with some complacency. "We control most of the world and are quickly expanding into the rest of it. Our system may lack the orderliness of a monarchy with a king and a hereditary nobility, but it spares us the government of pedigreed imbeciles. In Rome any man of great will and ability can shape the destiny of the world."

My confident words were purely for her benefit. The sad fact was that our rickety old Republic was fast coming apart. It was being destroyed by self-seeking megalomaniacs like Caesar, Pompey, and Gabinius, and, I hate to admit, by reactionary, aristocratic families like my own. We thought our-selves conservative because we steered a moderate course between the would-be Alexanders, but our maneuverings always had the goal of ex-panding our own clientage, holdings, and influence.

"Rome may be master of the world," she said, "but soon one of your great men must make himself master of Rome. There can be no other out-come."

The coming years were to prove her words prophetic.

THAT NIGHT A DREAM CAME TO ME. MOST people make far too much of dreams, attaching vast import to the most banal reflections of everyday cares, woes, and ambitions. I do not believe that the gods often put themselves to the trouble of sending prophetic vi-sions to individuals, and it is usually a mark of vanity to believe oneself the frequent recipient of such divine messages. When the gods wish to communicate with us, they speak to the entire community; and they do so through the medium of thunder and lightning, the flights of birds, and signs put in the heavens. We have officials and priests whose task it is to interpret such omens.

Personally, I have never believed that the entrails of sacrificial ani-mals have anything to do with it. That is mere Etruscan superstition.

Nevertheless, upon very special occasions, I experience a dream vision so remarkable that I think it must be sent by some divine agency, although perhaps not by a true Olympian. My vanity is not that great. Each of us, man or woman, is born with an attendant genius. These spirits watch over us and inspire us throughout life. It may be that they are in contact with other, equally supernatural beings and are able, at times of great import in our lives, to pass on messages from a world invisible to us.

However, it is the custom of the immortals to speak in signs, riddles, and conundrums when communicating with mortals; and so it was this time. For what it is worth, this was my dream.

I opened my eyes as from a deep sleep and discovered myself to be surrounded by clouds. In an instant I broke free of the clouds and saw below me a mass of brown and green surrounded by a deep blue-green. At first I could make no sense of what I was seeing. Then it came to me that I was gazing upon a great island lying in the sea. This, I understood, must be how the world looks to a soaring eagle. In the manner of dreams the great height at which I hovered did not alarm me, nor did it occur to me to wonder how I could be flying in the first place. Dreams take place in another world in which there is no past leading to the events we experience there.

I flew down toward the island (somehow I knew how to do this) and began to see details that had been invisible from higher up: ships upon the sea looking like children's toys, jewel-like towns with white walls and red roofs, and cattle no larger than ants grazing the hillsides.

I began to circle the island and, as I did, saw a disturbance in the wine dark sea perhaps a legionary mile offshore (distances are hard to judge when one is flying). There arose a great boiling and foaming, as if a volcano were erupting far below. The foam rose into a tower and began to take human shape. Soon there stood, larger than the greatest colossus, the form of a beautiful woman. She was, of course, the goddess Venus (well, Aphrodite, to be precise). She was still composed of semitransparent foam, for which I was grateful. To behold a real goddess would have blasted me to vapor even in my dream state. Such sights are not for mortals. I felt no fear but rather experienced awe of a purity I have seldom known in my long life.

Like a great cloud in motion, she strode across the waves, her feet indenting the water as if she walked upon a blue-green mantle thrown across a bed filled with the finest down. When she reached the coast, I expected to see great activity from the tiny towns: people rushing to see, songs of praise ringing out, a great stoking of altar fires. But I detected no reaction from the minute inhabitants of this place. They did not see her.

With a graceful gesture the goddess beckoned to me, and I followed her. Along the coastline of the island we went, passing many small coves, some of them lively with small fishing craft, some deserted. I was no longer at eagle-soaring height, though I was well above the tallest trees on the shore. I felt now more like a cruising gull, but that was because I was over water. As an attendant of Aphrodite, I suppose I was a dove, that bird being sacred to her.

We came to a part of the island that was different from the rest. A great district was denuded of trees, its soil gouged away into deep pits. Everywhere I saw columns of smoke rising to the heavens, as if a hundred farmsteads were burning.

The goddess arose from the sea and began to walk over the island, her toes just touching the crests of the hills as she strode inland. I followed, flying at the level of her perfect waist.

Inland the devastation was enormous. Whole hillsides and valleys were reduced to bare dirt and rock, furrowed with erosion, the stream muddy and foul. Everywhere the pits and tunnels made the island leprous. Gradually, light faded from the sky, and from the base of every column of smoke there came a sullen, red glow, as of a fire burning night and day.

We came to the other side of the island, and it was dawn again. The night had passed with the magical swiftness of dreams. The goddess walked out upon the waves once more. Below me the coastline was green and beautiful. Here no unnatural despoliation blighted the landscape, and all was serene perfection.

Aphrodite (if it truly was she and not some phantom in her shape) turned a last time and regarded me with a look of great sadness upon her wonderful features. Then she began to lose shape, to collapse in upon herself, returning to the sea until she was no more than scattered streaks of white atop the waves.

THE NEXT MORNING I WENT ABOUT IN A daze. The dream did not fade from memory as most of mine do but rather stayed sharp in all its details, and I had no doubt that it was a vision of utmost significance. But what did it mean? There are those who interpret dreams as a profession, but I had always doubted their gifts. In any case

I felt that the goddess had not spoken to me in riddles, but rather had shown me some real thing, though whether this was a reflection of the present or a prophecy of the future I did not know.

Leaving Hermes in the house to relay any messages from the naval base, I walked out into the town. The hour was early, but already it was abuzz with news of the murder. People eyed me warily, perhaps expecting some sort of violent vengeance from Rome, but I paid them no attention. For once my political and street senses were in abeyance. I had my mind on higher matters. Almost without conscious volition, my steps took me back to the Temple of Aphrodite.

"Senator!" The priestess Ione regarded me with some surprise. "You are back so soon?" She was supervising a bevy of her ever-charming acolytes who were hanging enormous, colorful wreaths all over the temple and its grounds.

"I hate to bother you when you are so busy preparing for the festival," I said to her. "But last night I believe your goddess sent me a vision." I added hastily, "Please, I am not the sort of person who has visions all the time. Quite the contrary in fact. That is why I hope you might be able to help me."

"Surely," she said, as if this were the sort of request she received every day. Maybe it was. She issued instructions to the white-robed women and asked me to accompany her. We went to a secluded part of the garden surrounded by a high hedge, its open side over looking the sea. I sat beside her on a marble bench supported by carved dolphins and told her of my dream. She followed this recitation with a look of deep seriousness, saying nothing until I was finished.

"This is most unusual," she said, when I was done. "Aphrodite very often appears in dreams. Most often it is because the dreamers are troubled in matters of love or fearful of barrenness or the dangers of childbirth. She has dominion over all these things. Here on Cyprus and some of the other islands she guides the thoughts and decisions of seafarers as well. What you saw in your dream is most uncharacteristic."

"Then perhaps it was merely a reflection of my own worries and the goddess had nothing to do with it," I said, almost relieved.

"No, what you saw was a true vision. I know this. Her appeararance as sea foam means she was Aphrodite of Paphos and no other."

"But what can it mean?"

"Do you have your purse with you, Senator?" she asked.

"I do."

"Then take out the smallest coin you have."

Mystified, I took the *marsupium* from beneath my tunic and rummaged through it. I drew forth a copper coin, the smallest minted in Rome. It bore the image of an augur from a previous generation, indifferently struck. I handed it to her, and she weighed it in her palm.

"What do you call the metal this coin is made of?"

"The Latin word is *aes*," I answered.

"And what is it called in Greek?"

I thought for a moment. *"Kyprios."* Then I made the connection. "It means 'Cyprian,' doesn't it?" And then it struck me that, in poems, Aphrodite is often called "the Cyprian."

"Exactly. Copper has been mined on this island since the days of the pharaohs. The copper mines of Cyprus have been the wealth of the island, as the silver mines of Laurium were the wealth of Athens. What the goddess showed you in your dream is the result of more than two thousand years of copper mining. The land is ravaged, its soil destroyed by digging and erosion, its timber harvested for wood to smelt the ore."

"How much of the island is ruined?" I asked her.

"Most of it," she said sadly. "What seems so fair from offshore is a wasteland just a short walk inland. This island has enriched pharaohs and Great Kings and Macedonian conquerors and now, it seems, it is to enrich Rome. But I do not think that if Aphrodite were to choose a home now, she would pick Cyprus."

I was shocked and saddened. If there is one thing that is sure to enrage an Italian, it is the destruction of productive land. We treat other people with great brutality at times, but we always respect and honor land. At heart we are all still small landholders, tending our few acres of field and orchard.

"Why did she reveal this to me?" I asked. "Surely there is nothing I can do about the ruination of her home."

"Someday you may be able to," she said. You are Roman, of a great family, and destined to hold high office. People say that Romans can do anything—that you divert rivers to serve your purposes, drain swamps to make new farmland, create harbors where there is only exposed shoreline. Perhaps such a people can restore Cyprus to the garden it once was."

"We admit to few limitations," I agreed. "It would be an intriguing project." I would never admit to her that anything lay beyond the powers of Roman genius. "When I return to Rome I will speak to the College of Pontifices. Caesar is *Pontifex Maximus,* and he is fond of undertaking projects in the name of Venus, since she is the ancestress of his house. Venus, or Aphrodite, was the mother of the Trojan hero Aeneas, who fled the burning city and settled in Italy. The Julian gens trace their descent from his son, Julus."

"I see. He is busy in Gaul, is he not?"

"Yes, but soon he will return to Rome. He will be incomparably rich and ready to undertake all sorts of extravagant things. That is his style. My wife is his niece."

"Ah, then there was good reason for Aphrodite to make her wishes known to you. Rome is the new master of Cyprus, you have a great future ahead of you as a Roman statesman, and you are related by marriage to the most glorious Roman of the age, who, it seems, is her many times great grandchild."

It always annoyed me when people spoke as if Caesar were the greatest man in Rome, but that was how he publicized himself so I suppose it was excusable.

I took my leave of Ione with many thanks and a gift for the temple. I fully intended to carry out my promise to approach the pontifices, whose pronouncements the Senate would follow, as soon as I returned to Rome.

It is not every day a goddess visits you and makes her wishes known.

8

By midafternoon the town was in full uproar for Silvanus's funeral. The house slaves were out in the plaza between the governor's mansion and the Temple of Poseidon, wailing fit to terrify an invading army. With military thoroughness, Gabinius had organized the whole affair. Carpenters were hammering away, erecting temporary stands for the local notables, men were roping off an area for the common spectators, women were bringing in heaps of flowers, and a funeral pyre of expensive, fragrant woods was being stacked in the center of the open area.

I thought it was clever of Gabinius to make such a show of it. Surely, whatever the state of anti-Roman sentiment, nobody would start a riot amid such solemnities. Everyone loves a good funeral. Just in case, though, Gabinius's hard-bitten veterans were everywhere to be seen. I even spotted a few on the roof of the temple. It pays to be cautious, but I couldn't catch even the sound of anti-Roman grumbling, and I've been in enough newly conquered cities to develop sharp ears for that sort of talk.

Seeing that everything appeared well in hand, I walked down to the market. The place was as busy as always and there was lively conversation about the demise of Silvanus, but the mood was not ugly and nobody cast evil looks in my direction.

I passed the stalls of the silk merchants, the glass sellers, the cutlery mongers, the sellers of bronze ware, and the rest. My nose led me to a section devoted to such things as perfumes, spices, medicines, and, naturally, incense.

The largest such stall was owned by a fat Greek who clearly did not share his countrymen's passion for athleticism.

"How may I help you, Senator? I am Demades, and I sell incense of all kinds and in all quantities. I can sell you a pinch to burn before your household gods or a year's supply for the largest temple in Rome. I have cedar incense from Lebanon, subtle cardamom incense from India, fir gum incense from Iberia, balm incense from Judea. I even have the rarest of all, an incense compounded with oil of sandalwood. It comes from trees that grow on an island far east of India. From another island of that sea I have incomparable benzoin, as useful for embalming as for burning before the gods. I have incense of myrrh from Ethiopia, famed for its healing properties. What is your pleasure?"

"Tell me about frankincense."

"Ahh, frankincense. The noblest of all the fragrances, and the most pleasing to all the gods. How much do you want?"

"Actually, I want to know about its history and where it is harvested and how it gets from its place of origin to places such as—well, here, for instance."

"You are a scholar?" he asked, somewhat puzzled.

"Of sorts. Immensely curious, in any case. And whenever I desire to learn about a subject, I always go to the one likely to know the most about it. When I inquired about frankincense, I was told that Demades was the very man I needed." Flattery costs nothing and often yields handsome results.

He beamed. "You were informed correctly. My family has engaged in the frankincense trade for many generations. There is no aspect of the traffic with which I am unacquainted." At his hospitable gesture, I took a chair at the rear of the booth, and he sat on a large, fragrant bale. He sent a slave boy off to fetch us refreshments.

"First off, I know that it comes from Arabia Felix, but I am a little hazy concerning the geography of that part of the world."

"Arabia Felix takes its name from its near-monopoly on the frankincense trade," he said. "If I had that monopoly, I would be happy, too."

"You said 'near-monopoly'?"

"Yes. The greater part of the frankincense gum is harvested in a small district near the southern coast of Arabia, but the shrub also grows in a small area of Ethiopia bordering the Red Sea. The greater quantity is harvested in Arabia, but the Ethiopian gum is of higher quality, almost white in color. It burns with a brilliant flame and leaves less ash residue. In both areas, local tribesmen harvest the gum, scratching the bark of the shrubs, letting the sap bleed forth and harden. These droplets, called 'tears,' are then scraped off, bagged, and carried on camels to the ports. The tribesmen are jealous of their harvesting grounds and trade routes. They fight fiercely to defend them."

"Where is it shipped from these ports?"

"Some travels eastward to India and to lands known only in legend and lore, but most is taken north up the Red Sea. From the Sinai it is carried overland to Alexandria, whence it is shipped all over the world. My own family resides in the Greek Quarter of Alexandria, and our business is based there."

"*All* of it goes to Alexandria?"

"Indeed. In the days of the Great King much went up the coast to Jerusalem and Susa and Babylon, but the first Ptolemy made the trade a personal monopoly of the Egyptian crown. Royal agents buy the gum at Sinai and sell it to trading firms like my family's at a great yearly auction in Alexandria."

"I take it that your trade routes are very old and established?"

"Oh, very much so," he assured me. "The traffic in frankincense is one of the few things that never changes through the centuries, despite alterations of dynasty and empire."

"How is this?" I asked him, fascinated as I often am by the words of a man who truly knows his business, especially when it is a subject about which I know all but nothing.

"Consider, sir. Frankincense is one of those rare commodities that is valued by all peoples. So is gold, but gold is stolen, hoarded, buried in Egyptian tombs, used to decorate monuments and wives. A great haul of gold, as when your General Lucullus sacked Tigranocerta, will depress the price of gold throughout the world.

"But frankincense is entirely consumed. That which is burned at a single ceremony must be replaced soon by the same amount. Where the amount of gold in circulation changes from year to year, that of frankincense remains almost constant. The trees are little affected by changes of rainfall; their number neither increases nor decreases. Only a freak storm on the Red Sea, sinking many ships of the incense fleet, is likely to alter the amount of the product delivered to Sinai. But the climate of the Red Sea and its winds at that time of year are almost as predictable as the rise and fall of the Nile."

He gestured eloquently. "Consider jewels. Everyone values them highly, but nobody agrees which are the most valuable. The emerald, the ruby, and the sapphire are valued in most places, but traders from the Far East scorn them. They want coral and the green stone called jade. You Romans use the colored stones for amulets and seal rings, but prize pearls above all to adorn your women. Everyone esteems amber, but as much for its reputed medicinal qualities as for its beauty.

"But every god must have frankincense. It is burned before the altars of the Olympian deities, in the groves of Britannia, in the great Serapeum of Alexandria, before the images of the thousand gods of Egypt, and the many Baals of the East. Herodotus affirms that, each year at the great festival of Bel, the Assyrians burnt frankincense to the weight of one thousand talents before his altar. Think of it! Thirty tons transformed to smoke at a single ceremony! Of old the Arabians yielded a like amount to Darius as tribute. The nameless god of the Jews gets his share, and each year I set aside a large consignment for the *Aphrodisia* celebrated here. A goodly poundage will go up in the funeral pyre of our late Governor Silvanus, too."

"Yours is a great and ancient trade," I acknowledged. "But surely your ships are often preyed upon by pirates, and this must represent a hazard of the business."

"Ah, but your General Pompey nearly eliminated that threat. And I understand that you, Senator, are here to put down the recent revival of that disreputable activity."

"Still, it seems such a desirable cargo. I would think that nautical miscreants would single out ships bearing frankincense as their natural prey."

He gestured eloquently, a combination shrug and spreading of palms that suggested a comfortable complacency. "As to that, sir, the two trades—one legitimate, the other felonious—came to an understanding many, many years ago."

At last we were getting to the important part. "How so?"

"The pirates, you understand, are—were, I should say, organized, rather like a corporation, almost like a small state in fact."

"Of course."

"This being the case, it has been possible to treat with them: representatives, bargaining sessions, business arrangements, the whole panoply of diplomatic arrangements between states was possible between the frankincense cartel and the pirates."

"And I take it that the Ptolemies formed one side of this arrangement?"

"Not directly," said the merchant. "After all, the frankincense is sold in Alexandria. Once at sea, what concern has the king what happens to it? The next year he will sell that year's delivery as always.

"No, all merchants who handle frankincense in bulk belong to the Holy Society of Dionysus. Each year, on the eve of the auction, we hold a banquet in the Temple of Dionysus in Alexandria, where we honor our patron deity and make our arrangements for the coming year's business. The society has envoys who handle all negotiations concerning the trade outside of Egypt. They deal with the authorities in the lands where we ship our cargoes, arrange for tithes, duties, and so forth. Among those they treat with are the pirates—*were* the pirates, I should say, since Rome has so beneficently driven that scourge from our sea after a fashion."

"So now your cargoes ride the sea-lanes safely, as long as weather cooperates and the timbers don't rot, eh?"

"Well, there is some slight danger of attack," he admitted with another small gesture. "You understand, sailors are a conservative lot, and in some ways they have not changed since the days of Odysseus. Sailors are, to put it bluntly, a rascally lot at the best of times. A ship with a crew of fifteen, for instance, meets with a smaller ship with a crew of only seven. The men of the larger ship take a careful look around, determine that there are no other ships in sight, take their weapons from their sea chests, and the next thing you know, seven unfortunate sailors are on their way to meet Poseidon, soon to be followed by their scuttled vessel, and the larger ship goes on its way, riding somewhat deeper in the water.

"These men are not pirates in the sense of the old, organized fleets. They are just ordinary sailors who see that Hermes has sent them a fine opportunity and are not about to anger the god by scorning his gift. These men seek only goods they can dispose of easily and without suspicion. They do not deal in slaves or ransom captives because they must have no witnesses to their nefarious deeds."

"This is most illuminating," I told him, and indeed it was. "Is this sort of naughtiness more common of late?"

He nodded, sighing. "Assuredly, Senator. And, while I would never speak ill of the glorious Republic of Rome, which you so ably represent and which all the world beholds with awe and wonder, much of this is your fault."

"How so?"

"In the old days the great fleets treated Poseidon's broad domain as their personal property. They were like eagles or great falcons, and when they found petty rogues poaching upon the waters, they behaved as the noble birds do when they espy ravens and magpies snatching game from their hunting grounds. Their revenge was swift and terrible. They were a scourge to many ships and most certainly a scourge to small, undefended towns along the coastlines and in the islands; but to those who could afford to treat with them, they afforded a security that has fled since they were banished from the sea."

"How unfortunate. And do you see in this latest outbreak of piracy a possible return to the security of the old days?"

"How is that possible, now that Rome is in charge? In any case, these new villains do not amount to a patch on the sail of one of the old triremes. They are too petty to treat with the Holy Society of Dionysus."

"Well, have no fear," I said, rising. "Soon Rome will be in firm control of the entire sea and its coasts, and Roman courts will soon deal with these seagoing rascals. Then the sea-lanes will be safe for everyone."

"I will sacrifice to Zeus, imploring him to speed the blessed day." I thought I detected a trace of irony in his smile.

Before leaving I thanked him profusely and bought a handful of frankincense, compounded with myrrh and benzoin, a very potent blend, to toss onto the funeral pyre of Silvanus.

Back at the home of the late governor, I found the statuary draped in black so that the sculptured figures could join in the mourning for their former owner. In Rome the figures of Silvanus's ancestors in the atrium would be thus draped, but here in a foreign place this expedient had to serve. The wailing was less extravagant, probably because the slaves were getting hoarse. Hermes spotted me and ran up.

"Any word from the harbor?" I asked him.

"No, praise all the gods. Maybe we'll have a reprieve." He looked around sourly. "Not that this place is a great joy to inhabit. Why don't we take lodgings somewhere else for a while?"

"No, just now I am exactly where I want to be. Where are Photinus and that Egyptian delegation?"

"I saw him in the garden awhile ago. What do you want him for?"

I walked past him. "Suddenly Egypt is in the air and on everyone's lips. I want to find out why this should be."

"If you say so." He followed me.

Photinus was seated by the pool, deep in conversation with Cleopatra. That was all right with me. I wanted a word with her also.

"Good to see you, Senator," said the eunuch, "even at such a sad time as this."

"Any time is a good one to renew so happy an acquaintance," I said with some jollity. Courtier and princess studied me with some wonder.

"You seem in a lighthearted mood today, Senator," Cleopatra observed.

"Indeed. I am feeling scholarly, and this afternoon I have been adding to my store of knowledge. There are few more agreeable activities."

"Are you well, Senator?" Photinus asked. "Try some of this date wine. It is mixed with ambergris and civet musk. Egyptians esteem it as the most fortifying drink in the world."

I tried it. "Wonderful stuff," I commended him. It tasted dreadful. "Photinus, my old and valued friend, I have been wondering about that pack of Roman merchants from Alexandria you've been shepherding about of late."

"Yes, Senator?"

"Would any of them happen to be in the frankincense trade?"

"I suppose some of them may have dealings in that particular business. Why do you ask?"

"He is asking," Cleopatra said, "because Governor Silvanus choked to death on frankincense." She eyed me warily.

"Princess, yesterday when we viewed the body of Silvanus and determined the extraordinary nature of his demise, you did not mention that your father owns a monopoly on the frankincense trade."

"I saw no reason to mention it. That is only within Egyptian borders anyway. It is the custom everywhere, when a luxury good passes through a nation, for the king to own a monopoly on its trade. Once it is sold at Alexandria, its new owners take it wherever they will. My father has nothing to do with frankincense on Cyprus."

"But, until quite recently, Cyprus was a Ptolemaic kingdom," I pointed out.

"Really, Senator," Photinus trilled, "you cannot think that the princess had anything to do with this awful murder."

"I did not say so, I just find the connection intriguing, and I must observe that, historically, the Ptolemies have displayed a taste for the most peculiar forms of murder."

"Are you trying to provoke me?" Cleopatra demanded. "I will remind you that I, too, am a guest in the house of Silvanus, and I am quite aware of the displeasure of the gods when the sacred bond of guest and host is broken by bloodshed."

"If you will forgive me, Princess," I said, "you Ptolemies have the most disgraceful record of incest, parricide, matricide, infanticide, and every other form of unnatural behavior in all the long, sorry history of royalty."

"It isn't easy being king," she said, seeming neither angered nor embarrassed. "For centuries we have been Greek rulers in a foreign land. Not only that, everyone else envies us and would like to conquer us. Royalty are not like the common run of humanity and should not be judged as such."

"Far be it from me to judge you," I assured her. "But I have a suspicious nature, and when I investigate a crime I look for—how shall I express this?—I look for correspondences, things that two otherwise unrelated events, persons, or circumstances have in common. Especially unlikely, obscure things. To wit, Governor Silvanus is dead, choked on frankincense, a method of homicide unique in my experience.

"A bit of inquiry at the marketplace today reveals that all the frankincense shipped over the sea comes through Egypt, where it is a royal monopoly. The princess of Egypt is a guest of the lamented Governor Silvanus. The First Eunuch of the court of King Ptolemy is a new arrival here, along with a delegation of Alexandrian merchants, some of whom may be aggrieved. I think you can understand why these things rouse my hunting-dog instincts."

"This is a most intriguing philosophical concept," she said seriously. "Were it not for the personal affront to myself, I should find it enthralling."

"I think, Senator," Photinus said frostily, "that you should confine your inquiries to the Alexandrian merchants. I shall be most happy to furnish introductions."

"Excellent idea," I said. "How soon can you get them together?"

"It had better be soon," he said. "Since the governor is dead, some of them are already making preparations to return to Alexandria."

"They'll do nothing of the sort until I am satisfied that none of them are involved. Call them together this evening after dinner."

"No one conducts business after dinner," he protested, scandalized.

"As you have said, time grows short."

SINCE THE HOUSE WAS IN MOURNING, I dined in my quarters. This was a relief because I needed time to myself. I had a great deal of information and experience through which to sort. In some investigations, the challenge is to find a likely suspect. In this one, it was to narrow down a field that was all too wide. I suffered from an over-abundance of suspicion. I had possible murderers vying with one another like so many charioteers in the Circus.

My two major suspects so far were Gabinius and Cleopatra. Gabinius was an exile, an ambitious general like too many Romans of his generation, desperate to get back to Rome and into the game of supreme power once more. True, he and Silvanus had been most friendly, but friendship is a notoriously elastic concept among politicians. He was here with a pack of thugs and was far too eager to seize control of affairs in Cyprus. A firm handling of the situation here might well raise his credit in Rome and speed his recall. And where was Silvanus's deputy anyway?

Cleopatra had ample reason to hate Rome. Rome had restored her father to his throne, but at a humiliating price. Rome had taken Cyprus from Egypt and driven her apparently beloved uncle to suicide. There was the fact that she had been the guest of Silvanus, but she came of a family that was sometimes capable but never scrupulous. In any case they had long since adopted the Egyptian practice of royal deification, pretending

117

to be living gods. Maybe she thought she could square things with the other gods later. And there was that business of the frankincense, whatever that implied.

But I did not want to suspect Cleopatra. I did not want this to turn into a major confrontation between Egypt and Rome. Our relations were tortured enough as it was and had been for centuries. Besides, I liked Cleopatra. She was an utterly unique woman, young though she was, and impossible to dislike unless she so desired it. Recognizing my own prejudice in her favor, I determined to be doubly suspicious of her.

And there were lesser suspects as well. The banker Sergius Nobilior and his salacious wife were playing a game of their own. The ever-elusive pirates might well have had cause to eliminate Silvanus. They always needed ports in which to dispose of their illegally gained cargoes and friendly officials to look the other way while they were doing it. Silvanus might well have indulged in such corrupt practices. Roman governors of that day were a venal lot. Despite what the First Citizen claims, they haven't improved much since either.

Photinus came for me personally, after allowing me a decent time to digest.

"Senator, since this house is in mourning, the party would prefer not to meet here. The high priest of the Temple of Poseidon has consented to let us meet in the temple." Once again he was all friendly courtesy. It is a courtier's special skill.

I could not blame them for not wanting to meet in a house of mourning. It is a well-known bringer of bad luck. And people often meet in temples. Even the Senate sometimes meets in the Temple of Jupiter or that of Bellona. It is commonly believed that people are less likely to lie in a temple, and it means you don't have to make a special trip if an oath must be sworn. Nevertheless, I put on my military belt with its sword and dagger. I had no special reason to fear treachery, but it would do no harm to remind these people of who I was. Hermes, as always in this place, was armed to the teeth.

We walked across the plaza before the mansion to the dignified old temple. The interior had been illuminated with lamps and folding chairs brought so we could all sit comfortably. To my surprise there were only four men waiting for us, and they seemed not to have brought any attendants. They all looked very different, but each wore the toga of a Roman citizen.

"I am Senator Decius Caecilius Metellus the Younger," I announced as I stepped within the sacred precincts. "I bear a commission from the Senate and People of Rome to stamp out piracy in these waters and am, at present, investigating the circumstances surrounding the death of Governor Silvanus." I looked them over. "I had expected a larger group. Are all here?"

"Each of these gentlemen," said Photinus, "represents a syndicate of Roman merchants dwelling in Alexandria. If I may introduce them—"

"Please do so," I said. "Citizens, I apologize for the abruptness of this summons, but my duties press me on all sides, and I have little time for niceties." All quite true and neatly sidestepping the awkward question of whether I had any authority at all.

"First," the eunuch twittered, "Marcus Junius Brutus of the Honorable Company of Wine Merchants." This was a bald-headed old fellow, clearly of a distant, plebeian branch of that famous patrician family.

"Next, Mamercus Sulpicius Naso of the Sacred Brotherhood of Hermes, grain exporters." This one was fat and oily and clearly another provincial. In Rome only the Aemilii used the praenomen Mamercus. I would watch this one closely. Any grain shipper is a speculator, always hoping for a shortage to jack up prices. They are dealers in other people's hunger.

"This is Decimus Antonius of the Guild of Hephaestus, importers of metals of all sorts save gold and silver." This one actually looked like one of the Roman Antonii. At least he had the distinctive features of that clan. That Roman political family was full of madmen and criminals though, but this one looked sane enough.

"And, finally, Malachi Josephides, leader of the Textile Syndicate." The man was tall and distinguished, his graying hair and beard groomed in the Greek fashion. I had met his like in Alexandria—what are called Hellenized Jews, meaning Jews who have adopted Greek culture in all things except religion. Even his name was rendered in Greek. Yet he wore a toga.

"How do you happen to be a citizen, Josephides?" I asked.

He smiled. "I was born in Massilia, where my family has resided for several generations. My father was the first to have the privilege of citizenship." A Jew from a Greek colony in Gaul with Roman citizenship; beat that for cosmopolitanism if you can.

"Gentlemen, be seated," I said. "We have been keeping the circumstances of Silvanus's death quiet for the moment, but you should know he was murdered. It was not done openly, and we are at a loss to know the killer's motive. I wish you to acquaint me with the business disputes and concerns you came here to discuss with him."

"You think, Senator," said Antonius, "that our problems are somehow connected to this murder?"

"I think nothing of the sort. But I cannot form any basis for a theory until I can understand the concerns surrounding the late Silvanus."

Josephides smiled again. "You sound more like a logician than a Roman official."

"I have been told so before," I acknowledged. "Just don't call me a philosopher. I wish to know one thing first: Did any of your worries involve *threats* against Rome, Roman citizens, or Roman interests?"

"You are most incisive, Senator," said Brutus. "There have been threats indeed: threats to our commerce, threats to our freedom, threats to our safety and our very lives!" The old boy was getting wrought up, having finally found a sympathetic ear.

"He exaggerates, Senator!" Photinus protested.

"I shall seek your counsel later, Photinus. For the moment I am listening to the Romans. What are the forms and origins of these threats, Citizens?"

"Credible threats against our commerce can have only one origin, Senator," Brutus went on, "King Ptolemy. He seeks to extort vast sums from the Roman merchants of Alexandria, sums that could well ruin us, and he enforces these extortions with threats of imprisonment, confiscation, even public flogging and death!"

Photinus was bursting to speak, but I silenced him with an upraised hand. "King Ptolemy threatens *Romans* in this fashion? Have you proof? I want details!"

"You may be aware, Senator," said Josephides, "that King Ptolemy incurred sizable debts in obtaining 'friend and ally' status, and further debts in regaining his throne?" He, at least, seemed able to retain his equanimity.

"So I've heard," I assured him.

"There was yet a further debt incurred in obtaining the services of General Gabinius to unseat his usurping daughter and her husband. You may have cause to wonder just how His Majesty ever expected to repay these tremendous sums."

"I assumed he would do it the way kings always have: squeeze his subjects until they cough up the money. Egypt is a famously rich land. Surely even a Ptolemy can make something of it."

"It is also the custom of kings," Josephides continued, "to victimize foreigners before fellow countrymen. Nobody loves Romans; therefore, the king incurs no wrath among the Egyptians if he robs the Roman community of Alexandria."

"It's preposterous!" I said. "Why would King Ptolemy, who owes his throne to Rome, turn against Rome? It would be suicidal! I have met the king, gentlemen. He is a fat, old degenerate who used to play a flute in a whorehouse, but he is not stupid."

"What is so stupid about it, Senator?" asked Antonius, the metal merchant. "When was the last time the Senate got indignant over the treatment of overseas merchants? We are *equites*, Senator. We are wealthy and we are often leading men in our communities; but those communities are not Rome, and our families do not serve in the Senate. People lump us together with the *publicani* and think we are all tax farmers. Some of us are moneylenders, and everyone hates moneylenders. When Lucullus curried favor with the barbarians by ruining the Roman moneylenders of Asia, who wept in Rome?"

"My colleague is bitter, Senator," said Naso, the grain speculator, "but he is quite correct. Lacking the gloss of *nobilitas*, we are despised in Rome. Since our wealth comes not from land but from trade and hard work, we are not respectable. King Ptolemy risks very little in attacking us."

There was much in what they said. Men of my own class committed untold villainies, but we belonged to ancient families and could count many consuls and praetors among our ancestors. Our wealth was decently inherited or wrested by force from our enemies, so we were eminently respectable, despite our frequent crimes and our ruinous ambitions.

The *equites* were so-called because of an archaic property qualification stating that men with wealth above a certain level were required to serve in the cavalry and supply their own horses. For centuries, though, it had been a mere property distinction. *Equites* could serve in the Senate if they could get elected, but for the last century, nearly all the senators had come from a tight little circle of about twenty families. Interlopers like Cicero were a great rarity. We called ourselves a republic, but in truth we formed an oligarchy as exclusive and as corrupt as any that ever ruled a Greek city-state. I was not about to acknowledge this to a pack of merchants though, especially in front of an Egyptian court eunuch.

"How great an assessment has he levied?" I demanded.

"The levy has been by association rather than by individual merchant," Brutus said. "Each of our associations have been assessed to the sum of one hundred talents in gold."

"A stiff sum," I commiserated.

"Per year," Antonius added.

I winced. "For how long?"

"Until the 'state of emergency' is ended," said Brutus, "which means until King Ptolemy is solvent, which means until he is dead."

"Solvency always seems to elude him," I agreed. "Now what about these threats?"

"Failure to deliver the stipulated sum at the proper date," Brutus said, "will result in the arrest of the officers of the association. Failure then to render the assessment, with penalties, will be punished by a public flogging of those officers and further penalties added to the assessment. After that, any failure to pay up will be punished by beheading."

"Ridiculous!" I said. "Photinus, what is your king thinking? Or is he thinking at all?"

"As for the special tax, Senator, it is perfectly just. After all, my king is allowing these people to trade freely in the greatest and richest port in the world. They owe him something for that. The tax would not have been necessary had Rome not been so astoundingly greedy. Your fellow senator, Gaius Rabirius, already has control of the grain revenue and several others, so His Majesty may not apply that to his debts."

This was true enough. "And threats to imprison, flog, and execute Roman citizens? We have gone to war over far less than that."

"Senator, you Romans tend to go to war over nothing at all. Possession of a full treasury draws the legions of Rome as a staked goat draws lions. But I think these men need have little fear on that account. It is customary for the successors of Alexander to specify the severest punishments for failure to comply with their will. It is mere form."

He spread his pudgy palms in an appeal to reason. "What is at stake here anyway? These men, who are already rich, will be a little less rich. In the age-old fashion of merchants they will raise the price of their goods, the loss will be passed along to their customers, and they will all be as fat as ever."

"He lies!" cried Sulpicius Naso. "We will be ruined! Our livelihood rides on each year's cargoes, at the mercy of war and weather. We are always on the brink of beggary!" Like most rich men, he had an infinite store of self-pity.

"Economics is not my field," I said. "Ask anyone at the Treasury, where I served my quaestorship. Why did you bring your complaints here to Cyprus instead of before the Senate in Rome?"

"Believe me, Senator," said Brutus, "a far larger delegation is on its way to Rome for just that purpose. We are here because we have business interests in Cyprus as well as Alexandria. This used to be a Ptolemaic kingdom, but since it is now Roman we sought assurances from the governor that King Ptolemy would not be able to seize our property here, which is considerable."

"And what did we find?" said Antonius, his face going red. "We found the governor in a cozy relationship with Aulus Gabinius, the stooge of Rabirius, the man behind Ptolemy's money woes! Not only that, but Ptolemy's daughter is his houseguest!"

"It does seem a bleak prospect for you," I agreed. So now somebody else had cause to kill Silvanus. In a way a Roman culprit would simplify things for me; the less foreign involvement the better.

"Of course," Josephides put in hastily, "we were as shocked and saddened as anyone when the governor was so foully murdered. Despite his unfortunate choice of friend and guest, he listened to our petitions with great sympathy and gave us assurances that our businesses and properties on Cyprus would enjoy the fullest protection. Now, in fact, our situation is once again uncertain. There seems to be no constituted Roman authority here."

"Unless you are the new governor," Antonius said.

It was time to change the subject. "How is it that you are here with Photinus?"

"At the king's insistence," Brutus said bitterly. "The only way we could get permission to sail was to leave surety for our return and take along a court minister. Our trading licenses are forfeit if we so much as hold a meeting without him present."

"As you observed, Senator," said the eunuch, "King Ptolemy is not stupid."

"So it would seem. One more thing, gentlemen, are any of you in the frankincense trade?"

They looked at me as if I were insane. It is a look I have learned to recognize.

"Frankincense?" Brutus said. "Why frankincense?"

"Indulge my curiosity. I have my reasons."

"In Egypt," said Antonius, "frankincense is a royal monopoly and the crown sells it for shipment abroad only to the Holy Society of Dionysus. That society is entirely Greek. No non-Hellene can even apply for membership, which is largely hereditary."

"I suppose that answers my question then. Gentlemen, thank you for coming, and you may return to your lodgings now. However, I will ask you not to leave the island until the murderer of Governor Silvanus has been found."

"Do you think," Brutus said, rising, "that we are anxious to return to Alexandria just now?"

9

THE NEXT DAY WAS LARGELY GIVEN OVER to the funeral of Silvanus. The weather was beautiful, and the hired mourners wailed superbly. The whole Roman population of Paphos and neighboring towns turned out for the occasion, and there were more of them than I had expected. The visitors from Alexandria were there, naturally, and Photinus represented King Ptolemy, dressed in court robes, wig, and cosmetics, adding a delightful note of the bizarre to the proceedings.

Since Paphos was a Greek city, a chorus had been hired for the occasion. They sang traditional funeral songs, plus a new one specially written by Alpheus. Gabinius, dressed in an impressively striped augur's toga (for he belonged to that priestly college), took the auspices, then sacrificed a couple of handsome calves. After the Greek custom, the fat and bones were offered to the gods. The rest would form part of the funeral feast.

Gabinius performed the oration ably, delivering an eloquent eulogy that, though formulaic, was so well crafted that I almost believed the departed had really possessed all those virtues and accomplishments. All the local dignitaries attended, and so did most of the town's population. It was an occasion out of the ordinary, a minor spectacle, and everyone appreciates a good show.

Silvanus was laid out in his whitest toga, wearing a laurel wreath I doubt he ever rated in life, rings winking from his fingers, cosmetics restoring his face to an almost natural color.

When Gabinius finished his oration, he took a torch and touched it to the oil-soaked wood of the pyre. In moments it was ablaze, its fragrant wood and burden of incense disguising the aroma of roasting governor. I tossed my own handful of frankincense, benzoin, and myrrh onto the blaze and surveyed the scene. No anti-Roman demonstrations so far, but the obtrusive presence of Gabinius's bullies, rattling with weapons and armor, seemed more of a provocation than a defense. I saw some of the rougher-looking elements of the crowd glaring at them with intense disfavor.

If there was to be trouble, I thought, it would be because the people here resented the insulting presence of these armed hooligans.

Even as the late governor went up in smoke, tables were being set up for a public memorial banquet. This agreeable custom seemed to put everyone in a fine mood. In no time people were taking their places at the long tables as slaves hired for the occasion heaped them first with great baskets of fruit, cheeses, and bread, then with plentiful courses of fish, more modest quantities of veal, lamb, fowl, and rabbit. The wine was indifferent and heavily watered, but only the fabulously wealthy can afford better for a public banquet. Knowing this, some of us took care to provide our own wine.

Most of the population were seated at long benches, but there were also special tables for the attending dignitaries and these had been provided with proper dining couches. I was, naturally, placed at one of these tables. On my right was Alpheus and on my left, none other than Flavia. I wondered, perhaps unworthily, whether she had bribed the majordomo to secure this arrangement.

"How goes your pirate hunt, Decius Caecilius?" she asked, apparently having decided that we were now intimate enough for her to drop my title and use praenomen and nomen only. I would have to be on my guard when she began to use my praenomen alone.

"Complicated by this lamentable turn of events," I admitted. "I shall be infernally distracted until the matter of Silvanus's murder has been put to rest. If this portends danger to Roman security on the island, the pirates may have to take second place in my priorities for a while."

"How would you deal with such a distraction?" Alpheus asked.

"Well, Gabinius has his veterans, and I have my sailors and marines under arms. There is a sizable body of mercenary material hanging about the bars and taverns, and doubtless a quick voyage to the mainland would net us a sizable force. If necessary, we could secure the island for Rome. I would just rather not."

"It seems a free-and-easy sort of military arrangement," said the poet. "I am no soldier, but I would think your Senate would frown upon such unauthorized adventures."

"Outside Italy," I explained, "there is really nothing to stop any citizen from raising an ad hoc army to deal with an emergency. As long as it is Roman interests he looks after, the Senate won't say a word in disapprobation. Some years ago Caesar, as mere quaestor, happened to be in Syria when he heard of an invasion from Pontus. He raised a personal army, marched to meet the invasion, and sent the enemy back across the border, all without so much as consulting the Roman governor of Syria. He suffered no censure for his high-handedness."

"It helped that he was successful," Flavia put in.

"It goes without saying that victory is essential," I affirmed.

"But why," Alpheus asked, "when your General Crassus was defeated at Carrhae, did Rome not immediately pursue that war? I would think that Parthia, not Gaul, would be your first priority."

"Crassus wanted a war with the Parthians to match Pompey in military glory. But the Parthians had done nothing to offend us, and the Senate refused to declare war. But Crassus was legendarily rich so he raised and paid for his own legions and marched out on his own. A Tribune of the Plebs named Trebonius laid a terrible curse on Crassus as he left Rome to join his army."

"It was the terror of Rome for a while," Flavia said. She drew a little phallus amulet from its resting place between her breasts and used it to make a complicated gesture, warding evil away from us. The tribune's infamous curse had been terribly potent, endangering the whole citizenry.

"So when Crassus was defeated," I continued, "most people said good riddance. We are under no obligation to avenge him and his army, and there has been no break in diplomatic relations with that kingdom, though young Cassius has been skirmishing a bit with them, or so I heard just before I left Rome. We would like to have the lost eagles back, and we want to free the survivors from captivity; but I suspect that when it happens we will just pay ransom."

"I doubt that," Flavia said. "Parthia is too rich a plum to resist plucking for long. When Caesar and Pompey are free of their current distractions, one of them will have a go at Parthia. Or Gabinius might when his exile is over. And none of them will blunder the way Crassus did, the senile old fool. Think how the plebs will love it when they see those freed captives marching in the Triumph, carrying their lost eagles."

"You may well be right," I admitted. I had known few women in Rome who were so politically astute. I looked around for her husband and saw him at a table next to some city dignitaries. Beyond him, at a table set for commoners, I saw Ariston. It annoyed me that he should expose himself in such a fashion and resolved to upbraid him for it. I turned to Alpheus.

"That was a very accomplished song you delivered," I commended. "Especially when you consider what short notice you had."

"You are too kind. Actually, it was just a variation on a funeral song I wrote years ago. I've employed it a number of times, making changes where necessary to fit the deceased. This was the first I've done for a Roman though. The real challenge was getting the chorus rehearsed. Luckily, I've had some experience in that art, and the chorus here is excellent. Of course, the whole citizenry sings, but these are the ones who take part in the theatrical productions."

"In Rome we have nothing like your Greek choral singing," I noted. "The closest we come is everybody piling into the Circus for a chariot race. The sounds we make there aren't very musical I'm afraid."

"So," he said, "you're thinking of putting off your pirate hunt until you've determined who killed Silvanus? That seems an odd sort of activity."

I explained to him some of the reasons why it was urgent that I set the matter to rest as soon as possible. "Of course," I added, "I cannot let an especially insolent or egregious act of piracy go unnoticed. It would be bad for Roman prestige."

"And for your political future," Flavia pointed out.

"Yes, there is always that. By the way, Flavia, while I realize your husband is a banker, does he, by any chance, ever deal in frankincense or have dealings with any who do?" It was clumsy, but I thought it worth a try.

She laughed. "Frankincense! Whyever would you ask that? Are you planning to go into the business yourself? Shame on you! And you a senator!" She went off into peals of laughter. Quite inappropriate at a funeral, but others were laughing as well. The wine wasn't good, but it flowed freely.

"Well, I suppose that answers me. Believe it or not, the question is pertinent to my investigation."

"I have little to do with my husband's business, but I'll ask him for you if you want. Frankincense, indeed!" She seemed to find the very idea inordinately funny. I doubted there was any aspect of her husband's business she didn't know about, but it was not unusual that she would deny it. Men were often suspicious of women who were too knowledgeable about such things as business, politics, and war. Of course, she had not been shy about flaunting her knowledge of the latter two subjects. Shyness was not among this woman's attributes.

Nor was she abstemious about the food or the wine. She put away large quantities of both, apparently one of those lucky women whose immoderate gustatory habits had no effect on her figure, which was voluptuous but not quite to the point of overabundance. Like me she had brought her own wine, and frequently signaled her slave girl for a refill. Each time she did this, she slid her hand along the young woman's body with the unconscious ease of a woman stroking a favorite pet. The girl seemed to take this quite naturally, and once leaned close to whisper into her mistress's ear something that set them both laughing uproariously.

"Will Silvanus have funeral games?" Alpheus asked.

"I don't believe he was that important," I answered him. "Ordinarily, *munera* are only held in memory of the most distinguished men, consuls at the very least. At one time only former consuls who had triumphed were allowed gladiatorial displays, but our standards have slipped somewhat of late. This is at Rome, you understand. In his hometown, his family may hold any sort of funeral games they wish. For all I know, Silvanus may have been the most distinguished man in Bovillae or Lanuvium or Reate or some such place. Senators who are political nobodies in Rome are often very important men in their ancestral towns. He may have provided for games in his will."

"He was from Ostia," Flavia said, her words beginning to slur a bit, "same as my husband. And yes, his family is a great one in that town. There's usually a Silvanus serving as one of the *duumviri*. I think he held the post three times. Yes, I think we can expect a good show after his ashes arrive home. I hope we're back in time to attend. I love the fights."

"You will be," I assured her. "Believe me, they take time to arrange. It will be a year or two before he gets his final rites. Look at Faustus Sulla. He celebrated the Dictator's games twenty years after his father died.

You're lucky you live in Ostia. Women aren't allowed to attend the *munera* in Rome."

"Rome is so stodgy and straitlaced," she said. "You should go to Baiae when there's a festival. I spend the summers there when I can. They do things there that would drop Cato and his tiresome crowd dead with shock."

"So I've heard," I said enviously. "I've never managed to be there when anything really scandalous was going on."

"Let me tell you what happened last time I was there," she said, her voice dripping musk and lasciviousness. She launched into a description of her adventures with several matrons of that free-and-easy resort town during the celebration of the *Priapalia*, a festival banned from Rome generations ago because of the licentious behavior that always accompanied the worship of that rustic deity, who in Rome is confined to gardens and brothels.

"You are an adventurous lady," I commended her, when the tale was done.

"On the island of Cythera," Alpheus said, "which also claims to be the birthplace of Aphrodite, there are very similar practices during their annual festival of the goddess; activity that even the inhabitants acknowledge as intolerable at other times become acts of pious worship during those three days."

"In Rome," I pointed out, "we men of the senatorial class have always wondered what our wives get up to during the annual rites of Bona Dea. Clodius once tried to spy on the rites dressed as a woman, but he was caught and expelled before he saw anything interesting."

"It's all very tame I am sure," Flavia said. "Roman women of spirit and imagination have to find their fun outside the City."

"Speaking of women," I said, "where is Cleopatra?" I looked around but did not see her.

"Up on the temple porch," Alpheus said, nodding toward the noble building. I looked and saw a long table where Cleopatra reclined next to Gabinius. The city archon, the high priest of Poseidon, and Photinus were at the same table.

"I would think you would be at the highest table," Flavia's tone was that of the devoted troublemaker. I pushed aside my own annoyance in recognition of the fact.

"Gabinius arranged the funeral," I pointed out, "and I am just a visiting military officer. The dining arrangements seem to be punctilious." Gabinius was using the practice to put me in my place, but I determined to settle the matter later. For now a united front was called for. "Where are Ione and the priestesses of Aphrodite?" I asked, to change the subject.

"With the *Aphrodisia* only days away," Alpheus explained, "they may not attend a funeral or enter a house of mourning. They would be ritually unclean, and the festival would have to be canceled for the year. It would be a terrible portent for the whole island."

"And this island has had all the bad luck it can handle," I said, "between Roman annexation, the pirates, and the copper trade, which has desolated large parts of it."

"Ah, you know how the island has been ruined by mining?" Alpheus said.

"I've heard something of it," I hedged.

"But it made the place rich," Flavia pointed out.

"It is the special genius of Rome," I said, feeling the wine a bit myself and growing expansive, "that we understand the proper path to wealth."

"What is that?" Alpheus asked. I had the distinct impression that he was humoring me.

"The way to get rich is not by ruining your own land to sell your resources abroad. Instead, you conserve your own land and go plunder somebody else's wealth." Flavia laughed like a jackass. Even Gabinius, on the temple porch, heard and glared in our direction. Well, his friend had just died. I tried to keep a straight face while he was looking my way.

When we had all gorged and swilled to repletion, people rose from their tables and began to circulate. Evening was drawing on and torches were brought out to illuminate the central part of the city. It was a great extravagance, but it is with these touches of excess that we hope to be remembered after we die.

Flavia, Alpheus, and I were fast friends by now, at least until the wine wore off; and like many others we began to walk off dinner, trying to make room for the sweets that had been brought out as the last course. At the funeral of Scipio Africanus, sweets were served and the extravagance was remembered for generations. His was a more austere time, and the island of Cyprus had access to such luxuries in abundance.

I met some of Flavia's friends, a number of whom seemed to be as debauched as she. Alpheus did a bit of business, arranging to compose songs for festivals in other towns. We came to a table set up on a side street off the main plaza and I stopped, my jaw dropping in shock. "What are you doing here?" I demanded.

131

Ion looked back at me, not at all dismayed. "All the resident foreigners in the city were invited to the banquet, Senator, just like you."
Looking along the table, I saw the crews of my ships, my marines, and the
hired mercenaries.

"You were to be at the ships, ready to sail on the instant!" I yelled.
"What are we to do if there is news of an attack?"

He looked me over. "Do you really think you're in any shape to
lead us?"

"I could be carried to the ships and sober up on the voyage out!" I
told him. "How I get into fighting shape is my business, not yours! What
are you laughing at?" This last was addressed to Alpheus and Flavia, who
seemed unreasonably amused by my embarrassment.

"Suppose the pirates were to strike the city right now!" Flavia
whooped. "How would it sound in the Forum, when Pompey's men spread
the word that Metellus and his whole crew were gorged and besotted at
the banquet tables when the enemy came calling!"

"If Themistocles and his men had been like this the night before
Salamis," Alpheus put in, "I'd be composing verses to Ahura-Mazda in
Persian right now!"

"No one attacks at night," Ion asserted, refilling his cup. "We'll be
ready to sail at dawn, and a sailor who can't put to sea with a hangover is
a poor excuse for a seaman anyway."

"Well, not much to be done about it now," I said, my indignation running out like wine from a punctured skin. Just be ready to sail at first light."

"Let's be away from here," Flavia urged, pressing a great deal of
soft flesh against my side. "It's noisy in this place. My litter is somewhere
around here. Let's go find it. Come along, Decius." There it was: the
praenomen.

I looked for Alpheus and saw him making a discreet exit. The man
was the soul of diplomacy. Joining Flavia in some secluded nook seemed
like a fine idea, which shows the condition I was in. Abruptly, the soft
flesh pressing against me was replaced by hard muscle on both sides.

"Why, here you are, Captain!" said Ariston, taking one arm in a
steely grip.

"Better come along with us," Hermes said, gripping the other. "Tomorrow comes early, as you keep reminding me." He turned to Flavia.
"My lady, we have to get the master to bed."

She looked him over, then she gave Ariston an even longer look, up and down. "That sounds like an excellent idea. Why don't we all find a place to relax away from this crowd? I know a house just two streets away that provides all the amenities we could wish."

Hermes leaned close to my ear and whispered, "Julia could be here tomorrow." That did it. He might as well have cast me into icy water.

"Flavia," I said, "much as I appreciate your generous offer, duty comes first for an officer of the Senate and People. I must be ready to sail at daylight."

She looked at me with great disfavor. "I had hoped better of you, Decius." She turned and walked away. I sighed after her twitching, Coan-veiled buttocks.

"There goes a shipwreck in woman's form," said Ariston. "Come along, Captain. Plenty more where that one came from and much better time for them than tonight."

My two faithful if somewhat insubordinate followers hoisted me off to my quarters.

"UP!" SOMEBODY SHOUTED. "GET UP and get dressed!"

"Why?" I asked, not entirely sure where I was. I was fairly certain that I wasn't in Rome, but that left a lot of territory to be considered. Gaul? Alexandria? Somehow I felt not. I knew it would come to me, given time.

Hermes yanked me to my feet and pulled my military tunic down over my shaky body. I was on military duty, that was clear enough. "What is going on?" Even to my own ears I sounded querulous as a used-up old man.

"The pirates have been seen!" Hermes said. "They sailed right past the harbor mouth, bold as purple-assed baboons!"

"Pirates!" I cried. "Thank the gods! For a moment there I thought the Gauls were attacking. Well, by all means, let's go kill these pirates so I can get back to bed."

Somehow Hermes got me fully dressed, armed, and halfway presentable and, accompanied by the redoubtable Ariston, we hurried down to the naval harbor.

Ion had the ships in the water and fully manned, although many of the men were cradling their heads or vomiting over the sides or collapsed at their benches. I clambered onto my ship and gave orders to push off. Cleopatra's ship came smartly alongside.

"We have been waiting for you," she said, seeming a bit indignant. "They went past about an hour ago, sailing southward. My own lookout spotted them."

"Did you see them with your own eyes?" I asked.

"I did."

"How did you get down here in time?"

"I slept on my ship, as you should have done! And I kept my crew here as well. No banqueting allowed. Now we will lose them!"

"Don't scold me. I have a wife for that. How many ships?"

"Three."

I tried to force rational thought through the fog within my thundering skull. "Just three? They must have split the fleet. All right, then. Oars out and let's be after them. Timekeeper, as soon as we are in open water, I want you to set us a quick pace."

Groaning and complaining, the men set to their oars. At first their strokes were so ragged that they might as well have been untrained landlubbers. Soon, though, they were back into their usual rhythm and began to sweat out the previous night's wine. I ran the marines through boarding drills and catapult drills until they, too, were sweating in their armor, and I made sure that the men on the other ships were doing the same. By the time the pirate vessels were in sight, I felt that the worst was over. My head was almost clear, my stomach had settled down, and the strength was returning to my limbs.

We were close to shore, near a stretch of beach I had not seen in my previous outings. It was rocky and deserted, except for some ruined old buildings that looked as if they had not been inhabited in centuries. It was an ill-favored place, fit haunt for harpies and Gorgons.

"They're coming about," Ion said. Ahead of us, the three lean vessels had dug in their oars, halting their forward motion. Then, with the port and starboard oars working rapidly in opposite directions, they spun on their axes and presented their rams to us.

"Prettily done," Ariston noted. He had come to stand beside me in the prow of the *Nereid*.

"That's right," agreed Ion. "And I think we had better do the same, Senator."

"Why? We came here to catch them, and we are still four to their three, however well they row."

He looked at me with disgust. "And how long do you think that will last. If three of them think they can take on four warships, their friends can't be far away. They've laid a trap for us, Senator."

"Do you think I am totally dense? Hung over or not, I knew they were luring us out when I heard they'd traipsed past the harbor in something less than full strength. I was sent to bag these brigands, and I intend to do it. If their remaining ships will just come out from behind whichever headland they are lurking, I will give battle right here. Just remember to take some of them alive so that we can find out where their base may be."

Ariston laughed. "Maybe the Senate sent out the right man after all."

Ion shook his head. "I still have my doubts."

As the ships drew nearer, I saw what the island woman had meant when she said the pirate ships had been "the same color as the sea." The hulls were painted a deep shade of blue-green. With yards lowered and masts unstepped, they would blend with the surrounding water, making them difficult to discern at any distance. My own ships, painted in their traditional naval colors, were visible from far away. Cleopatra's, with all its gilding, could be seen as far as the horizon on a sunny day and was tolerably visible by moonlight.

"Down with the yards and masts!" Ion bellowed, as if reading my mind. Quickly, the crews of all four vessels lowered the yards, then lifted the masts from their footings and laid them upon the grooved wooden blocks on the decks. It is customary to do this before going into battle because otherwise the ships would be top-heavy and inclined to wallow during fast maneuvers. In place of the mast, they raised a shorter, thicker post with a pulley at its top. This was to be used as a crane for raising and dropping the *corvus* when we got within boarding distance.

Thinking of this caused me to note an odd discrepancy in the ships fast approaching us. "Why are their masts still up?" I wondered aloud. I could now see this plainly, and that their yards, though lowered, lay athwart the deck railings, a most inconvenient arrangement for combat.

"They must mean to hoist sail and run for it," Ion speculated, "but there's little sense to that. In this weak breeze we'd catch them easily. And where are their reinforcements? We ought to have seen them by now."

"Ariston," I said, "any suggestions?"

"They can't mean to fight," he said. "The odds aren't right, and they haven't rigged for it. It must be a trap, but what sort?"

I was beginning to have a terrible feeling about this, but what choice did I have? With my four warships I simply could *not* run from three scruffy pirate vessels. I'd be the laughingstock of the Forum. I'd be dubbed "Piraticus" in derision, as the elder Antonius had been named Creticus after that lowly regarded island people beat him in battle.

"Captain," shouted a sailor, "we're taking on water!"

"What!" Ion and I shouted at once. Then we saw. Water was bubbling up through the stones that ballasted the ship's hull.

"Impossible!" Ion said, wonder tinging his voice. "I've seen to every inch of this hull! There's no rot, and we'd have felt it if we'd scraped a submerged rock."

"Senator," shouted one of the other shipmasters just a few paces to our starboard, "we're shipping water! We have to beach before we sink!" The skipper just beyond him reported the same problem.

Cleopatra pulled up to our port side, and she came to the rail. "What is wrong?"

I knew that my face was flaming as purple as a *triumphator*'s robe. "We've been sabotaged! Our hulls have been bored through and we're sinking! Clearly you are not. We have to get these tubs on shore and repair them before it is too late. You will have to cover us while we retreat."

"There are three of them and one of me, Senator," she said. "I am not the one who left his ships abandoned all night! Queen Artemisia had a way out of this sort of situation, remember?"

I remembered all too well. Artemisia of Halicarnassus and her ships had been attached as allies to the fleet of Xerxes. When she saw that the Greeks were going to win the battle of Salamis, she rammed and sank a Persian vessel so that the nearby enemy would think her ships were Greek. As soon as she saw a way clear, she hoisted sail and fled from the battle.

I was not going to argue with a subordinate officer, which was what she had wanted to be. "Keep between us and those ships until we are safely beached. Then you can pull for Paphos. If your rowers are as good as you say they are, you'll have no trouble outdistancing them."

Ion began a brisk series of orders, and our rowers got to work. In the bows of the ships, men with long poles probed the bottom, feeling for submerged rocks. All the rest, sailors and marines, bailed frantically with buckets of wood or tarred leather, with cooking pots and with helmets. The pirate ships drew closer, but Cleopatra stayed with us. When the poles touched bottom, Ion turned the ships so that our rams were seaward, and we began backing water, moving sluggishly now as the hulls filled.

The men with the poles moved to the sterns by the steering oars and began calling off the depth as we neared shore.

"Rocky bottom, rocky beach," Ion groused. "I'd never go ashore in this place except the alternative is to sink."

"Captain," Ariston said, "they may have their main strength ashore. We'll be vulnerable as we leave the ships."

"We'll have to chance it," I told him.

The blue ships held off, just out of catapult range, grinning faces lining the rails. I looked for a large, long-haired figure, but there were several such, and I could spot no man I might positively identify as Spurius. Seldom in my life had I felt so frustrated and mortified. It did, however, beat being drowned.

With a teeth-rattling grate, our stern crunched onto the stony bottom. We were within twenty feet of dry land, a bit of luck. The prospect of leaping full-armored into chest-deep water and wading a hundred yards to shore has been known to cool the combative ardor of the bravest soldiers.

"Swing the *corvus* around," I ordered, "and drop it onto the beach. No man should have to get his shoes wet. I am going to take half the men ashore and set up security. When I've done that, we can unload the ships and haul them ashore for repair." I ordered the archers and catapult handlers to stay in the bows, just in case the pirates should try to attack us, and lined up the rest of the marines to rush ashore.

The ponderous gangplanks swung around and dropped, their bronze spikes crunching into the rocky beach, the ships shivering with the impact. Immediately the marines double-timed down the planks and ashore. They fanned out and established a semicircular defensive perimeter, shields to front, spears slanting outward.

"They're leaving," Ion remarked. I saw the yards ascend the masts of the blue ships, the sails dropping to hang slack for a moment, then filling with wind, billowing like pregnant bellies as the pirates laughed, hooted, and cheered.

"Anyone inland?" I called. A few curious goats studied us from the rocks, but nobody saw so much as a single human form. I was so frustrated that I almost wished for an attack. No one, however, wanted to oblige me. "Ariston, Hermes, take some men and scout inland. Raise a shout if you see anyone. Everyone else, stand to arms until they come back."

I sat on a convenient rock, already sure they would find nothing. Spurius did not want to trap me. He wanted to humiliate me. Trust a

Roman to know that men of my class preferred death to ignominy. Actually I could take quite a bit of humiliation before I considered death preferable, but this could mean the end of my political career. Beached on Cyprus by a pack of scruffy criminals who never had to shoot a single arrow my way.

"Cheer up, Senator," Ion said, reading my expression. "You still have your ships and your men. You've lost nothing but a little reputation, and you didn't have all that much to begin with." I sensed that he meant this kindly, but it galled me anyway.

"Why," I said, "didn't the rowers notice the ships were getting heavier?"

"I intend to find out. Soon as I get a look at the hulls, I'll tell you."

Cleopatra was rowed ashore in her golden skiff, and slaves carried her onto the beach so she would not get her golden sandals wet. If she had some cutting remark prepared, she changed her mind when she saw my face.

"Gabinius did this to me," I said to her.

"How?"

"He invited my sailors and marines to the funeral banquet, then he sent men to sabotage my ships while they were deserted. He is in collusion with Spurius. For all I know, he could *be* Spurius! All it would take is a wig and a false beard."

"That is far-fetched," she protested. "But collusion, perhaps. But why?"

"Any number of reasons, simple profit being the most obvious. He likes to live well, he has a minor army of thugs to pay, and he had a bad reputation for extortion when he was a governor. Even Cicero couldn't get him an acquittal, so that has to say something."

"Gabinius strikes me as the sort of man who would simply kill you if you displeased him."

"Perhaps he's learned subtlety out here in the East. He wants to dishonor me and perhaps humiliate my family in the process. Maybe he's planning to go over to Pompey."

Her eyebrows rose. "More Roman politics?"

"It gets more complicated than this, believe me. With me out of the way, he might get the Senate to appoint him governor of Cyprus. Then the island would be his to loot. It will do until I can think of a more plausible reason. But whatever the reason, Gabinius was the only man with the means. He used his friend's funeral banquet to send me out to sea with a hungover crew rowing leaky ships."

She shrugged. "Maybe it is true. What will you do now?"

"First, I have to assess the damage. I suppose it's too much to hope that the ships can be made seaworthy quickly. You may have to go back to Paphos for supplies."

"Why don't you go with me?"

"No, I'll not return without my ships and my men. He'll be waiting at the harbor with a smirk on his face. Just say publicly that my ships struck submerged rocks and have to be repaired. He'll have to go along with it or admit his complicity."

"Kings do more foolish things to save face. I shall do as you ask."

Ask, I thought. So much for her being my subordinate officer.

An hour later Hermes and Ariston returned. They had seen no one save a few goatherds, and the goatherds had seen only other goatherds in the last year or more. So I had the men down arms and set to unloading the ships. This done, we dragged them ashore. Ion winced at the sound of the keels grating on the stony beach.

"Neptune will not forgive me for treating good ships like this," he lamented. Then he examined the hulls. With a blunt finger he began prying a sodden mess of fibers from between the siding planks. He carried a handful of the repulsive stuff to me and held it up.

"This is goat hair, just like we use to caulk the seams, only they've mixed it with wax instead of with pitch. It's waterproof for a while, but hard rowing and the ship working softens the wax and it gives way all at once. That's what they did, and that's why the rowers didn't notice. It wasn't a slow leak. All the seams gave way at once. It's a miracle we didn't just sink immediately." In disgust he hurled the loathsome mass out to sea. "They scraped out my careful caulking with gouges and replaced it with this. We've a job ahead of us, Senator."

"So it's just a matter of recaulking the hulls? That sounds simple enough." I looked at the animals on the rocks. "Goat hair should be no problem anyway."

"You wouldn't have any pitch on you, I don't suppose?"

CLEOPATRA RETURNED TWO DAYS LATER with the needed supplies, which turned out to be considerable. I learned that you don't just take handfuls of pitch and slap the ugly stuff onto the hulls. It has to be heated in pots first, and that takes firewood. The place where we were stranded turned out to be as denuded of trees as the Egyptian desert beyond the pyramids. Once heated, it must be mixed with goat hair and stirred, then taken out with special, paddle-shaped tools and worked carefully into the seams of the wood, then pounded in with wooden mallets. After all that, the entire hull must be sealed with a coating of pure pitch, without the hair. It takes a lot of pitch and a great deal of work.

When I say that Cleopatra returned with the supplies, I do not mean to imply that she sullied her royal yacht with such a foul-smelling cargo. No, in her wake came a tubby merchantman bearing the goods. The fat-bellied freighter could not be hauled onto such a beach as could a galley, so it was another job to unload tubs of pitch, sacks of reeking hair, bundles of firewood, heavy copper pots, and other, less objectionable supplies using our skiffs.

In charge of the naval supplies was Harmodias. He made me sign for all of it.

"It's a good thing for you," he informed me, "that the ship chandlers are willing to extend credit to Rome."

"They'd better," I said, not in the best of moods.

"Seemed a little odd though. We heard you'd run onto rocks, but you didn't need wood or nails just caulking material."

"They were unusual rocks."

He walked over to one of the ships. It lay almost on its side, exposing a flank all the way to the keel. "Wax caulking, eh? I thought that was what it might have been. It's an old trick, Senator. Usually done by some merchant to destroy a rival. The ship just sails off and, if the trick works as planned, is never heard from again."

"And where were you on the night of Silvanus's funeral banquet, Harmodias?"

He grinned within his beard. "I know what you're getting at. Fact is, I was at the banquet like everyone else. It's my job to oversee naval stores not to guard your ships, Senator."

I turned around, saw the copper cauldrons already heating over the wood fires, smelled pitch melting in them.

"Let's get to work," I said. "I want to sail into Paphos by sundown tomorrow."

10

We had a fair wind for the voyage back, so most of the sailors got a little rest after the arduous labor of repairing the hulls, then dragging the ships back into the water and reloading them. I had little to occupy my mind except for my problems and my predicament.

Gabinius was my enemy, that much was clear. I had allowed myself to be distracted by the exotic image of a Roman pirate chief, trying to invent a character and a past to explain him, when in all probability he was just one of Gabinius's old soldiers and still obeying the commands of that failed, scheming general.

But that must mean that it was Gabinius who had Silvanus killed. Something was wrong there. I have seen false friendship in plenty. Everyone has. I would have sworn that there was genuine affection between those two otherwise unlikable men. Of course, even family affection counts for little where great wealth and power are concerned, as witness Cleopatra and her family. And a sense of betrayal can turn love to hatred in an instant.

There remained that business of the frankincense. Most likely, I thought, it was just another piece of irrelevant nonsense thrown in to confuse the investigation.

I half expected to see laughing, jeering crowds lining the wharfs, ready to pelt us with rotten fruit and offal as we skulked in, cowed and humiliated. Nothing of the sort. In fact nobody paid us much attention at all. We had become a familiar sight, and it looked as if word of the trick that had been played upon us had not spread.

I amended that thought. That "trick" had been no lighthearted prank. The sabotage of our hulls might have cost all our lives, had we been farther from shore when we discovered it. Or had we been opposite sheer cliffs instead of a shelving beach. Or had we caught up with the pirates and in the middle of a sea fight when our ships went down beneath our feet. No, it was no minor jest that had been played upon us.

The question was: What to do about it?

When the ships were secured, I assembled the men on the pavement before naval headquarters, where they had taken their oath of service.

"Our situation has changed," I announced. "From now on every man bunks here at the naval base. That includes me. Any man who needs to go into the town must get permission from his skipper and must on no account be away for more than two hours. Anyone who leaves must return by nightfall, and no one leaves after dark. We now know that we have enemies in the town." Their looks darkened. "I have complete faith in you men," I continued, "and I know that there has been no treachery among us. For one thing, no man is such a fool as to go to sea aboard a ship he knows will sink.

"We have taken on a task and we will complete it. Those pirates are laughing at us now. You will have the opportunity to laugh at them when they hang on crosses. I want no loose talk. The time to boast is after we have conquered. In the meantime nobody needs to know what we are thinking or doing. We are through with play and with half measures. We now commence serious operations. Be ready."

They heard me out in silence, and I detected no insolence in their manner. That suited me well enough. The ability to inspire men has never been my gift. Caesar and Pompey were the masters of that art, and it has always been a mystery to me.

I sent Hermes and a couple of sailors to the house of Silvanus to get our gear, which didn't amount to all that much. I was not afraid to go myself. Gabinius would not try an open attack. He had done that once and failed on the night I had reeled back from the waterfront tavern with Cleopatra and Alpheus. It had been an uncommonly clumsy attempt for a crafty old campaigner like Gabinius, but he had not expected very stiff resistance, and he had not dared to use his own men. He had not counted on the presence of Ariston, who had eliminated three of the attackers. And, of course, he had made sure that neither of the men who left the fight alive survived to talk about who had hired them.

The more I thought about it, the more comfortable I became with the idea of Gabinius as my enemy. It was in the long tradition of war between members of the senatorial class, an extension of our everyday activities in the Forum and in the streets of Rome. Gabinius had a private game to play here on Cyprus and I was interfering, so he had to eliminate me. I had been sent to get rid of the pirates, so I needed evidence to put before the Senate tying Gabinius to their plunderings. It should not prove difficult now that I knew what to look for.

He must have an agent, a go-between to do his will while keeping his hands clean. It would have to be someone well-placed, accustomed to moving large sums without arousing suspicion. Nobilior? He was a banker and a Roman, but he had as much as told me that Gabinius was behind all the problems on Cyprus, in Egypt, and in the East generally. Cyprus was a commercial crossroads and full of merchants, financiers, speculators, and others who would fit Gabinius's needs perfectly.

I told Cleopatra of my new arrangements.

"I can make quarters for you on my ship," she offered. "You will be much more comfortable there than in these austere barracks."

"All too tempting," I said. "But I must beg off. It might be bad for morale if I insist that my men live here while I enjoy palatial accommodations. All the most successful generals make a point of sharing the same hardships as their men during a campaign. Caesar's tent is little more capacious than those of his men, and half the time he keeps the army marching days ahead of their supply train anyway. Then he sleeps on the ground wrapped in his cloak just like any common trooper."

"Really?" She seemed enthralled. "You must tell me more about Caesar."

That is what it was like in those days. All anybody wanted to hear about was Caesar.

Hermes returned with our gear. "All's quiet at the mansion. The funeral's done, so the loud mourning is over. They're packing up, waiting for word from Rome as to what's to be done next."

"What is the feel of the place?" I asked him.

He shrugged. "The way it usually is when the master's dead and nobody knows who is going to take over. It's an anxious time for slaves. They may go right on taking care of another house, or they might be handed over to a cruel master, or they could be parceled off and sold who knows where. Working in a big, rich house with a fairly easygoing master is about as good as a slave's life gets, so they're not expecting any improvement."

"Was Gabinius there?"

"I saw no sign of him or his men."

"He has an estate somewhere outside the town. Find out where it is."

"What do you have in mind?"

"Just do it. You never know when information like that may be of use. The messengers should know, or anyone who makes deliveries."

"I know how to find out. I just hope you're not planning anything reckless."

"Don't concern yourself with my plans. You'll know soon enough." He walked away grumbling. I cursed myself for being so short with him. For one thing, it meant that I was letting my feelings show, and that can be deadly. Emotion has no business intruding on politics and revenge. But my pride had been hurt, and I was angry as I had been few times in my life. What was it Cleopatra had said? The only emotion a king could fittingly display in public was great rage. It was the same for a senator on the *cursus honorum*. This insult would have to be repaid at a high rate of interest.

HERMES RETURNED THAT AFTERNOON with his report. "Market gossip is all about the *Aphrodisia*. It's the big event of the year for the people here. It's getting crowded in town, by the way. People are arriving by the shipload from the other islands and from the mainland. All the inns and taverns are full. People are renting out rooms in their own houses. You could probably make some money by renting out space here in the naval station. It's mostly empty."

144

"I don't doubt Harmodias has been doing exactly that every year. What about Gabinius's house?"

"It's about a mile south of town on the coastal road. It's built near the beach and has its own little wharf."

"That's convenient."

He sighed. "What are you planning?"

"Tonight we are going to pay the illustrious general a little visit. We'll go by water. That way nobody will see us leave through one of the city gates."

"Just you and me?"

"We'll take Ariston. He's a good man in a tight spot, and besides, he can row, which neither of us can. Go find him and send him here. Then get some sleep. We may have a long night ahead of us." He sighed again as he went to do my bidding. He knew better than to argue. Sometimes he acted more like my caretaker than my slave, but I suppose he had to look after his own well-being. After all, where would he find another master as sweet tempered and reasonable as I?

AN HOUR AFTER SUNDOWN, WE GOT INTO the skiff. The three of us wore dark tunics, and Hermes and I wore soft-soled sandals. Ariston, as usual, was barefoot. He had also covered his startling, blond hair with a scarf. He set to the oars in near silence, having already expertly muffled the tholes with scraps of cloth. We crossed the naval harbor and slid among the ships in the commercial basin as silently as an eel gliding along the surface. As we passed Cleopatra's yacht I saw lights burning in her little cabin. On deck, her crew went about their tasks as silently as we.

Not for the first time, I wished I could trust the princess, but I knew all too well how foolish it would be to do so. In so many ways she seemed like a civilized human being: cultured, staggeringly well educated, high-born, and charming beyond all common understanding of the term.

She was also an alien, an Orientalized pseudo-Greek, and the royal progeny of centuries of incest. On top of that she was a willful child and, should she become queen, might well remain a willful child all her life. Such people are supremely dangerous. They are mercurial, self-centered, and usually lack a conscience, as the rest of us understand such things. No doubt she believed herself to be something of a goddess. Even if she was my staunch ally and supporter at the moment, she could easily change her allegiance the next day, should the mood take her.

Once past the harbor mole, Ariston began rowing hard, pulling us southward with long, powerful strokes. The moon was nearly full, and I remembered that the *Aphrodisia* would commence upon the full moon. Curious, I thought, that Aphrodite's festival would be governed by the moon, which is the realm of Diana, or rather Artemis, since we were in Greek territory. But then, Aphrodite was a sea-goddess here. Perhaps, in the days of the world's youth, the gods and goddesses were not so strictured in their aspects as they have become since men began raising temples to them.

"Should be near here somewhere," Ariston said in a low voice, after he had rowed for the better part of an hour. I scanned the shoreline for the wharf. Even as I looked, I saw a flame making its way from the beach out onto the water. It was someone bearing a torch, and it looked as if he was walking along a jetty. At the end of the structure, the flame began waving back and forth. Behind and above this vision, a line of perhaps ten more torches appeared, spaced evenly to illuminate what had to be a path or stairway leading from the wharf to the bluff above, where I judged the general's house to be.

"Now what—" I barely got the words out before Hermes gripped my shoulder.

"A ship!" he said, in an urgent whisper. Immediately, Ariston shipped his oars and turned to look.

"You have better eyes than mine," I said. "Where?" But then I heard it: the steady, two-note piping of a *hortator* setting time for ship rowers. A low, shadowy form slid across our line of sight perhaps half a bow-shot ahead of us. I could just hear the low call of the poleman in the bow calling out the depth.

"A penteconter," Ariston reported, this being a ship with only a single bank of oars, much favored for raiding and smuggling. It has a limited cargo capacity but needs only half the crew of a Liburnian.

"Think they've seen us?" I asked him.

"Doubt it. Approaching shore like that, in the dark, all eyes are straight ahead."

"But they've got a light to bear on," Hermes said. "Doesn't that tell them they're on course?"

"They'll take no chances," he replied. "Ships get nightbound on the water sometimes, and people ashore light false beacons to lure them onto

146

the rocks so they can take the cargo. Coast guards will do the same thing to lure smugglers in. They'll feel for rocks and keep their hands on their swords until they're safely tied up and sure of whom they're dealing with."

"Ariston," I said, when they were past us, "bring us to shore just to the north of that wharf. I want to work my way close to them. Can you beach us without being heard or seen?"

"Depends on how alert they are." I saw the flash of his teeth in a quick grin, then he had the oars out and was turning us, pulling for shore. The noise of the muffled oars seemed loud to me, but doubtless could not have been heard ten paces away.

When we nudged the shore, Ariston sprang out and held the prow steady against the light surf. "We'll have to pick it up and carry it onto shore," he said. "They'll hear if we drag it." So Hermes and I took off our sandals and climbed out to either side. The boat was much heavier than it looked, and I felt the strain from my belly to my chest as we heaved it onto the gravelly beach.

"What now?" Hermes asked, as we sat to put our footwear back on. "We weren't expecting a visiting ship."

"We weren't *expecting* anything," I reminded him. "We came out here to see what was to be seen, and this is it. If, as I suspect, these are his pirate friends calling on him, this may be all I need to put an end to Gabinius and his schemes."

"You'll just walk in and arrest him?"

"Let me worry about that. Ariston, wait here with the boat. If we're running when we return, start dragging it to the water as soon as you see us."

"If you say so, Captain." He seemed disappointed to be missing out on the fun.

Hermes and I set off. After our nighttime scouting expeditions in the Gallic forests, approaching the wharf was child's play. We moved quietly, but the sound of the sea covered any noise we might have made. The surf of the sea is feeble compared to the roaring waves of the ocean beyond the Pillars of Hercules, but it makes sufficient sound to mask lesser noises.

By the time we reached it, the ship was secured to the wharf. I could see by the light of the moon that it was riding high, so it was not here to discharge cargo. Even as I had this thought, I saw a line of men making their way up the torch-lined path. At its top I could now see an imposing house upon the bluff, its white marble making it seem to glow.

I could make out a mutter of voices and wanted mightily to be able to hear what they were saying. The only way to do that was to get closer.

Sizable shrubs grew almost down to the water, meaning that this area was goat-free. That suited my purposes to perfection, allowing us to work our way nearer until we were almost beneath the wharf. At the spot where I was able to get the nearest, its walkway was just above the level of my head. Men were now returning from the house, laden with what appeared to be weighty bags on their shoulders.

"This will make for an easier voyage back," said a rumbling voice. "She's been wallowing from being so lightly laden." The language was Latin and the accent was Roman, or very nearly so. There are subtle nuances by which you can tell the speech of a City man from one raised elsewhere. He sounded like a man of the better class, but from one of the nearby towns, not Rome itself. The accent was familiar, but I could not place it.

I couldn't quite distinguish the man who was speaking, but I could make out two who stood close together not far from me, keeping clear of the men carrying burdens. They were well away from the illumination of the torches, and the light cast by the moon was not strong enough to make out details of feature or dress. I tried to work my way to a position where I might be able to see both of them to best advantage.

"This must be the last cargo for a while." That voice was unmistakable: Gabinius. "Things are too volatile here. We'll have to desist for a while."

The other chuckled. "You mean that fool and his play navy?"

"That and other things. I've warned you. I won't warn you again."

"Your business isn't just with me," said the other, "and you know it." Now I could see the two silhouetted against the moon and stars. The outline of Gabinius was as unmistakable as his voice. I thought at first that the other wore a cowl drawn over his head, then I realized it was his long hair falling below his shoulders: Spurius.

"Nonetheless, our business is concluded until I say otherwise. I'm giving you a letter to deliver along with your cargo. If you'll take my advice, you'll vacate these waters for a season or two. I hear the shores of the Euxine are a good prospect for a man of courage and enterprise."

"I'll determine my own destination," Spurius said. "Besides, I've a notion to attend the festival. It is famed all over the world, and here I am, so handy to Paphos. It would be a shame to miss it."

"Then your blood is on your own head. You'll end up on the cross soon if you don't clear out."

"You know that isn't going to happen." I could hear the smile in his voice. But what was he referring to? Crucifixion or his departure for fairer waters?

"But," Spurius went on, "I think it's time for me to be out of this business anyway. Perhaps this should be my last voyage for you."

There was a pause, then, "That might be best," Gabinius said. At that point the two began to walk toward the house. I yearned to follow them, but there were too many men about, and there were more torches alight. I could see that some of them were held by Gabinius's bullyboys, who wore armor and weapons. There was precious little trust on display that night.

I tapped Hermes on the shoulder, and we began to work our way carefully back into the bushes, then along the beach. There was so much more I wanted to know, but I had already pressed my luck as far as it would go. I have been a gambler all my life, but it is only money that you lose at the races.

Ariston loomed out of the night like an underworld demon sprung from a hole in the ground. "Are any of them after you?"

"If they are, they're quieter than I am. Where is the boat?" Now that I had determined to leave, I wanted to be away quickly, as if this was the most dangerous phase of the operation. Stealthy activities often affect me that way.

"You're almost standing on it. Help me carry it, and we'll be away." He had disguised it with brush, anticipating an all-night wait. We cleared away the boughs, picked it up once more, and carried it down to the water. Getting it back into the water proved to be more difficult than taking it out had been, perhaps because the waves, though small, were now trying to force us in the opposite direction. The result was an unavoidable splashing and scraping among the stones of the beach. I expected an alarm to be raised at any moment, but with strenuous effort we were soon afloat again.

When Ariston had rowed us some distance from the shore, I told him to stop. We rested for a moment, listening hard. Torches lined the wharf and the path to the house, so the pirates were still loading their ship. Whatever they had come for, there was a lot of it.

"Were you ever on any errands like this?" I asked the ex-pirate.

"It sounds like smuggling. I always felt that was beneath a pirate, but, as I've told you, these are a pretty sorry lot."

"What would Gabinius be smuggling?" Hermes asked.

"Good question," I said. "Come on, let's get back to the base. Ariston, do you think we can get back in time to get the ships underway, return here, and bag this lot? We'll never have another chance like this."

"Speaking of chances, there isn't any. They'll have that ship loaded and away from here long before daylight, else there's not much point in coming here at night. Even if you two could row, we wouldn't have the ships crewed and launched and back here before midmorning. We wouldn't catch a glimpse of their mast going over the horizon."

"This mission lies under a curse," I said to no one in particular. I dipped my fingers in the water and touched them to my lips to let Neptune know I wasn't complaining about him.

Rosy-fingered Dawn was performing her daily act as we pulled up by the naval wharf. Ariston worked his arms and shoulders as we got out of the boat. Being sole rower in a three-man boat had taxed even his strength.

"Rest today," I told him. "Spurius isn't likely to strike until he's delivered whatever he picked up to whomever it goes to."

"What about me?" Hermes said. "I was up all night."

"You did nothing but ride in a boat. Oh, all right, go ahead and get some sleep. I have work to do." I watched him trudge off toward his bed and thought I was being too lenient on the boy. At this rate I was going to ruin his character.

The good thing about a city getting ready for a festival is that the food vendors are out early, not wishing their town to be disgraced should a visitor die of hunger. A short walk and a few coins provided me with bread hot from the oven and dipped in honey, some grilled sausages, and heavily watered wine, warmed and spiced.

I found a comfortable bench near the water, shaded by an ivy-draped arbor, and engaged in one of the most profitable of all human activities: I sat and thought. Philosophers can make a living doing this, but I find that even a man of action can sometimes find no better use for his time. So, watching the fishing boats raise their sails and set out for their day's work, I munched on my breakfast and considered the ramifications of what I had learned.

First, Gabinius and Spurius were deep in it together. No real surprises there. I had suspected Gabinius from the first.

Second, Spurius was definitely a Roman, if not from Rome itself. This may have been the meaning of his "that will never happen" remark. Citizens cannot be crucified. That most degrading of punishments is inflicted only on rebellious slaves and foreigners.

So much for the certainties. There were still many questions left to answer. What, precisely, was the relationship between the two men? I had assumed that Spurius was one of Gabinius's officers or clients, but the pirate's manner was not in the least subservient. He spoke as an equal. That, of course, could be bluff and bluster. I have known many soldiers, strong-arm men, and politicians who salved their pride and raised their own credit by putting on a fierce, I-bow-to-no-man front when dealing with their betters. Such men invariably find other, more subtle methods to cringe and toady. That was a definite possibility.

And just what was going on out there at Gabinius's estate. Smuggling? If so, what? The ever-mysterious frankincense? It seemed bizarre, but so much about this business was baffling that I felt compelled to retain it as a possibility. Another thought struck me: suppose Spurius was stashing his loot on Gabinius's estate. That might leave him free to continue his depredations in the area without having to repair to some distant island base. He would know it was safe, protected by his patron or partner, as the case might be. This was a definite possibility. I liked it.

The more I thought about it, the more sense it made. He might have come back to fetch it because he was feeling safe, having beached and humiliated me. Toy navy, indeed!

Gabinius, clearly, was building a stake to finance another grab at supreme power and providing himself with the nucleus of a naval force while he was about it. While Silvanus was alive, he could provide them all with the protection they needed as well. That thought drew me up short. That being the case, why was Silvanus dead? Well, doubtless all would be made clear in time. I just needed more facts.

It has always been my habit, when investigating, to gather all the facts I could, to have them at my disposal when time came for the trial. It was this little mania of mine that made me such a curiosity to my contemporaries, most of whom never let facts get in their way. In Rome the traditional way to sue a fellow citizen was to haul him before a praetor's court and loudly accuse him of every criminal depravity you could think of, leaving him to prove himself innocent. This he usually did by bringing in as many high-placed friends as he could to swear what a fine, upright, honest fellow he was. The prosecutor would reply by bringing forth "witnesses" who would swear before all the gods that they had personally seen the accused performing every perversion from incest to bestiality. In the end, each would vie to outbribe the jury.

Even Cicero, who was more scrupulous than most, indulged in this sort of buffoonery. I have already mentioned his scurrilous characterization of Gabinius. At an earlier date, he had attacked a senator named Vatinius for wearing a black toga, calling it a degenerate insult to the revered Senate, where white togas are the rule except when in mourning. Later, when Cicero defended Vatinius in a lawsuit, he blandly proclaimed that the black toga was a pious austerity demanded by Vatinius's Pythagorean beliefs.

It was all great fun and wonderful public entertainment, but I could never see that it led to anything resembling justice.

There was also the little problem that this was not Rome. Had it been, I could have at least made my accusations, backed and protected by my family's many clients. Before his exile, I could even have called on Milo's gang as bodyguards. Here, on Cyprus, I was not in a position of strength, despite my military status. I had sailors and marines of doubtful loyalty. Gabinius had his veterans, and he might have far more of them than I had seen thus far. And there were the pirates. I had a feeling that they were seldom very far from Cyprus. For all I knew they hid their ships in some nearby cove, and the taverns of the city might be full of them.

No, this was not yet the time to throw half-baked charges in Gabinius's craggy face.

These ponderings lasted much of the morning. They also called for a bit more of that watered wine to help them along. Before I knew it, it was time for lunch. I repaired to a dockside place with a fine view of the harbor, where I laid in a substantial meal. Despite the crowding of the place brought about by the upcoming festival, I leaned back in my bench, resting my back against the whitewashed wall, intending only to meditate for a while, and soon was contentedly asleep. Well, it had been a long night.

I was awakened by a loud clamor. Somewhere, great trumpets were sounding. A great shouting came from the direction of the waterfront, and the tavern's patrons had sprung to their feet. I shook my head, lurched to my own feet, and pushed my way to the front. All eyes were directed out to sea. Beyond the harbor mole the water seemed to be covered with sails. There were ships out there, many of them. And they were huge.

"Neptune preserve us," I said, "we're under attack!" Surely there weren't *that* many pirates. And why such enormous ships?

A man standing next to me laughed at my expression. "Calm yourself, friend. No enemy in sight. It's the Roman grain fleet, bound for Alexandria."

Embarrassed and relieved at the same time, I walked down to the waterfront to enjoy the spectacle. Now I saw that the ships had multiple masts and triangular topsails like merchantmen. But these grain ships were far larger than the usual cargo vessels, with five or six times their capacity. They were the biggest of all seagoing vessels, exceeded in size only by the Ptolemies' monster river barges.

In Italy the annual grain fleet had an almost religious significance. From the time it sailed to the day of its return, there was a collective holding of breath. Impressive as they were, the ships could all be lost in a single storm. If that happened, there could be hungry times ahead, so dependent had we become on Egyptian grain. When the returning fleet came safely to harbor, beacon fires were lighted the whole length of the Italian peninsula, and there was celebration in every town. Even if the Italian crop should fail, nobody would starve. When Pompey was given a five-year oversight of the grain supply, with a free hand to root out corruption and inefficiency, he was given the greatest trust the Roman people could bestow, as prestigious as any military command.

It took much of the afternoon for the ships to lower their sails and make their way to anchorage under oars. While they were doing this I returned to the naval base, washed up, shaved, dressed in my best clothes, and assembled a group of my most handsomely equipped marines to act as an honor guard. With Hermes likewise turned out in his best, hovering attentively behind me, I returned to the main wharf of the commercial harbor.

I was just in time. The flagship of the fleet, a truly immense vessel painted white and trimmed with gilding, an arching swan's neck at her stern and a towering spray of carved acanthus leaves at her bow, was inching up to the stone pier. The city dignitaries were out in force to greet the arriving officials, and they made way for me and my gleaming escort. I got there just as a gangplank big as a trireme's *corvus*, complete with a protective railing of gilded chains supported by fish-tailed Cupids holding toy tridents, was lowered to the pavement.

First down was the senatorial official in charge of the fleet, a quaestor named Valgus. I had been a quaestor myself, once, in Rome. In Rome a quaestor held the lowest elected office, was little more than a glorified clerk, and was accorded little respect by the citizenry. Outside Rome, a quaestor was regarded with almost the same awe as a promagistrate. Then came some senators bound for the Alexandrian Embassy, some of whom I knew. Then there were the distinguished passengers.

"Decius!" Julia waved like an excited girl from the ship's rail. Then she was on the gangplank, restraining herself to a formal, patrician descent. Then she stood before me, embraced me chastely, and gave me a peck on the cheek.

I patted her bottom. "You can do better than that."

She dug an elbow into my ribs. "Of course, but not here in front of respectable people." She caught my men grinning between the cheekplates of their helmets. The grins disappeared beneath her glare. "Somebody else you know came with us."

Then I caught sight of the big form stalking down the plank. "Titus!" I whooped. Milo bounded the last few steps to the wharf and grabbed my hand in both of his. His palms were still as hard as wood.

"You see, Decius, I brought your lady safely to Cyprus, fighting sailors and senators away from her the whole voyage. You look better than when I saw you last. Sea air must agree with you."

"I was wasting away in Rome. It's too peaceful there now, and you're missing nothing. I need you here, though, and desperately. Just the sight of you raises my spirits." In truth I was somewhat shocked at Milo's appearance. His hair had gone completely gray, and his once godlike face was deeply lined and almost haggard. I had to remind myself that he was near my age, for he looked far older. His limbs seemed to be as powerful and his gait as lionlike as ever, but he was gaunt, as if all the surplus flesh had been burned from him. Well, there was gray in my hair as well.

He clasped Hermes by the shoulder. "Hermes! Hasn't this vicious tyrant manumitted you yet? I thought I'd see you in a toga by now."

"I want to sell him," I said, "but no one will make an offer. Come along, I'll show you our quarters." I hoped he did not catch the look in Hermes's eyes. Hermes had worshipped Milo since boyhood, and he was as appalled as I but less schooled in hiding it. Julia was not traveling alone, naturally, so I left some men to escort her slaves and baggage to the base when they had it unloaded.

"I am so glad we had such wonderful sailing weather," Julia said, as we walked toward the base. "I was afraid we wouldn't be here in time for the *Aphrodisia*. This is perfect timing. Have you visited the temple?"

"I have. I'll take you to see it tomorrow and introduce you to the high priestess Ione herself."

"Wonderful! I so want to—" she paused as she saw the cluster of plain, functional, military buildings ahead of us. "Decius, I thought you would have engaged more suitable lodgings for us. Do you expect me to live among sailors and marines?"

"Actually, my dear, until a few days ago I was living in the governor's mansion and looking forward to introducing you to its luxuries."

"Then why are you not living there now?" I knew that tone all too well.

"Actually, my sweet, there has been a bit of a complication. The governor is dead. Murdered, in fact; and since I might well be next, I thought more secure accommodations were in order."

"Murdered?" Milo said happily. He cared nothing for luxury, but he liked excitement. At least that much had not changed.

"I had hoped this would be a more productive posting," Julia said. "You are getting too old and dignified for this sort of squabbling among criminals and cutthroats. You are one of Rome's rising men, in line for the next praetorship election. You should leave investigative duties to your subordinates. What have you been training Hermes for all these years anyway? Give him his freedom and let him go around poking into dangerous places among low company."

"If you two don't stop this, the boy is going to start getting ideas." I knew I was on safer ground though. I had her hooked. Despite her patrician protestations, she loved this sort of thing. She was, after all, a Caesar; and politics played for life-and-death stakes excited her above all things. Most Roman women were utterly shut out from this masculine arena, but I sometimes let her help me with my investigations, another of my little eccentricities.

As we reached higher ground overlooking the harbor, she paused and pointed. "What is that beautiful ship? We passed it coming in to the anchorage."

"That's Cleopatra's yacht. It's part of my little fleet, actually."

"Cleopatra? Ptolemy's youngest daughter? Isn't she a bit young for a naval command, besides being female?"

"Royalty do things differently, and I desperately needed another ship. But she may have killed the governor, so be careful around her."

"Decius, why can't you ever lead a normal life?"

I showed her the austere suite of rooms I had commandeered. In other times they had been used by the Roman naval commander when he was on the island. They were comfortable enough, but the government spent little on amenities for military officers, who were expected to provide for themselves.

"I want to take a look at your ships, Decius," Milo said, beginning to show the old nervous energy that kept him forever in motion.

"Go ahead," I told him. "I'll join you shortly."

"My lady," Hermes said, when he was gone, "has Titus Milo been ill?"

"I was wondering the same thing myself," I said. "How was he acting on the voyage?"

She looked wistful. "I've never liked Milo," she began, "and made no secret of it; but now I almost feel sorry for him. Strife and struggle for power were the breath of life to him, and he almost had the laurels in his grasp when it all came crashing down around him. He rose from nothing, just a common street thug. He would have been consul if it hadn't been for the murder of Clodius. Now he is an exile. His gang is scattered, and with no family he has no support in the Senate. He was Cicero's man, and Cicero's star is fading fast."

"Surely he can expect to be recalled," I protested. "When I am praetor, I'll exert pressure on the tribunes to . . ."

"There is no chance, Decius," she said gently. "Your family's power is fading, too, and you know it. Caesar is to be the new power. When he returns from Gaul, he will be dictator in all but name. And Clodius was Caesar's man. Caesar will not forgive Milo, not even for you, and Caesar truly likes you. Fausta has left Milo, did you know that?"

"No, but it does not surprise me. Milo in the ascendant was the prize catch of all the men in Rome for Fausta. Milo descending is of no interest to her. She'll make a play for Caesar next. You might advise Calpurnia to have someone test her food and drink from now on."

"Fausta is not that ambitious and cold-blooded, but neither is she going to be married to a failure and be exiled from Rome. Not the Dictator's daughter."

"You think that is what's turning him into an old man before his time? It isn't some inner illness eating him away?"

"For Milo," she said, "it is the same thing."

That evening, when Julia and her girls were settled into their quarters and Milo was satisfied with the ships, we had dinner outdoors, enjoying the cool, offshore breeze. Over dinner I told them of everything that had happened so far. Of course, I left out certain small details concerning Flavia. Julia, as always, was most interested in my strange dream. Like most Romans, she loved portents, omens, and dreams. Milo barely bothered to hide his contempt. He had no use for intangible things, although, like all politicians, he was happy to use them for his own purposes. He had been known to hold up debates and votes endlessly by claiming to have seen bad omens.

"We need to commence social activity immediately," Julia said. "I want to see Cleopatra. She may be a scheming Ptolemy with dynastic ambitions, but she's little more than a girl and I'll sound out her intentions."

"She's young," I cautioned, "but she's no girl. It won't be easy to match wits with her."

"Have you forgotten? I am Julius Caesar's niece. She's eager to know all about him. I'll wring her out like a sponge. And I want to meet that banker and his scandalous wife."

My scalp prickled. Had I let something slip? "Why?"

"This Nobilior is a rich *eques*, a banker, and was a friend of Silvanus. Corruption always involves money, so he'll know what the governor was up to, and his wife will know what her husband is up to. She may like to play with sailors when she is away from home, but she is very aware of her social position and will want to better it. She'll be flattered by the attentions of a patrician lady from the Republic's oldest family." Julia could always strip away the dross and get down to the essentials. And she was more than willing to make shameless use of her pedigree.

"Excellent plan," I said, although with some reservations I did not voice. "We'll commence the social assault in the morning, as long as I don't get a pirate alarm and have to sail to Bithynia or some such place."

"Leave the pirate hunting to me for a few days," Milo said. "I'll whip these Greek sluggards into shape. You've been too soft on the rowers.

I know every malingerer's trick in their trade. I'll double the speed they've been giving you. They've been rowing you like bargemen, not man-o'-war's men. I'll pop the whip on those carpenters, too. Your catapults and ballistas should have been finished days ago. They're dragging out the job because you're paying them by the day. They're not laborers; they're supposed to be craftsmen, paid by the job. I'll break a few fingers and teach them wisdom."

"I am not sure the Senate would approve my delegating command to you. To go to sea as my assistant, maybe, but . . ."

"I am an ex-praetor. My conviction keeps me out of Rome and out of office, but my fitness for military command was never questioned. You've been given a free hand out here. Use it."

"He's right," Julia told me. "You have to understand that when the Senate gives you an overseas commission, even a small one like this, you get to define your own powers until they send someone else out with a bigger commission. This paltry business will be over with long before the Senate wakes up from its collective nap and takes notice."

"Agreed, then?" Milo said.

It was a little disconcerting to have these two gang up on me. Usually they were on opposite sides. "All right."

"Excellent. While I'm at it, I'm going to wring some answers out of this man Harmodias, the one in charge of the base and its stores."

"I don't doubt he's turned a few sesterces peddling government property while nobody was looking," I said, "but I've never met a low-level official who didn't. Or a high-level one either, for that matter."

"Nonetheless, he has a few things to answer for. That damned paint, for instance."

"What? Unlike the ships, the rations, and almost all the arms and supplies, the paint is the one thing that's *there!*"

But Milo would say no more on the subject.

11

WE BEGAN AT THE TEMPLE OF Aphrodite. I had left my little fleet to the fearsome attentions of Titus Milo and well might they tremble. His reputation had spread even to these eastern waters.

Julia wanted to see the temple and told me that all the most important people on the island would be there this near festival time, but I knew that she had another reason for being so anxious to attend. The Caesars were a famously infertile family, bearing few children, most of whom died at birth or in infancy. The children who lived were mostly girls. Years later it was for this reason that, needing an heir, Caesar was reduced to adopting his sister's grandson.

Julia had yet to conceive, and this worried her endlessly. I had long since assured her that I would never divorce her on grounds of infertility. There were far too many Metelli as it was, and men of my class adopted sons more readily than they bred them. Nonetheless, she felt that her failure to conceive diminished her. Patrician women had a nasty habit of snobbing each other over the number and health of their children. Julia hoped that attending the annual ritual of Aphrodite would bestow fertility upon her. My dream vision had reinforced this hope.

The resident and visiting notables were out in force, as were the expected local peddlers, beggars, and idlers, most of the latter offering themselves as guides. Having already had the tour, I was able to show her everything myself.

"It *is* a rather strange statue," she said, when she got a look at the cult image.

"At least this way," I told her, "you don't have hawkers constantly trying to sell you miniature copies of it, the way they do at every other famed temple site of my experience."

"I suppose. But it is very moving nonetheless." We emerged from the dim interior, and I took her to see the golden nets. In the garden I pointed out Ione, who was speaking with a group of very well-dressed people.

"Oh, what a lovely woman!" She all but clapped her hands with delight. "Come and introduce me." The little crowd parted for her, as crowds always seemed to do before members of her family. She made a grave bow before Ione, and the priestess took her hand.

"I see the senator's wife has arrived." I made introductions and the rest of the group, sensing that Ione wished to give a private interview, drew off a little way.

"I am deeply honored," Julia said. "I aspire to become a priestess of Venus in time."

"But surely you hold that position already. Is there not a family connection?"

"Our family is devoted to the aspect of Venus named Genetrix. The priestesses of Venus Genetrix are patrician, and they must have at least one living child." She paused. "It is concerning this that I wished to speak with you."

Ione smiled, still holding Julia's hand. "Come with me, my dear." She led her farther into the garden, and they were soon all but invisible beneath the shade of the beautiful trees.

"Do you realize," said a voice next to me, "that you and your wife are receiving more personal attention from the high priestess than visiting kings and queens? There are several here, you know."

"Good day, Flavia." She was dressed as before in her priestess's gown and blonde wig. "I suppose we must just be interesting people, nothing more. And Romans are the new power here. The authorities of temples are generally careful to stay on good terms with the people in power."

"When Silvanus came here she did no more than greet him. She has shunned Gabinius entirely. When Cato was administrator, she avoided him despite the fine gifts he brought. And Cato is a genuinely pious man."

"He is that. He is also one of the most unpleasant, insufferable men in existence. I, on the other hand, am intensely likeable; and Julia, besides her many other charms, bears that magic name."

"I heard she arrived yesterday with the grain fleet. I also heard that the famous Titus Milo was on the same ship."

"Your sources of information are impeccable as usual. Titus is one of my oldest friends. He's come here to assist me in my naval duties."

"Really? I hope this means he is returning to Rome's good graces. It was so unjust to banish him just for killing an evil wretch like Clodius."

"Actually, Titus didn't kill him. There was a brawl between their supporters, and Clodius just sort of, well—he ended up dead." This was not something I wished to discuss. "But I am confident Milo will be back in the thick of it soon. I will personally agitate for his recall. I'll be standing for next year's praetorship you know."

"So I understand. My husband has quite a large clientele, and he always takes them up to Rome for the elections. Who are you supporting for the quaestorships? We always want to have an agreeable grain quaestor at Ostia." Now we were back on a sound, familiar footing: the old game of votes and favors. Here we were, on a foreign island pursuing vastly differing purposes, and we were dickering over the next elections. That is how it was back when we had a genuine republic.

In time Julia returned, her face glowing. Whatever Ione had told her, it agreed with Julia.

"My dear, this is Flavia, wife of Sergius Nobilior of Ostia and a priestess of Venus assisting here at the temple. Flavia, my wife, Julia Minor, daughter of Lucius Julius Caesar, granddaughter of Caius Julius Caesar, and so on back to Aeneas."

Julia beamed. "I am so glad to meet you, Flavia. Pay no attention to my husband's sarcasm. He has no gift for it. But he has told me so much about you."

"He has?" Flavia was nonplussed but covered it well. "We've been so looking forward to your arrival."

"I wish I could invite you to our house, but my husband has us living in a *barracks,* if you can believe that. I simply can't have people of quality in to visit."

"Nonsense! You've just arrived, and we've been here for ages. You must have dinner with us this evening. I know that Sergius has already invited the archon of Paphos, and a visiting Ethiopian prince, whose name I can't pronounce. Cleopatra will be there, too, if she doesn't have to go off chasing pirates with your husband."

"Oh, it would be so unfair to ask you to have us over at the last minute like this. I am sure your couches are already full."

"Not at all! If they are, we will just bring in more couches! This isn't Rome after all."

"Then we will be delighted."

"Wonderful!" Flavia fairly glowed. Julia was right. This shameless female reprobate was flattered at attention from a patrician. She turned to me. "Senator, please ask your friend Milo to come as well. Having the three of you in my house will make me the envy of Paphos." Such are the demands of social life in the provinces. As for Milo, I felt no apprehension about introducing him to the voracious Flavia. He was a match for anything save the massed hostility of the Senate.

"Now," Julia said, as we walked back toward the center of the town, "we must hire a litter to take us to their house this evening, if there's one to be had in this town."

"There won't be one for hire, not with every snob in the eastern sea come to visit. I'll talk to Doson, Silvanus's majordomo. He'll lend us one for a small bribe. The household staff have nothing much to do now anyway."

"Good idea. Then you must take me to see Cleopatra."

"Yes, dear." I was not being timidly compliant. It was just that Julia, besides being single-minded, was fearsomely competent at this sort of operation.

Our litter-arranging mission accomplished, we found Cleopatra aboard her ship. In fact her golden boat was waiting for us at the dock. "She stationed a slave to ambush us as soon as we came in sight," Julia commented. "Wasn't that thoughtful of her?" She seated herself amid the colorful, scented cushions. I remained standing, trying to project the image of the salty naval commander, and actually managed to retain my feet all the way to the spectacular ship.

"Julia!" Cleopatra cried, as my wife was lifted aboard expertly by a team of solicitous slaves. "How wonderful to see you again!" Julia tried to bow, but Cleopatra swept her up in a sisterly embrace.

"Princess, you overwhelm me. You can scarcely remember me. You were just a little girl, and my husband was a mere assistant to the Roman envoy." I was a bit nettled, but Julia always knew how to do the proper thing in situations like this. I clambered up the ladder after her and held my tongue.

"I remember you wonderfully well, don't speak nonsense. You and your friend Fausta were the first Roman ladies I ever met, and you made a profound impression on me."

I'll bet Fausta did, I thought. I said nothing. She seated us at a table on the fantail beneath a striped canopy, fanned by slaves equipped with palm-fiber fans. These are far more efficient than the beautiful but ineffective ostrich-feather fans affected so much by those who wish to ape Oriental standards of luxury.

"You flatter me, Princess." I noted that Julia was ever so slightly deferential. She was Roman aristocracy, but Cleopatra was Greek-Egyptian royalty.

"Not the least. I've lived most of my life among the royal and noble ladies of my part of the world. Most are as silent, cowed, and ignorant as peasant women, only far sillier. Roman ladies are so much more intelligent and assertive. I long to visit Rome and be introduced to your society. I will feel that at last I am among equals." The woman's grasp of flattery was phenomenal.

"I would ask you to stay with us while you are in Rome," Julia told her sadly, "but our house is far too humble. My father's house is far finer, but you really must stay in my uncle's house. When he is in Rome he lives in the great *Domus Publica*. It is actually owned by the State, but as Pontifex Maximus it is his for life and he always puts it at the disposal of visiting dignitaries and royalty."

"Ah, yes. The great Julius Caesar is your uncle, is he not? You really must tell me all about him. The whole world is fascinated by Caesar." There went the hook.

I gave half an ear to their talk while a wonderful lunch was set before us. As I munched on the delicacies, I looked out to the open sea past the harbor mole. Out there, Milo was drilling my crews. He had them rowing in dashes, and once I could have sworn I saw a ship leap clear of the water under oar power, like a fish chased by a shark. And I thought *I'd* had them rowing well.

As always, when seeing such a thing, I wondered how one man can inspire such obedience while another, I for instance, could not. How did a long-haired dwarf like Alexander get men to follow him all the way to India? How did Hannibal, scion of a nation of merchants, weld a polyglot horde of Gauls, Spaniards, Africans, and others, all armed differently and none of them knowing a word of Punic, into an army that consistently defeated larger Roman forces? And how did he keep them together and fighting for twenty years without a whiff of mutiny? How did Caesar do what he was doing, which I had seen firsthand and still was at a loss to describe? I could never put a finger on it. But Titus Milo, in his own way, was a man as unique as Caesar, and men did his bidding almost joyously, breaking their backs and hearts for him. He was one of those men who could inspire fear and love at the same time.

Whatever it was, I was not going to argue with it. Just having Milo there with me was an enormous relief. It meant that I could leave the naval duties to one of the few people in the world I trusted utterly. It meant I could devote my attention to finding out who had murdered Silvanus. And I was certain that that, in turn, would tell me who was profiting from this little upsurge of piracy in the East.

THE LITTER WAS A BIT LARGER THAN THE ones common in Rome. This was because most Roman streets were so narrow that comfortably wide conveyances were impracticable. The litter slaves knew their job and the trip to the house of Nobilior was a pleasant one, though slowed by the throngs in the streets. Julia and I had taken an afternoon nap after Cleopatra's reception and were now ready for an evening of entertainment and intrigue.

Julia had sounded Cleopatra out about Flavia, whom the princess had described as "a dreadful woman but great fun." She had also learned a great deal about Cleopatra's mission on Cyprus. It turned out that Ptolemy had narrowly survived an attempted coup, was conducting a ruthless purge of his guards and nobles, and wanted his beloved daughter to be well out of it.

"I commiserated with her about Berenice," Julia said, meaning Cleopatra's ill-fated older sister. "I truly liked her, silly woman though she was. Do you know what Cleopatra said? 'The duties of royalty are terrible.' She insisted that her father grieved for the daughter he had to execute as deeply as she did herself. I suppose it must be true."

"Ah, well," I said, "we always have old Brutus. He ordered the execution of his own sons for the good of the State. Inconsolable afterward, so they say."

We climbed from the litter, and the carrying slaves squatted beside it patiently. I had no fear that they would sneak off and get drunk because I had not come alone. Having been attacked once and knowing that I had a superfluity of local enemies, I had brought along twenty of my marines as an escort. I had left Hermes to keep an eye on the naval station. I wanted no more acts of sabotage, and I didn't trust my men as fully as I pretended.

"Senator! Julia! Welcome to our house!" Flavia was turned out in her usual Coan gown, expensive cosmetics, and several pounds of gold, pearls, and jewels. Crowning her was a blonde wig dressed in a towering basketwork of interwoven locks, threaded through with strings of seed pearls and powdered with gold dust. She peered past us. "Was your friend Milo not able to come?"

"He'll be along presently," I assured her. "He had some affairs to attend to at the naval base and sends his apologies for his lateness."

"Oh, wonderful! Now you must come along and meet our other guests." She seized Julia's arm and spirited her away, leaving me to follow them onto a broad terrace overlooking the sea. In the center of the terrace was a pool, now drained, where Cretan dancers performed. All around it the guests stood and conversed while servers circulated among them. Sergius Nobilior beckoned to me, and I joined him. He stood with two other men, one of them I recognized: Antonius the metal trader. The other was a very tall, thin man dressed in rich, colorful robes. His face was fine featured and very dark, with huge, black eyes. This had to be the Ethiopian prince Flavia had mentioned. Looking around, I saw that Flavia had plunged with her catch into a group of well-dressed ladies, Cleopatra among their number.

"Greetings, Senator," Nobilior said. "Flavia will be impossible to live with now. She has Julius Caesar's niece all to herself."

"Whose niece?" asked the Ethiopian.

"At last," I said, "someone who has never heard of him. I think I am going to like you."

"Senator, I believe you have already met my friend Decimus Antonius. This is Prince Legyba of Ethiopia. He is here to attend the festival."

"You've traveled far, Prince," I said. "I know Homer speaks of the 'pious Ethiopians,' but you are the first I have met who travels to honor the gods."

He flashed a smile full of brilliant teeth. "My people are always curious about the gods and religious practices of other people, but I am actually on a trade mission on behalf of my father the king." He spoke excellent Greek, but with the strangest accent I had ever heard, an almost musical singsong.

At that moment a tall, mournful-looking man joined us. I recognized him as Nearchus, the archon of Paphos. On Cyprus that meant the head man of the city council. As usual in Hellenistic cities, he was one of the richest landowners.

"Senator," he said, "while I hate to bring business to a social occasion such as this, might I have a few words with you?"

"By all means," I said. "My friends, will you give us leave?"

"As long as you're with us for dinner," Sergius said. "It will be ready shortly, Nearchus, you'll be in a better position to wring concessions from him after he's had a bit to drink."

We went a little aside to a quiet corner by some large, potted shrubs.

"Senator, our council meetings have come almost to a standstill. With Governor Silvanus dead, it is not at all clear who is the Roman authority on the island. We are stymied. General Gabinius behaves as if the mantle has fallen on him, but he is no more than an exile, although a prestigious one. You would seem to be the ranking Roman official here, but your commission is naval and you have not come forward to take control. What are we to do?"

"I really can't administer the island," I told him, "since I may be called away at any time to pursue pirates. Gabinius, however, has no standing. If he tries to give you orders, simply say that you are awaiting word from the Senate. They should have sent out an assistant governor long since, and perhaps they'll speed up the process now. But on no account should you regard Gabinius as the man in power here. He is a noted plunderer, and you have to be pretty bad to get expelled from Rome for robbing foreigners." I would not have said this earlier, but seeing Gabinius conferring with Spurius had changed my view of him.

He looked more mournful than ever. "This is most distressing." I had to sympathize with him. It is always upsetting to see infighting among the conquerors. "I hardly know what to do."

"Take my advice: just shut down operations and enjoy the festival. If Gabinius prods you further, tell him the goddess forbids official business until the next full moon. That's how we do things in Rome."

"I shall take your words to heart. Thank you, Senator." From his look I had provided him with little comfort, but comfort was not in the commission I had received from the Senate.

At that moment Milo arrived. He had dressed impressively in a fine toga complete with a broad praetor's stripe to which he was not really entitled, but who was going to argue with him on Cyprus? He immediately became the center of attention, and I was called upon to make introductions. Changed though he was, he was still a tremendously impressive man, diminished only in the eyes of those of us who had known him in the days of his glory. And when he turned on the charm, he was as magnetic as Marcus Antonius on his best day.

I saw Julia, with Flavia clinging to her like a barnacle, talking with the Ethiopian prince. He was pressing some sort of gift on her, with many graceful gestures. Then the majordomo announced dinner. We trooped into the triclinium and flopped down for the first course.

Dinner was a great success. Flavia, it turned out, had cleverly selected dishes that had some connection to Aphrodite. Some came from plants or animals sacred to the goddess; others were mentioned in the legends of her life and exploits. The wines were all from vineyards connected to her most famous temples and shrines.

After dinner we retired once more to the terrace to catch the cool, evening breeze and clear our heads of wine fumes. Julia came to check on me.

"Why you've restrained yourself," she said, finding me sober. "I'm so pleased. I was speaking with that Ethiopian prince before dinner, such an elegant, delightful man, and so exotic! Look, he's given these to all the ladies here." From somewhere within her gown she produced a small, plump bag of snowy white cloth, bound with a ribbon. Its sweet scent was familiar.

"Let me see that!" I snatched it from her and tugged at the ribbon.

"Don't you dare spill any!" She snatched it back. "Let me open it. You're so clumsy with anything except dice." She opened the top to reveal a cluster of tear-shaped drops from which a lovely fragrance arose. They were white, almost transparent. "Why, it's frankincense!"

"Exactly. Governor Silvanus met his end through a surfeit of the common, yellow variety from Arabia Felix. This is the white, Ethiopian

tached herself to Julia. Good luck to her, I thought. No man who had spent years married to Fausta had anything to fear from a social-climbing bacchante like Flavia.

Before long the dice were out, and I pitched in with a will. Things were beginning to come together in my mind, and I was able to give the little cubes the full attention they require.

"You're doing well," Flavia noted, looking over my shoulder. She had temporarily lost Milo.

"I usually do. If there are no races or fights going on, I can always rely on the dice. Where is Alpheus tonight? I thought he never missed a party in this town."

"I've no idea. I sent him an invitation, but he probably found another, more profitable party somewhere else. As you can imagine, this is the height of the entertaining season in Paphos."

"Well, you've scored a great success, even without him." I rolled the dice and won again. Everybody else groaned.

"Oh, yes! Cleopatra, Julia Caesar, and Titus Annius Milo, what a list!" Her voice dripped satisfaction. It wasn't common to give any woman a cognomen, but I knew that Flavia would refer to her thus when talking about her. She would want to leave nobody in doubt *which* Julia had come to her event.

In time I packed away my winnings and collected my wife and Milo and made my farewells to all the guests and to my host.

"You must come again, Senator," said Sergius Nobilior. "I want a chance to win back some of my losses."

Milo put a hand on my shoulder. "With Decius, never use his dice and always take his tips on horses and gladiators."

"Don't worry, Sergius," I assured him, "you'll see plenty more of me."

"How much did you win?" Julia asked, as we rolled into our litter and were lifted to shoulder height.

"Roughly nine hundred sesterces in staters, drachmae, darii, minae, and some sort of Arabian silver coin I've never seen before. Six rings, one of them set with a small emerald, two strings of pearls, and a jewel-hilted dagger."

"Oh, let me see the pearls!" She pretended to study them in the dimness. "Isn't Flavia the most wonderfully vulgar woman? A Coan gown! You could see that she rouged her nipples!"

"Never glanced in that direction."

169

"Liar. But Cleopatra was right. She is loads of fun. She's promised to show me the town tomorrow. Will that be all right?"

I thought about it. "Tomorrow morning and afternoon, fine. But be back well before nightfall. After tomorrow, you had better stay away from her."

"Why?"

"Because I am going to have to arrest her husband soon."

"Really? On what charges?"

"I'm not sure about all of them. And I *am* sure that he's not alone, so I can't proceed precipitately. When dealing with a conspiracy, you know, it is always a bad idea to attack it piecemeal. You should try to bag everyone at once."

"That makes sense."

Back at the naval base I tipped the bearers and sent them back to the house of the late governor. Milo, minus his showy toga, joined us in the triclinium, where Julia made extravagant use of candles and lamps so she could examine her new pearls. I sent Hermes to fetch Ariston.

"How are the men shaping up?" I asked Milo.

"I have them under control. We'll have a viable force when the time comes to smash these bandits. First, we have to get rid of their colleagues here in Paphos."

"We'll be ready to start that soon," I told him.

"Good. I want to seize Harmodias's account books, but I don't want to tip him off too soon."

"I should have done it as soon as I took command here," I admitted.

"Just as well you didn't. You'd've had your throat cut before you went out on your first patrol."

"So Harmodias is in with them?" Julia said.

"Certainly," Milo answered. "It wasn't that so much had been taken by Pompey's agents for the war in Gaul. It was that *everything* wasn't seized. It's my guess that only the larger ships and their gear and the war engines were taken, maybe some of the arms. But it was the paint that first roused my suspicions."

"I should have seen it," I said, "as soon as that woman on the island said their ships were 'the same color as the sea'. They have no use for Roman naval colors, have they? They don't want their ships bright and showy."

"Same with the naptha and the rams," he said. "Pirates don't want to sink or burn ships; they want to take them intact. The arms that were left behind are a mixture of types and nationalities unsuitable for the legions. Most of the pirates probably already had their own arms, so Harmodias didn't have to strip his arsenal bare. Easy enough to claim that Pompey seized it all to send to Caesar. Who's going to call them to account?"

Hermes arrived with Ariston.

"Have a seat," I told the ex-pirate.

He sat. "Are we going out on another late-night scout?"

"Not this time," I said. "Describe for Titus Milo the ship we saw out there at Gabinius's estate."

"A penteconter: typical pirate craft, favored by smugglers, too. It's light, fast, draws little water, and can go into almost any creek or inlet. Rides low, hard to see. Can't go head-to-head with a trireme, not enough men or power. If there's to be fighting, three or four penteconter skippers can gang up on a bigger ship."

"And this one was riding high in the water," I said.

"Looked like it to me, but I didn't get as close as you did. Looked like it was wallowing a bit, too."

"At Gabinius's estate, they took on cargo. Might it have been frankincense?"

He frowned and thought. "Doesn't make sense. Any sort of incense is a light-weight cargo. Even if he was going to pack his hold with it, he'd've come ballasted. It's unsafe making any sort of crossing with too little weight in the hold. Whatever he picked up, it was heavy enough to make the ship stable for the voyage to wherever they took it.

"That was my own thought," I said, "but I don't trust my knowledge of nautical matters. Titus, Cyprus produces in abundance one very heavy product: copper."

"So why is Gabinius stockpiling copper in his house and smuggling it out?" he mused. "It's a legitimate trade."

"Good question. But we know already that there are a number of people involved in this matter. Spurius said, 'Your business isn't just with me and you know it.' I am certain that Nobilior the banker is one of them. But who are the others?"

"I hope not Cleopatra," Julia said. "I like her, and besides, anything touching Egypt is always dangerous."

"Say that again," Milo said.

"Say what?"

"What Spurius said. You were imitating his accent, weren't you?"

"I suppose I was. I've been trying to place it since I heard him. It's from somewhere near Rome, I'm sure."

"Repeat everything you heard him say. I'm sure I know that accent."

So I repeated everything the man had said, which wasn't all that much. Milo stopped me a few times to get the pronunciation of certain words.

At the end of it, he grinned. "The man is from Ostia! I ought to know since I spent so many of my younger years there."

I slapped the table. "Why didn't I realize it! It's the way you talked when I first met you, back before you became more Roman than Cincinnatus!" Things began to connect more firmly. "Silvanus was from Ostia, and so is Nobilior."

"I wonder if Spurius meant what he said," Hermes put in.

"About what?" I asked him.

"About attending the *Aphrodisia*."

I looked at him. "Surely the gods would never be so good to me."

12

T HE TOWN WAS PACKED. THE HARBOR WAS jammed with ships of every size and description. The Roman grain fleet was still in harbor, loading supplies for the final leg of its long journey down the coast of Syria and Judea, past the Delta of the Nile, on to Alexandria. Although predominantly Greek, the crowds featured people seemingly from every nation of the world. There were Arabs in desert robes, Egyptians in linen kilts, Africans in colorful skins, tattooed Scythians, and people from no country I had ever heard of. I even saw some Gauls in checked trousers.

Flavia had arrived early to carry Julia off for their tour of the city. It may seem foolhardy to trust her to the wife of a man whose execution I might well demand, but to have begged off at the last moment might have roused too many suspicions. Anyway, violence aimed toward me would come from some other direction. Flavia's awe of Julia's family would keep her safe.

Leaving Milo to crack the whip over my men, I took Hermes and plunged into the festivities. Everywhere, people decked in flower wreaths sang Greek hymns and poured libations at the town's many small shrines to Aphrodite. Businesses that used her name or her image on their signs were decked out in flowers and other decorations and offered free drinks and food to passersby. Processions carried her images and sacred emblems through the streets, and people from widely separated cities and islands offered the sacrifices and performed the rituals of the goddess that prevailed in their own locales. A few of these were genuinely orgiastic, but most were fairly sedate. Of course, it was still daytime.

"Gabinius's men," Hermes said, as we came to the market where I had inquired about frankincense. I saw a cluster of tough-looking specimens, some of them armored, all of them draped with weapons.

"That is a very unbefitting sight on a holy and festive occasion," I said. They were glaring toward me, but nobody was making a hostile move yet. "Come along, let's try the public garden." I had received an invitation to a reception being held there by the city council for all officials and distinguished visitors.

The garden was laid out in imitation of the Academy at Athens. Every Greek city has one of these groves. Like most of them, the one at Paphos was used primarily by the city's schools, for Greeks do not believe in confining boys indoors except in bad weather. Its plantings and fine statuary had been donated by successive generations of rich residents, and there was a beautiful gymnasium and palaestra attached to it. On this day it had been commandeered by the city council for its annual celebration in honor of the town's goddess.

On entering the grove I was handed a cup, and I poured a small libation before taking a healthy swig. As I handed the cup back, Nearchus came to greet me.

"Welcome, Senator. I am so glad your duties have not kept you away."

"I wouldn't have missed it." I scanned the crowd. "Is Gabinius here?"

"We have not seen the general yet. Doubtless he will come in time. This reception will be open until late in the afternoon when the great procession goes up to the temple."

"If you should see him, tell him that I would like to speak with him." I wanted to confer with Gabinius, but only in a public place, preferably one where a lot of important men were gathered. Safer that way. Under no circumstances was I going to his house, nor would I meet with him in some deserted place.

"I shall see that it is done. In the meantime please enjoy the hospitality of the city and the company of our many distinguished guests."

I saw the quaestor Valgus from the grain fleet, standing with a group of well-dressed Romans. I walked that way and introduced myself.

"How good to meet you, Senator," Valgus said courteously. "All Rome speaks glowingly of your aedileship. I think you may know some of these gentlemen. This is Salinius Naso of Tarentum, who is in overall command of the fleet." This man was not a ship's captain, but rather the man charged by the Senate with responsibility for the fleet and its cargo.

"I believe I know the name. You have had this command before, have you not?"

"This is my fourth voyage to Alexandria, Senator." He looked more than competent. Such a trust probably made him the most prestigious man in Tarentum.

"And this," Valgus said, "is Marcus Furius Marcinus, once a Tribune of the People." This was a large, pale-faced man who took my hand and nodded formally. "An honor," he said, in a deep voice.

"And this," Valgus said, "is Senator Manius Mallius, just arrived this morning, who came to Cyprus to be Governor Silvanus's assistant and now, it seems, is to be governor himself."

"If the Senate approves it," Mallius said. He was a young man with the look of the inveterate Forum politician. I had the look myself, with a few more years on it.

"You were quaestor two years ago, weren't you?" I asked.

"I was."

"Nearchus and the council will be overjoyed that you are here," I assured him. "The situation has been complicated, but with a clear commission from the Senate you should have little trouble."

"Such is my hope. I was not expecting this. May I call on you for a briefing on the situation here?"

"Please do so. As a matter of fact—" I excused us from the little group of Romans and took him aside. "What is the Forum gossip about Gabinius?"

"Gabinius? I'd heard he was here helping Silvanus. What about him?"

"Is there agitation to get his exile rescinded?"

"Well, naturally. He has many friends, you know. He was convicted in Cato's court on the charge of extortion. But Cato opposes Caesar, and

175

Gabinius is Caesar's supporter. Pompey and Caesar are allied at the moment, so it is only a matter of time before he's recalled. The tribunes had it up before the Plebeian Assembly when I left Rome, and you know who has the power in that assembly these days. His recall letter may be on the next ship. Why do you ask?"

I gave him a judiciously edited version of the way Gabinius was trying to take control of Cyprus, minimizing my own questionable acts. I knew that Mallius was an experienced man and would know well poisoning when he heard it, especially since my family's shift toward the anti-Caesarian faction, but he would be on his guard against Gabinius anyway.

"How go your operations against these pirates I was told about?" he asked.

"I expect to smash them utterly within a few days," I told him, smiling. He expected no other answer of course. "In fact I happen to know that several persons here in Paphos are in league with them, and I may need you to lend me your authority in arresting them and bringing them to trial."

"That seems reasonable, but I just got here and I need to learn exactly what resources I have. The city guard will be under my command, I suppose. Arresting some Greek conspirators, trying and executing them right at the outset of my administration—yes, that might just set a good tone for my government."

"Actually, Governor, some of the people I need to arrest are Roman citizens."

He didn't exactly turn pale, but his attitude changed noticeably. "Citizens? You mean to arrest Roman citizens in a newly annexed territory, then take them back to Rome for trial? A process that can consume years? This is not reasonable, Commodore!"

"I am afraid it will be necessary if I am to suppress piracy in these waters, Governor," I insisted.

"Nonsense! Find them, destroy their ships, find their base, and bring the surviving wretches here to me, and I will be most happy to crucify them for you. If there are Romans here in league with them, go back to Rome and indict them. I won't begin my administration by disgracing citizens before foreigners!" Well, I hadn't expected it would be easy.

I circulated for a while, limiting my wine intake and checking from time to time to assure that my weapons were handy. As I left the garden to see what was happening elsewhere in town, a familiar voice hailed me.

"Senator! Decius Caecilius!" It was Alpheus, already tipsy, a laurel wreath slightly askew on his head. He was with a little group of similarly festive companions. "Come join us!" I meandered over to the joyous band.

"I thought you would be taking part in the ceremonies," I told him.

"There is nothing left for me to do. I have taught and rehearsed the sacred chorus, but there is no role for me in the rest of the ritual, so now I am just enjoying the festivities like everybody else. Have a drink with us. There is a high-class tavern near the Temple of Hephaestus that is giving away Judaean wine flavored with rose petals, this day only."

"What is it called?"

"The Hermaphroditus. The statue in front is worth the trip by itself."

This intrigued me. I had never seen a really convincing depiction of the double-sexed offspring of Aphrodite and Hermes, and was curious to see how this statue interpreted the difficult subject.

"Hermes, run, find Julia, and tell her to join us there."

"I'd rather not leave you by yourself."

"Don't be an idiot. I'm among friends, and nobody is going to cause trouble at this festival. Anyone who tries to spoil the fun will be torn to pieces by the crowd as a sacrifice to the goddess."

"I still don't like it. How will I find her in this mob?"

"Easily. They'll be at one of the town's more famous locations, and Flavia will have the biggest, showiest litter in sight. It will stick up well above the crowd. Off with you now."

He left us and Alpheus introduced me to his companions, who had Greek names that all sounded the same: Amyntas and Amoebeus and Admetus or something of the sort. I knew I would not remember the names the next day so I made no effort to sort them out. Probably tavern acquaintances, I imagined: sworn brothers today, forgotten tomorrow."

"Will you be staying much longer on Cyprus, Alpheus?" I asked, as we set off for our destination.

"As soon as the ceremony ends tomorrow, I'm off for the next island."

"That is unfortunate. I was looking forward to—" I stopped when I saw five well-armed thugs pushing their way through the crowd toward us, their beady eyes fixed on me. Immediately, I regretted sending Hermes away.

"Gabinius's men. Alphaeus, do you know how we can lose them?"

"Are you feuding with Gabinius? And you Romans are always chiding us Greeks for infighting. My friends here know the town well. We ought to be able to lose a pack of iron-bound Romans easily. Come on."

So we ducked into a narrow alley, which featured a turn into an even narrower alley where there was a ladder propped against a wall. We scrambled up to a flat rooftop and pulled the ladder up after us, then across two or three roofs and down a set of stairs into a courtyard where about a hundred naked people were worshipping the goddess in her most basic ritual, after an astonishing fashion that Alpheus assured me was a most pious observance in Phrygia. They invited us to join them, but I was forced to decline.

"Why couldn't I have visited this place ten years ago?" I complained. "Or even five? You and your friends can stay if you like, Alpheus. I can probably find my way to the Hermaphroditus."

"Nonsense. We're just resting up. The real celebration starts after nightfall, and you need to keep up your stamina if you hope to last until sunrise."

So we went out onto a side street, and I realized that I had no idea where we were.

"This way," Alpheus said. We went down a long stairway between two rows of houses. "Now through here." We entered a tunnel that bored into one of the buildings, into a large, dim room.

"Where are we?" I asked. "I think you took the wrong—" I was stopped short by the dagger that appeared beneath my chin. A hand plucked my own dagger from beneath my belt.

"He's got a *caestus* under his tunic," Alpheus said.

No, I definitely shouldn't have sent Hermes away. "Alpheus! I was suspicious of everybody else, but I thought you, at least, were my friend."

"You mean I wasn't important enough to be involved in any of the great matters of international concern, don't you? Well, that was the idea. But please don't take this personally. I truly have enjoyed your company, and I regret that your stubborn persistence has led you to this dismal fate."

"Well, what now? I take it you plan to kill me." I didn't plan to go without a fight, not that there was much I could do in my predicament, but I suspected he had something else in mind for me. People who intend to cut your throat usually do it before you know they have a knife.

"No, I was told to keep you here until someone joins us. Please don't get your hopes up though."

"So I am going to get to meet your employer?"

"One of them. You see, a traveling poet makes an ideal agent, spy, and broker. No one is suspicious of our wanderings because our art takes us wherever there is a demand for us. There is always a festival someplace that needs a new hymn, a funeral someone wants to make memorable with an elegiac ode, and so forth. My employer needed a base on Cyprus, and so he sent me ahead to scout the place out and pass the requisite bribes. It is an added bonus that I am always in demand in the houses of the rich, so nobody thinks it unusual to see me in the company of the highest authorities. Poets are very fashionable guests."

"My compliments. You've achieved an elegant balance in your double career. I take it the poet's art does not pay well?"

"Alas, no. But that's no matter. One practices art at the bidding of the muse, not for gain. But I do like to live well, and for that a supplemental income is necessary. The old fleets used to use actors for this purpose, but they were not welcome in respectable households except as entertainers, so a poet is a better choice."

"I am getting dense in my old age," I said bitterly. "It was you who suggested giving Ariston the oath at the Temple of Poseidon, then you excused yourself while I was distracted by Flavia disporting herself with her sailors. That was when you arranged the ambush, wasn't it? Then you led us there at a deliberate pace with your poem about Orpheus and Eurydice—it was not at all a bad poem, by the way—and you held your torch high when the attack began to make sure nobody mistook you for one of the intended victims."

My eyes were adjusting to the dimness, and I could see we were in a large cellar that was used for storage, with bales and jars stacked all around. I could see no way out except for the way we had come in. The Greeks whose names I had already forgotten bound my hands behind me and thrust me against a bale, forcing me to sit.

"Now stay there and don't try to stand, Decius," Alpheus said, "or I'll be forced to nail one of your feet to the floor with a dagger."

"I'm not going anywhere just yet. I truly want to meet your master." A brave show harms nothing when you are helpless.

"Employer," he corrected. "I have no master."

At that moment a large form blocked the light from the door. Then a man entered with more men at his back. He wore a toga and blinked in the dimness for a moment. It was the pale-faced man from the public garden. Mentally I cursed myself.

"I should have known the second I saw your pasty face! But you were with other Romans, so I assumed you'd arrived with the grain fleet. But you should have been deeply tanned after such a voyage, and I didn't catch it. When did you cut your hair and shave off your beard? This morning?"

"Yesterday. Actually, I've been arranging passage away from here on the flagship." The rumbling voice was unmistakable. If he'd just spoken a few more words in the garden, I would have caught the Ostian accent. By such small chances are great opportunities lost.

"I knew Spurius couldn't be your real name. Are you really the ex-tribune Marcinus?"

"I am indeed."

"And I suppose you were one of Gabinius's officers in Syria and Egypt?"

"That, too. What are we to do with you, Decius Caecilius?"

"We kill him and get away from here," said another voice I recognized. A pudgy man pushed forward and glared at me with his fists planted on his hips, Sergius Nobilior. "Why couldn't you have kept chasing after the pirates as the Senate told you to? Did you have to poke your big Metellan nose into *everything* that was happening on this island? Some of us were doing very well here until you began stirring things up!"

"Nobilior! And our wives have become such good friends!"

"Yes, and a very good time they're having today, if I know Flavia. And don't worry, she'd never let me harm a Caesar. You, however, have to go." He looked at one of the Greeks. "Cut his throat." Nobody moved.

"My men don't take orders from you," Marcinus said. "His wife is a Caesar?"

"Niece to the great Caius Julius," Nobilior affirmed. "But don't let that concern you. He'll be glad to have her a widow. He'll be able to marry her off to someone far more important."

"If he's murdered, there could be a lot of trouble for you," Marcinus said. "His family is one of the greatest, even if he doesn't amount to much. But don't let me stop you. I won't be here. I'll be on a leisurely voyage to Alexandria, then home. But do your own throat cutting."

Nobilior stood there and fumed for a while, then Alpheus spoke up. "Must you Romans be so crude and brutal? He need not be murdered at all."

"My thought exactly," I said.

"This is festival time, a time when all the usual strictures on community behavior are relaxed. What more natural than a veteran tavern crawler like Decius Caecilius Metellus should have a bit too much to drink, topple into the harbor on his way back to the naval base, and drown? Let's get some wine in him and on him, wait until nightfall, and carry him down to the water. The distance isn't great, and nobody takes notice of men carrying a drunk at a time like this."

They were discussing my death, but I did not protest. Anything to keep breathing a while longer. Who could tell what might happen? I was working at my bonds. They had used leather straps, and they had a little give to them. I might be able to work them loose if I had long enough. A man was dispatched to search for some wine, which should prove no great quest on that day.

"I am curious," I said. "Which of you killed Silvanus? And why? You all seemed to have such a cozy arrangement here. Did he get a little too greedy? Or was he frightened of being found out and impeached in Rome? There have been some pretty savage prosecutions lately for unauthorized plundering."

"Don't look at me," Marcinus said. "I had nothing to do with that killing."

"Don't tell me you scruple at murder," I said. "You nearly wiped out an island just to frighten people so they wouldn't cooperate with me."

He shrugged. "It isn't like they were citizens. These islanders are little more than cattle. I didn't know then I'd be quitting the business so soon, or I wouldn't have bothered."

"Yes, rather hard on them, wasn't it? Nobilior, a few days ago you mentioned your great and good friend Rabirius, financial adviser to King Ptolemy and the man in charge of collecting on those colossal loans. I recently learned that Rabirius had seized the grain revenues and 'several others' as partial payment on the debt. Might one of the others be the frankincense monopoly?"

"So you figured that out," Nobilior said, "Yes, that is right. But Rabirius discovered that the frankincense deliveries were being diverted elsewhere before they reached Alexandria. They were being taken up through Judea and Syria, then brought here to Cyprus, and Silvanus was transferring it to the Holy Society of Dionysus for shipment all over the world."

No wonder, I thought, the merchant Demades, member in good standing of that society, had mentioned nothing about a cessation of shipment to Alexandria. "Judea and Syria?" I said. "That's Gabinius's old territory.

"Yes," Nobilior said. "He reopened the Great King's old trade routes for frankincense and silk, as they were in the days before the Ptolemies. He and Silvanus conspired in this, and Rabirius was furious. He told me to put an end to it and even specified how Silvanus should die."

"So it was you? And Gabinius had nothing to do with it?"

"I should hope not!" He said. "They were friends!"

I was a little crestfallen that my favorite suspect was not the murderer after all. This did not let him off the hook though. There was no mistaking his hostility toward me.

The man returned with a skin of wine. A hand grabbed the hair at the back of my head and tipped it upward. The reed nozzle of the skin was thrust into my mouth and the bag given a squeeze. I swallowed rapidly, then gagged and spit as the man jumped clear.

"You fools!" I said, when I could speak. "Nobody will believe I was drinking that cheap stuff!"

"It all smells the same the next day," Marcinus assured me. "Give him some more." The skin was reapplied, then reapplied again. The last try was counterproductive, causing me to vomit spasmodically.

"Now we'll have to do it all over again," said the Greek with the skin. He took a drink himself.

"He doesn't have to be really drunk," said Alpheus. "He just needs to look and smell that way, and he does already."

"We're wasting time," Nobilior said. "Why not just knock him on the head? He'll still look like he drowned after being in the water all night."

"That might leave a mark," Alpheus pointed out. "But smothering would do the same thing and," he held up a finger for emphasis, like the chorus master he was, "it will give him the bug-eyed, black-faced aspect of drowning."

"Excellent idea," Nobilior said, nodding. "Who has strong hands?"

The time had come for desperate action, and I couldn't think of a thing to do. I had one possible move. They had not bound my feet. I could be up in a single bound, smash my head into Nobilior's fat face, then sprint for the door. At least I would die knowing that Nobilior would regret ever having known me, every time he saw his own reflection. I began, carefully, to gather my feet beneath me, leaning forward slightly.

"Careful, he's planning something," Alpheus said. They began to turn my way, then the doorway was crowded with people again. I could see armed, hard-faced men, Gabinius's. Come to kill everybody in sight, I figured. They would be near blind coming in from daylight. Alpheus whirled and came for me with his dagger.

I was off the bale in an instant, but not to butt anyone in the face. I dived and rolled, catching Alpheus just below the knees, toppling him and sending his wreath rolling across the floor to be trampled beneath the scuffling feet. There were shouts and muffled groans and the familiar, butcher-shop sound of blades plunging into bodies and chopping against bone. Light streaming through the doorway glittered on bared blades and glowed redly from the sprays of blood that saturated the air. Among the droplets, flowers and leaves from the festival wreaths drifted to the floor.

Alpheus tried to rise, but I doubled up my legs and let him have both feet beneath the chin. His head snapped back and cracked into an amphora, breaking the heavy clay and spilling poor-quality olive oil onto the floor. If I couldn't defeat a poet, even with my hands tied behind me, I deserved to die.

"Metellus," somebody bellowed, "where are you?" I recognized the voice of Aulus Gabinius, come to do me in just like a *flamen* killing a bull, although just then I felt more like a second-rate sheep, one not even worthy of sacrifice. I looked toward the door, measured the distance, scrambled to my feet, and leapt over a pair of struggling bodies. Even as I did, I saw more people crowding into the doorway. Just my luck.

But one thing was certain: I did not want to linger another minute in that cellar. I ran for the crowd, hoping to bull my way through and keep running. A sword rose, lanced toward my belly, then several strong hands stopped me as solidly as if I had run into a wall.

"A man could get killed rushing onto sharp steel like that," said Ariston, grinning. One of his hands rested against my chest. The other held his big, curved knife. So he was with them, too? Then I saw who was holding the sword that just pierced the cloth of my tunic: Hermes, his face gone so white I could not help laughing.

183

"Hermes, if you could see yourself!"

"You're something of a sight yourself," Titus Milo said. His were the other hands that had stopped me so abruptly. Milo never carried weapons because he never needed them. Hermes resheathed his sword with a shaky hand.

"What," I asked, "is going on?"

"You've led us a lively chase, Captain," Ariston said. He spun me around and slashed my bonds with a single stroke. "Your boy came running to the base, said you'd been abducted, and we should all turn out and look for you."

"I knew something like this would happen," Gabinius said, walking toward us. He was wiping blood from a sword that looked as natural in his fist as a finger. "That's why I've had my men watching you all day. When they said they'd seen Furius Marcinus in town with his hair cut and his beard shaved, I suspected he'd want to take care of some unfinished business and sent them to bring you to me. They saw Alpheus make off with you, so I set them to combing the town. One of them spotted the man they sent out for wine and followed him back here, then ran to fetch me. Why didn't you just bring your suspicions to me, Metellus? It might have simplified things."

"I thought you were trying to kill me." I looked over the room. There were bodies everywhere, lying among the leaves and petals, in a mixture of oil and blood. All of Alpheus's men lay dead. Alpheus himself looked dead. Marcinus and Nobilior were certainly dead, their throats decorated with gaping wounds. "I see you've eliminated your partners."

"Metellus," he said, "I am showing forbearance out of respect to Caesar and your family; but if you accuse me of complicity in the murder of my friend Silvanus, I may just make a clean job of it right here."

"Let's not be hasty now," Milo said, smiling his most dangerous smile. Hermes and Ariston let their hands fall to their sheathed weapons.

"We have more than a hundred armed men just outside," Hermes said.

"So have I," Gabinius answered.

Suddenly I was very tired. "There's been enough bloodletting today," I said. "Let's not have Romans fighting each other in a new territory. The civil wars ended twenty years ago. Come on, let's get away from this slaughterhouse and talk somewhere where there's clean air."

"Good," Gabinius said, handing his sword to one of his men. "By preference, in a place where you can get a clean tunic."

An hour later, washed up and dressed in a clean tunic, I walked out to the terrace before my quarters. Gabinius was there, and Milo and Mallius, the new governor.

"Hermes," I'd asked as I bathed and dressed, "how did you know to summon help so quickly?"

"I found Julia only two streets away from where I left you. I gave her your message, and Flavia said Paphos had no tavern named Hermaphroditus. I knew that woman would know what she was talking about."

"It's a good thing you did. If you hadn't been there, Gabinius might have gone ahead and killed me just to be rid of the annoyance. He could have claimed that he got there too late."

Now as I went out to talk with them, I was fairly certain I had most of the facts. Milo sat with some scrolls and tablets in front of him. Gabinius looked supremely confident. Mallius looked bemused. I took a seat.

"This shouldn't take long," I said. "Then we can all get back to the festival. Aulus Gabinius, tell me why I should not charge you with murder and piracy and a number of other charges before a praetor's court?"

"Furius Marcinus was tribune in the same year I was. He supported me in passing the *lex Gabinia* that gave Pompey his command of the whole sea to sweep it clean of pirates. In return, when I had my propraetorian command in Syria, I took him along as legate. When I agreed to put Ptolemy back on his throne, it was Marcinus I used to recruit the bulk of the mercenary army I took to Egypt."

"That included recruiting among the aforementioned pirates, then settled in villages inland?"

"Right. After the war, when we set about collecting the enormous debt Ptolemy had incurred, several merchant organizations came to protest Ptolemy's extortions. He was trying to raise the money from foreigners so he could keep the Egyptian population docile. Among these was the Holy Society of Dionysus. Rabirius had seized control of the frankincense trade, the most lucrative of the Ptolemaic monopolies."

"Rabirius was trying to collect that debt, too," I pointed out.

"For himself and his own cronies. I wanted to be sure that my own part, and that of my supporters, got paid back. To foil Rabirius, Ptolemy sent word to Ethiopia and Arabia Felix not to deliver the stuff while he had no control of it. This was unthinkable. The Society of Dionysus agreed to advance me the money to buy the incense and get it to them secretly somewhere other than Alexandria. Marcinus told me he had two acquaintances from Ostia: Nobilior the banker and Silvanus, a prominent politician, on Cyprus. Silvanus was an old friend of mine, and Cyprus was a perfect location. I gave Marcinus the job of setting up the route. It was then that I was called back to Rome to stand trial. This petty little exile resulted. Naturally, I decided to spend my exile on Cyprus. By the time I got here, the business was going along nicely."

"I seized Harmodias's books and clapped him into a storage shed under guard," Milo reported. He picked up a scroll. "As I suspected, Pompey's agents took only the triremes and the better equipment. They weren't interested in the smaller ships. The first ships he turned over to Spurius, as he was called, were the penteconters. Then Spurius wanted the Liburnians as well. Nobilior brokered the deal, with Silvanus well-paid to look the other way."

"Marcinus was an adventurous man," Gabinius said, "not really suited to ordinary military duties and administrative work. At first, he used the penteconters. They were ideal for smuggling, at which he branched out far beyond our incense trade. Then that became too tame for him. He wanted to try his hand at piracy, and that called for real warships. I had nothing to do with that, I assure you. I advised Silvanus against all such dealings, but so much wealth so easily had is difficult for a man to pass up."

"Then," I said, "Rabirius got wind of what was happening and was very angry with his 'friend' Sergius Nobilior?"

"Yes. The trade was too big to keep hidden. Rabirius has agents everywhere. He gave Nobilior one chance: redeem himself by returning his profits to Rabirius and killing Silvanus with a fitting gesture. Otherwise Rabirius would ruin him with the Ostian bankers and the whole banking community. For a climber like Nobilior, that was death. I got word of it too late."

"You didn't scruple to keep employing Marcinus for your own smuggling."

"Just for the one last cargo. And I advised him to get out of the business while he could, although you may not believe me."

"Oh, I believe you," I said. "By the way, what were you smuggling? Copper?"

His shaggy brows went up. "You must be brighter than I thought. Yes, it was copper. I've been investing my profits in copper right here at the source, where it's cheap."

"Copper? Mallius said. "Why smuggle copper? There is nothing illegal about the trade."

"I am shipping it to my agent in Syria to be struck into coins to pay my troops when I get the eastern command. That had to be kept quiet."

"I thought it might be something like that," I said. "You are very confident."

"It has all been arranged. I am to be recalled to Rome soon, cleared of all charges, restored to the Senate with all my estates and other property returned, and given the eastern command. I will raise, equip, and pay the legions and *auxilia* myself, so I haven't been idle here."

Mallius's ears seemed to have grown to twice their usual size. "This sounds like, ah, privileged information."

"So it is," Gabinius agreed. "A wise man might well prosper mightily being privy to such affairs."

"I was not entirely satisfied. It was awfully convenient for him that Marcinus, Nobilior, and Alpheus were all dead. And there were those two men who had attacked me in front of the Temple of Poseidon who had died mysteriously. But I had nothing solid against him. If he was guilty of something, all our other politician-generals were guilty of far, far worse.

"Now," Milo said, "if this is all over, why don't we get to work cleaning up Marcinus's fleet? I'm in the mood for a little fun. It's going to be too easy though without him in command."

I rose, then remembered something. "Aulus Gabinius, Manius Mallius, if you would, I have a little ceremony to conduct here tomorrow morning that requires three citizens as witness. Could you join me and Titus Milo just after sunrise."

"Certainly," Mallius said. Gabinius nodded.

"And Manius Mallius, just forget all those awful things I said about Aulus Gabinius."

He looked at me a moment, then shrugged. Politics.

THE AFTERNOON WAS AS BEAUTIFUL AS they had all been since I had arrived on Cyprus. Julia and I took our privileged position in the forefront of the crowd at the Temple of Aphrodite.

frankincense, the purest and finest sort. I've become quite an expert on this stuff as you can see. Where is that prince?"

He wasn't difficult to find, and it was easy to draw him aside, as everyone else was watching a wonderful Syrian magician who could do amazing things with flames, live birds, large serpents, and even more unlikely props.

"Prince," I said to him, "I am curious about the gift you gave my wife."

His eyes went wide. "Was this improper? If so I am very sorry and must plead ignorance of your customs."

"No, no, it was perfectly delightful. But we seldom see white frankincense in our part of the world. It seems an extremely extravagant gift."

He gave me that dazzling smile again. "Oh, not at all! We have so much of it this year, since we are not sending it up the coast to Egypt. I thought it would be perfect for small guest gifts. It is easy to carry, and everyone loves it."

"So they do, so they do. Ah, you said that you are not shipping it to Egypt this year? Might that be because of King Ptolemy's troubles?"

"Yes, yes." He smiled and nodded vigorously at the same time.

"Is there trouble between Ethiopia and Egypt?"

"No, no," now smiling and shaking his head with equal vigor. The sudden changes in direction of those flashing teeth were making me a little dizzy. "No, it was King Ptolemy who asked us to hold back certain things we have always traded directly with the royal house: ivory, feathers, a few other things. And, of course, the frankincense. He said these things would be stolen from him."

"Stolen? Because of the unrest in his country?"

He looked embarrassed. "Why, please forgive me, Senator, I do not wish to give offense, but he said it was because of you Romans."

I nodded too, much more slowly and without smiling. "I see." And indeed I was beginning to see. "Thank you, Prince, both for your gift and for your information."

"I have not offended?" He seemed genuinely concerned.

"Not at all. And I think that very soon things will be back to normal between ourselves and King Ptolemy and your father's kingdom."

This time he *really* smiled, an ear-to-ear stretch of ivory bright as a bucket of pearls. "Wonderful! My father will be so pleased!"

Flavia, I saw, was now hanging on Milo as eagerly as she had at-

Next to us stood Hermes, looking decidedly uncomfortable in his new toga and Phrygian bonnet. That morning, with Gabinius, Mallius, and Milo as witnesses, I had given him his freedom, conferred upon him full rights of citizenship, and given him his freedman's name: Decius Caecilius Metellus. He would always be Hermes to me though.

My recent experience had reminded me how fleeting life can be and that I might not have a chance to conduct the ceremony myself should I wait too long.

Cleopatra stood nearby, surrounded by her entourage. She caught my eye and nodded, smiling. I was unutterably relieved that she had not been involved in the sordid business on Cyprus. At least, not in any way I could prove. If she was involved, she'd showed more circumspection than she displayed later in her life.

Then the chorus began to sing the hymn composed by the late Alpheus, whom I was going to miss. He'd had his faults, but he had been excellent company. Then the priestesses came out of the temple, draped in the golden nets and nothing else. Last of all came Ione. In procession they passed us while the people bowed their heads.

When she came near us, Ione paused. Timidly, Julia stepped forward, reached out a hand, and touched Ione's flesh through the net. Then the procession went on, and we fell in behind. Other women came from the crowd and touched the lesser priestesses, but no other was allowed to touch Ione.

When the procession reached the seashore near the temple, the crowd lined the beach and carpeted the hillsides and bluffs nearby. The priestesses paused for a moment at the water's edge, then slowly walked out into the water. First to their knees, then to their waists, then to their shoulders. Then, just as the chorus swelled to the last notes of the hymn, their heads disappeared beneath the water. There was silence for the space of ten heartbeats.

Then the priestesses emerged smiling from the waters, and the people raised a truly ancient Greek hymn of praise in which we visitors joined. The nets were gone. Dressed only in the sea-foam the priestesses returned to their island renewed, reborn.

These things happened on the island of Cyprus in the year 703 of the City of Rome, the consulship of Servius Sulpicius Rufus and Marcus Claudius Marcellus.

GLOSSARY

(Definitions apply to the year 703 of the Republic.)

Arms   Like everything else in Roman society, weapons were strictly regulated by class. The straight, double-edged sword and dagger of the legions were classed as "honorable."

The *gladius* was a short, broad, double-edged sword borne by Roman soldiers. It was designed primarily for stabbing.

The *caestus* was a boxing glove, made of leather straps and reinforced by bands, plates, or spikes of bronze. The curved, single-edged sword or knife called a *sica* was "infamous." *Sicas* were used in the arena by Thracian gladiators and were carried by street thugs. One ancient writer says that its curved shape made it convenient to carry sheathed beneath the armpit, showing that gangsters and shoulder holsters go back a long way.

Shields were not common except as gladiatorial equipment. The large shield *(scutum)* of the legions was unwieldy in narrow streets, but bodyguards might carry the small shield *(parma)* of the light-armed auxiliary troops. These came in handy when the opposition took to throwing rocks and roof tiles.

Campus Martius   A field outside the old city wall, formerly the assembly area and drill field for the army, named after its altar to Mars. It was where the Popular Assemblies met during the days of the Republic.

Centuriate Assembly   The Centuriate Assembly was a voting unit made up of all male citizens in military service. It seemingly dealt with major policy decisions, but by the Roman historical period the votes were largely symbolic and almost always positive, usually taken when decisions had already not only been made but sometimes even acted upon. The body was divided into five different parts based on wealth; the result was that the highest level or two always won and the lowest classes were not even called upon to vote.

Circus   The Roman racecourse and the stadium that enclosed it.

College of augurs   Augurs had the task of interpreting omens sent by the gods, usually thunder and lightning and the flights of birds. An augurate was for life and new augurs were co-opted by the serving priests. The augurate was largely a political appointment and was a mark of great prestige. Augurs could call an end to official business by interpreting unfavorable omens and this became a potent political tool.

Crucifixions   The Romans inherited the practice of crucifixion from the Carthaginians. In Rome, it was reserved for rebellious slaves and insurrectionists. Citizens could not be crucified.

Curia   The meetinghouse of the Senate, located in the Forum, also applied to a meeting place in general.

Cursus Honorum   "Course of Honor": The ladder of office ascended by Romans in public life. The *cursus* offices were quaestor, praetor, and consul. Technically, the office of aedile was not part of the *cursus honorum,* but by the late Republic it was futile to stand for praetor without having served as aedile. The other public offices not on the *cursus* were censor and dictator.

Duumvir   A duumvirate was a board of two men. Many Italian towns were governed by *duumviri.* A *duumvir* was also a Roman admiral, probably dating from a time when the Roman navy was commanded by two senators.

Eagles   The eagle was sacred to Jupiter, and from the time of Gaius Marius gilded eagles were the standards of the legions. Thus, a soldier served "with the eagles."

Equestrian   *Eques* (pl. *equites*) literally meant "horseman." In the early days of the military muster, soldiers supplied all their own equipment. Every five years the censors made a property assessment of all citizens and each man served according to his ability to pay for arms, equipment, rations, etc. Those above a certain minimum assessment became *equites* because they could afford to supply and feed their own horses and were assigned to the cavalry. By the late Republic, it was purely a property class. Almost all senators were *equites* by property assessment, but the Dictator Sulla made senators a separate class. After his day, the *equites* were the wealthy merchants, moneylenders, and tax farmers of Rome. Collectively, they were an enormously powerful group, equal to the senators in all except prestige and control of foreign policy.

Families and Names   Roman citizens usually had three names. The given name (praenomen) was individual, but there were only about eighteen of them: Marcus, Lucius, etc. Certain praenomens were used only in a single family: Appius was used only by the Claudians, Mamercus only by the Aemilians, and so forth. Only males had praenomens. Daughters were given the feminine form of the father's name: Aemilia for Aemilius, Julia for Julius, Valeria for Valerius, etc.

Next came the nomen. This was the name of the clan (gens). All members of a gens traced their descent from a common ancestor, whose name they bore: Julius, Furius, Licinius, Junius, Tullius, to name a few. Patrician names always ended in *ius*. Plebeian names often had different endings.

The stirps was a subfamily of a gens. The cognomen gave the name of the stirps, i.e., Caius Julius Caesar. Caius of the stirps Caesar of gens Julia.

Then came the name of the family branch (cognomen). This name was frequently anatomical: Naso (nose), Ahenobarbus (bronzebeard), Sulla (splotchy), Niger (dark), Rufus (red), Caesar (curly), and many others. Some families did not use cognomens. Mark Antony was just Marcus Antonius, no cognomen.

Other names were honorifics conferred by the Senate for outstanding service or virtue: Germanicus (conqueror of the Germans), Africanus (conqueror of the Africans), Pius (extraordinary filial piety).

Freed slaves became citizens and took the family name of their master. Thus the vast majority of Romans named, for instance, Cornelius would not be patricians of that name, but the descendants of that family's freed slaves. There was no stigma attached to slave ancestry.

Adoption was frequent among noble families. An adopted son took the name of his adoptive father and added the genetive form of his former nomen. Thus when Caius Julius Caesar adopted his great-nephew Caius Octavius, the latter became Caius Julius Caesar Octavianus.

All these names were used for formal purposes such as official documents and monuments. In practice, nearly every Roman went by a nickname, usually descriptive and rarely complimentary. Usually it was the Latin equivalent of Gimpy, Humpy, Lefty, Squint-Eye, Big Ears, Baldy, or something of the sort. Romans were merciless when it came to physical peculiarities.

First Citizen   In Latin: *Princeps.* Originally the most prestigious senator, permitted to speak first on all important issues and set the order of debate. Augustus, the first emperor, usurped the title in perpetuity. Decius detests him so much that he will not use either his name (by the time of the writing it was Caius Julius Caesar) or the honorific Augustus, voted by the toadying Senate. Instead he will refer to him only as the First Citizen. *Princeps* is the origin of the modern word "prince."

Forum   An open meeting and market area. Roman citizens spent much of their day there. The courts met outdoors in the Forum when the weather was good.

Freedman   A manumitted slave. Formal emancipation conferred full rights of citizenship except for the right to hold office. Informal emancipation conferred freedom without voting rights. In the second or at least third generation, a freedman's descendants became full citizens.

Games/*Ludus* (pl. *ludi*)   Public religious festivals put on by the state. Games usually ran for several days. They featured theatrical performances, processions, sacrifices, public banquets, and chariot races. They did not feature gladiatorial combats. The gladiator games called *munera,* were put on by individuals as funeral rites. *Ludi* were also training schools for gladiators, although the gladiatorial exhibitions were not *ludi.*

Gymnasium, palaestra   Greek and Roman exercise facilities. In Rome they were often an adjunct to the baths.

Hospitium, hospitia   *Hospitium* was a contract of mutual obligation between individuals and families. When a hospes visited the home of another, the provider was obligated to provide him with food and shelter, medical care if sick, aid in the law courts should such be necessary, and a proper funeral and burial should he die when visiting. *Hospitium* was symbolized by an exchange of tokens, and it was hereditary. An Athenian, for instance, who appeared at a Roman house with a *hospitium* token had to be given hospitality, even if the tokens had been exchanged by great-grandfathers a century before.

Imperium   The ancient power of kings to summon and lead armies, to order and forbid, and to inflict corporal and capital punishment. Under the Republic, the imperium was divided among the consuls and praetors, but they were subject to appeal and intervention by the tribunes in their civil decisions and were answerable for their acts after leaving office. Only a dictator had unlimited imperium.

Lex Gabinia   Roman military commands and governorships were apportioned by laws introduced to the Plebeian Assembly by the tribunes. Each law bore the name of the tribune who introduced it. The *lex Gabinia* gave Pompey his extraordinary command of the whole Mediterranean for his campaign against the pirates. The law was introduced by the tribune Aulus Gabinius.

Legatus, legati   When a praetor or consul stepped down from office and went out to govern a province, he could name a *legatus* as his assistant. The *legatus* had to be approved by the popular assemblies. If he was engaged in a major war, as Caesar was in Gaul, he might have several *legati*. The duties of a *legatus* were determined by the governor.

Legions, legionaries   In the Republic, a legion was a Roman army consisting on paper of 6,000 men, but the real number was usually closer to 4,000. Legionaries were citizens and fought as heavy infantry. A legion was usually accompanied by a roughly similar number of noncitizen auxiliaries who usually supplied the archers and slingers, light-armed skirmishers, and cavalry.

Munera   Special Games, not part of the official calendar, at which gladiators were exhibited. They were originally funeral games and were always dedicated to the dead.

Naval forces   In the Roman navy, sailors were hired civilians. Marines were soldiers assigned to the ships, usually with lower pay and lesser status than legionaries. Rowers were also hired freemen. Despite *Ben-Hur*, Roman galleys were never rowed by slaves or convicts. That was a practice of the Middle Ages and Renaissance. Coast guards were usually provided by local officials and served primarily to foil smugglers.

Naval Titles

   Admiral   The Roman title was *duumvir*. A *duumvir* was appointed by the senate to command a fleet.

   Commodore   In the Romen navy, any officer in command of a flotilla. The word "commodore" is modern.

   Hortator   The coxswain of a rowed vessel. He kept the rowers in time by voice, flute, or drum.

Leadsman   A sailor whose task was to determine the depth of the water beneath the ship with a weighted rope knotted at intervals.

Poleman   A sailor charged with wielding a pole to keep the ship from scraping against the wharf or another ship.

Skipper   An informal term for the captain of a ship. The term is modern, from a Dutch word meaning "shipman."

Nobiles, Nobilitas   Rome had no official aristocracy, but families that counted consuls among their ancestors were classes as *nobiles*.

Offices   A tribune of the people was a representative of the plebeians with power to introduce laws and to veto actions of the Senate. Only plebeians could hold the office, which carried no imperium. Military tribunes were elected from among the young men of senatorial or equestrian rank to be assistants to generals. Usually it was the first step of a man's political career.

A Roman who embarked on a political career had to rise through a regular chain of offices. The lowest elective office was quaestor: bookkeeper and paymaster for the Treasury, the Grain Office, and the provincial governors. These men did the scut work of the Empire.

Next were the aediles. They were more or less city managers who saw to the upkeep of public buildings, streets, sewers, markets, and the like. There were two types: the plebeian aediles and the curule aediles. The curule aediles could sit in judgment on civil cases involving markets and currency, while the plebeian aediles could only levy fines. Otherwise, their duties were the same. They also put on the public games. The government allowance for these things was laughably small, so they had to pay for them out of their own pockets. It was a horrendously expensive office, but it gained the holder popularity like no other, especially if his games were spectacular. Only a popular aedile could hope for election to higher office.

Third was praetor, an office with real power. Praetors were judges, but they could command armies and after a year in office they could go out to govern provinces, where real wealth could be won, earned, or stolen. In the late Republic, there were eight praetors. Senior was the *praetor urbanus*, who heard civil cases between citizens of Rome. The *praetor peregrinus* (praetor of the foreigners) heard cases involving foreigners. The others presided over criminal courts. After leaving office, the ex-praetors became propraetors and went to govern propraetorian provinces with full imperium.

The highest office was consul, supreme office of power during the Roman Republic. Two were elected each year. For one year they fulfilled the political role of royal authority, bringing all other magistrates into the service of the people and the City of Rome. The office carried full imperium. On the expiration of his year in office, the ex-consul was usually assigned a district outside Rome to rule as proconsul. As proconsul, he had the same insignia and the same number of lictors. His power was absolute within his province. The most important commands always went to proconsuls.

Censors were elected every five years. It was the capstone to a political career, but it did not carry imperium, and there was no foreign command afterward. Censors conducted the census, purged the Senate of unworthy members, and doled out the public contracts. They could forbid certain religious practices or luxuries deemed bad for public morals or generally "un-Roman." There were two Censors, and each could overrule the other. They were usually elected from among the ex-consuls.

Under the Sullan Constitution, the quaestorship was the minimum requirement for membership in the Senate. The majority of senators had held that office and never held another. Membership in the Senate was for life unless expelled by the Censors.

No Roman official could be prosecuted while in office, but he could be after he stepped down. Malfeasance in office was one of the most common court charges.

The most extraordinary office was dictator. In times of emergency, the Senate could instruct the consuls to appoint a dictator, who could wield absolute power for six months. Unlike all other officials, a dictator was unaccountable: He could not be prosecuted for his acts in office. The last true dictator was appointed in the third century B.C. The dictatorships of Sulla and Julius Caesar were unconstitutional.

Patrician   The noble class of Rome.

Plebeian   All citizens not of patrician status; the lower classes, also called "plebs."

Pontifical College   The pontifices were a college of priests not of a specific god (see Priesthoods) but whose task was to advise the Senate on matters of religion. The chief of the college was the *Pontifex Maximus,* who ruled on all matters of religious practice and had charge of the calendar. Julius Caesar was elected *Pontifex Maximus,* and Augustus made it an office held permanently by the emperors. The title is currently held by the Pope.

Popular Assemblies   There were three: the Centuriate Assembly *(comitia centuriata)* and the two tribal assemblies: *comitia tributa* and *consilium plebis*.

Praetor's court   The standard Roman law court. Praetors were judges.

Priesthoods   In Rome, the priesthoods were offices of state. There were two major classes: pontifices and *flamines*. College of Pontifices were members of the highest priestly college of Rome. They had superintendence over all sacred observances, state and private, and over the calendar. Head of their college was the *Pontifex Maximus*, a title held to this day by the Pope. The *flamines* were the high priests of the state gods: the *Flamen Martialis* for Mars, the *Flamen Quirinalis* for the deified Romulus, and, highest of all, the *Flamen Dialis*, high priest of Jupiter. The *Flamen Dialis* celebrated the Ides of each month and could not take part in politics, although he could attend meetings of the Senate, attended by a single lictor. Each had charge of the daily sacrifices, wore distinctive headgear, and were surrounded by many ritual taboos.

Technically, pontifices and *flamines* did not take part in public business except to solemnize oaths and treaties, give the god's stamp of approval to declarations of war, etc. But since they were all senators anyway, the ban had little meaning. Julius Caesar was *Pontifex Maximus* while he was out conquering Gaul, even though the *Pontifex Maximus* wasn't supposed to look upon human blood.

Publicani (sing. *publicanus*)   Every five years censors were elected who let the contracts for public work: tax collecting, road building, etc. The bidders on these contracts were known as *publicani*.

Rites, Festivals

Aphrodisia   A festival dedicated to the goddess Aphrodite. They were held everywhere, but the one at Cyprus, putative birthplace of Aphrodite, was especially famous and splendid.

Cult of Dionysus   An uproarious, orgiastic cult that traveled from city to city throughout the ancient world. The female devotees of Dionysus, called maenads or bacchantes, were rumored to enter homicidal frenzies at the climax of an orgy and rip men to pieces with their hands and teeth. The cult was often suppressed in Italy but kept coming back.

Eleusinian Mysteries   The most famous mystery cult of antiquity, its initiates included many famous men, including Cicero, who described its rites as very moving. It was forbidden for anyone to describe the ritual, but it seems to have involved resurrection and rebirth.

Festival of Bel   The great annual Babylonian ritual in honor of the god Bel. According to Herodotus, its magnificence quite eclipsed anything done in the West.

Priapalia   An agricultural rite in honor of the ithyphallic god Priapus, protector of gardens and fields.

Rite of Bona Dea   Bona Dea "the Good Goddess" was honored in Rome with a special service presided over by the wife of the *Pontifex Maximus,* during which no male of any species could enter the house. All the participants were highborn married women. Clodius violated the rite when Caesar's wife presided. See *SPQR III: The Sacrilege.*

Temple of Ephesian Diana   One of the Seven Wonders of the ancient world. Actually dedicated to the goddess Artemis, whom the Romans equated with Diana, it was located in Ephesus, in modern Turkey.

Rostra (sing. rostrum)   A monument in the Forum commemorating the sea battle of Antium in 338 B.C., decorated with the rams, rostra of enemy ships. Its base was used as an orator's platform.

Senate   Rome's chief deliberative body. It consisted of three hundred to six hundred men, all of whom had won elective office at least once. It was a leading element in the emergence of the Republic, but later suffered degradation at the hands of Sulla.

Ship chandlers   Chandlers purveyed all the supplies required by a ship: cordage, pitch, paint, sails, etc.

Shipping-Related Terms

Harbor mole   A seawall built out from land to protect the harbor and narrow the passage through which ships could enter.

Jetty   A small pier built out into the water for the use of small craft.

Ships   A variety of ships were used in the ancient Mediterranean. Some were:

Cutter   A light, narrow vessel used for carrying dispatches, intercepting smugglers, etc.

Flotilla   A varying number of ships detached from a fleet.

Liburnian also bireme   A lighter warship with two banks of oars. It was named for the Liburni, a piratical Illyrian people who were believed to have been the first to add a second level of oars, to give their predatory pirate ships extra speed.

Merchantmen   Capacious vessels with a much greater width to length ratio than warships. They were propelled by sails rather than oars, though they used oars to maneuver in and out of harbor. They ranged from quite small vessels to huge grain ships for hauling the Egyptian grain harvest to Italy.

Penteconter   A Greek galley with fifty oars on a single level.

Skiff   A small rowboat.

Trireme   The standard warship of the time. It was rowed with oars arranged on three levels, or "banks." With so many rowers it was the fastest and most powerful ship, capable of ramming an enemy vessel. They carried marines for boarding the enemy, manning the catapults, etc.

SPQR Senatus Populusque Romanus   The Senate and the People of Rome. The formula embodying the sovereignty of Rome. It was used on official correspondence, documents, and public works.

Toga   The outer robe of the Roman citizen. It was white for the upper class, darker for the poor and for people in mourning. The *toga praetexta*, bordered with a purple stripe, was worn by curule magistrates, by state priests when performing their functions, and by boys prior to manhood. The *toga picta*, purple and embroidered with golden stars, was worn by a general when celebrating a triumph, also by a magistrate when giving public games.

Temple of Bellona   A unique temple located in Rome outside the walls of the city. Its priests, the *fetiales*, solemnified a declaration of war by casting a spear into a plot of land before the temple designated as enemy territory.

Triclinium   A dining room.

Triumph   A ceremony in which a victorious general was rendered semidivine honors for a day. It began with a magnificent procession displaying the loot and captives of the campaign and culminated with a banquet for the Senate in the Temple of Jupiter. Every general wanted a triumph and it was a tremendous boost for a political career.